NEWFOUNDLAND
NES
ELITE SECURITY

NES*SERIES

Risky Vengeance

RHONDA BREWER

Acknowledgments

So many people have made my writing and publishing journey possible. A simple thank you never seems like enough to convey my gratitude.

To the wonderful ladies who help me make my stories better, Amabel Daniels, Michelle Eriksen and Abbie Zanders, I don't know what I would do without your advice, suggestions, keen eyes and encouragement. To my dedicated betas and dear friends, Jackie Dawe Ford, Nancy Arnold-Holloway, and Karie Deegan thank you for always being there when I need you. To Corey Majeau of Majeau Designs and Golden Czermak of Furious Fotog for making my covers so amazing.

Last but not least thank you to my husband, children and grandchildren, I would never be able to do what I love without your love and support. You all mean the world to me, and I love you with all my heart.

Dedication

This book is dedicated to my wonderful family who lifted me up when I was struggling and gave me the confidence to push ahead.

I love you all.

Prologue

Eleven-year-old Abigale Martin lay on the floor of her living room with a scowl on her face and reading a schoolbook. She was grounded and not allowed to do anything else. Her mother, the mean Claire Martin, would not allow Abigale to go outside before she finished her homework. Of course, if Abigale had just done it and not yelled at her mother, she would probably be out with her sister.

Laurie was outside, but she didn't have her homework done. She was older and always got away with more than Abigale did. It was why she got so frustrated and screamed at her mom, telling her how unfair it was that Laurie could go out, but Abigale had to read a stupid book she didn't like.

Laurie was having fun with their friends Dana Sampson and Belinda Carter. That was another thing making her angry. Dana and Belinda were Abigale's best friends, but Laurie stuck her nose in *and now they always tried to exclude Abigale from things they did together, or that was how it seemed.*

"Why are you lying on the floor, Monkey?" Abigale's father entered the living room and got down on the floor with her.

"I'm doing my homework," Abigale replied as she rolled her eyes.

"What book are you reading?" He smiled.

"Diary of Anne Frank*," Abigale answered.*

"I read that when I was your age." He nudged her with his shoulder.

"I have to read it if I want to go outside before I'm old like you," Abigale grumbled and dropped her head on her arms.

"Old like me, huh?" Her father laughed, but she didn't find it funny.

Her father poked her, and she raised her head. She focused on the name tag on his overalls. Darren. It was weird when people called him that because most everyone around called him Hammer. Abigale had overheard the story of why her father had the nickname, and it had something to do with people he nailed. When she asked her mother about it, her mother said she'd understand when she was older.

"Mom said you talked back to her." Her father raised an eyebrow.

"It's not fair. Laurie can go out, but she didn't do her homework." Abigale complained.

"Maybe not, but that doesn't mean you can be rude to your mother, does it?" Her dad had a way of talking to her without shouting and making her feel she had to apologize.

"No." Abigale sighed.

"Laurie doesn't have school tomorrow, Monkey. That's why she was permitted to go out." He kissed her forehead and then hopped up on his feet.

"Abigale, can you run around the corner and tell your sister supper is ready?" Abigale's mother shouted from the kitchen.

Abigale held down her urge to remind her mother she was grounded because it wouldn't make the situation any better. Instead of getting herself in more trouble, she shoved her book back in her backpack and headed out of the house.

Abigale shuffled along as she made her way the two blocks to Dana's house. Laurie told their mother she was going there to hang out with Dana. If Abbie had to go out to get Laurie, she wasn't going to rush. That way, she'd get as much time outside as she could.

As she turned the corner, she spotted Dana and Laurie on the sidewalk by Dana's house. They seemed deep in conversation, and she hurried toward them to see if she could hear what they were saying. When Laurie saw Abigale, she waved, causing Dana to turn around.

"What took you so long?" Laurie asked.

"I had to do homework, unlike some people. Mom sent me to tell you supper is ready," Abigale told her sister.

"Are you coming back out after supper?" Dana asked them.

"I doubt it. I'm grounded." Abigale grumbled.

"Why?" Laurie tilted her head in confusion.

"I got mouthy with Mom." Abigale shrugged.

"You will never learn." Laurie rolled her eyes.

They talked for another few minutes before they began to head home. Abbie's mother would come looking for them if they took too long or worse, she would send their father. He would toss both of them up on his shoulders and carry them back home.

"Call me if..." Dana's words stopped when Laurie shoved both Dana and Abigale.

"Watch out," Laurie screamed.

Abigale tumbled to the ground and landed hard on her side. A sudden surge of pain shot up her arm, and all she could hear was someone screaming. She tried to get up, but her arm hurt too much, and she cried out in pain.

"Jesus, Christ," a woman shouted.

"Stop him," a man yelled.

"He's fucking drunk," another person roared.

Abigale felt sick, and her head started to hurt along with her arm. Everything spun around her, and she closed her eyes. When she opened them again, her mother was next to her, tears streaming down her face, and her shirt covered in something red.

"My arm hurts," Abigale cried.

"It's okay, Abigale. We're going to get you to the hospital." Her mother glanced behind her.

Abigale lifted her head to see a car on the sidewalk, and a crowd of paramedics around it. It was hard to figure out what they were doing, but when she locked eyes with her father, she realized something was seriously wrong.

"Mom, where's Laurie?" Abigale asked.

"She's hurt, honey." Her mother trembled, and her voice cracked.

Abigale didn't get a chance to ask another question as more paramedics surrounded her and her mother stepped back. Her dad wrapped his arms around her mother, and they followed Abigale to the back of the ambulance.

"You go with Abigale. I'll go with Laurie," Abigale heard her father say.

"Darren," her mother choked.

"She's going to be fine," he whispered, and they were the last words she heard when the ambulance doors closed.

Abigale had some x-rays, and her arm was placed in a cast. The doctors put stitches on the back of her head and bandaged a small cut on her knee. She was woozy because they gave her some medication to help with the pain.

It didn't prevent her from overhearing the conversation outside the curtain between her mother, father, and Dana's mom. They talked about Laurie and how there was nothing the doctors could do for her. Laurie's brain was dead.

"Hey, Monkey, would you like something to drink?" Her father walked into the room holding a paper cup.

Abigale nodded and he helped her sit up. As he held the cup to her lips, she stared up at him. His eyes were red, and it looked as if he was crying. The sight made it hard to swallow the juice and she carefully pushed away the cup.

"Dad, is Laurie's brain really dead?" Abigale whispered.

Her dad dropped his head, and when he lifted his eyes to meet hers, she saw tears. Abigale saw her dad cry once before, and that was when his mother died. If he had tears in his eyes, it meant something was bad.

"Monkey, your sister was hurt when the car hit her. There was nothing the doctors could do." Her father took her uninjured hand.

"She pushed Dana and me," Abigale remembered.

"What do you mean?" Her dad tilted his head.

"She screamed and told us to watch out. Then she pushed us hard." Abigale swallowed hard.

"She saved you." Her dad's voice cracked as a tear slipped down his cheek.

"Is she… you know." Abigale didn't want to say the word.

"Yes, Monkey. I'm afraid so." Her father ran his hand over the top of her head.

Abigale couldn't stop the tears if she tried. Her sister was dead, and she knew what that meant. She just didn't realize that it happened to someone as young as Laurie. Older people died, or that was what she thought.

When they got home, Abigale sat in her room, staring at her sister's empty bed. It still had her bookbag on it, and her school uniform tossed on the floor.

Death was a hard thing to understand, and listening to her mother sobbing hysterically was difficult for Abigale to hear. She'd never seen her parents cry so much, and although her arm started to hurt her again, she wouldn't ask for anything. Abigale didn't want to cause any more trouble for her mother and father.

Over the next few days, Abigale heard everyone talk about the man who hit them. He was drunk and tried to leave without helping. Some men in the neighborhood caught him and held him until the police showed up.

She didn't know what would happen after this. Abigale knew she would never see her sister again, and she felt as if part of her heart was gone. She didn't know if any of them would ever get over losing Laurie.

Chapter 1

Ben Trunk Murphy ended the call he'd received and made his way to the third floor of the Health Science Center. It was the largest hospital in the city of St. John's, and he despised the place. Still, when his boss assigned him to a job, he didn't question the location.

Trunk's boss, Keith O'Connor, ensured his clients were always given top-rate help from Newfoundland Security Services, but these clients were especially important. The two women were close friends of the family.

Keith's brother, Mike, wanted his girlfriend's friends safe. Billie Carter had been going through a tough time over the last few weeks. One of her friends was murdered and two were now in hospital after they were trapped in a fire. Trunk was assigned as security for the women until the threat was neutralized.

Keith and Dean Bull Nash owned the high-end security firm. The company dealt mostly with private security for politicians, dignitaries, and VIPs but also were hired from time to time as bodyguards. Keith and Bull were great friends and Trunk loved working for them.

Trunk loved the job and got along well with his co-workers. Since the company was relocated back to Newfoundland from Yellowknife, the entire staff were more like family than people who worked together. There was also the perk of living rent-free in a bunkhouse Keith built on his property.

Keith's six brothers had quickly become close friends with Trunk and the rest of the men who worked for NSS. Between Keith, his brothers, cousins, parents, aunts, uncles, and their quirky grandmother, it was like having a huge extended family.

Trunk stepped off the elevator and immediately locked eyes with John O'Connor. Keith tended to work side by side with the police for the most part and since four of his brothers were with the Newfoundland Police Department, it became a necessity. Although sometimes the scales of justice were tipped if it was in the best interest for the person they were protecting. The client's safety was always the most important.

Trunk's assignment was to protect two of Billie's friends. They were caught in a fire that the police believed was set by the same people after Mike's wife. It didn't matter who was after the women, Trunk's job was to keep them safe, and that was what he would do.

"So, you're saying some sicko is obsessed with Billie and to get her attention, he's killing, or attempting to kill people she cares about?," one woman asked.

"That's the theory, but John doesn't want to take chances. The fire probably destroyed any evidence, but you never know," Mike explained.

Trunk could hear the conversation from outside the partially opened door as he waited for the okay to go inside. John was on the phone and nodded when Trunk motioned to the door.

"But you're saying until they find out, we'll have someone following us around," the same woman said, but she didn't seem happy about the situation.

"Abbie, it's for our safety." The other female voice was soft.

"I don't want some goon following me around," Abbie snapped and then coughed.

Trunk figured both women were still choked up from the smoke they'd inhaled. At least the second woman sounded concerned, but the one she called Abbie seemed pissed.

The conversation stopped when Trunk stepped inside the room, and partially drawn curtains blocked them from his view. It took a few seconds before Mike noticed him standing there and nodded.

"Hi," Trunk said.

"Don't be afraid, Trunk." Mike smirked. "I'm sure Abbie

won't bite."

He wasn't worried about being bitten, but he had a feeling Abbie wasn't going to take kindly to security. As he stepped forward into view of the girls, he wasn't surprised by their reaction to him. After all, he was a big guy, not to mention his fitted T-shirt clung to his muscled body and revealed a sleeve of tattoos down his right arm.

"Abbie and Dana, this is Ben Murphy, but we all call him Trunk," Mike introduced him. "Trunk, Abbie is on the left, and Dana's on the right."

"Nice to meet you, ladies." Trunk folded his hands as he studied the two women.

"Holy, mother of Jesus. It's a real-life Adonis." Abbie gasped as she practically undressed Trunk with her eyes.

"Not quite, but thanks for the ego boost." Trunk chuckled, but she was eyeing him so intensely that it gave him a peculiar feeling in the pit of his stomach.

"How in God's name do you need an ego boost? Do you have a mirror at home?" Dana raised an eyebrow.

"Yes, I do." Trunk smirked.

"Okay, the name Trunk, is it because your arms are the size of tree trunks?" Abbie's eyes dropped to his crotch, and Trunk prayed she didn't see his dick twitch.

"Not even close." Trunk chuckled.

"Oh, is something else as big as a tree trunk?" Abbie wiggled her eyebrows.

"You're going to be trouble, aren't you?" Trunk pointed at the attractive woman.

"Yes, she is," Billie interjected.

"I'll be good if you tell me why they call you Trunk." Abbie's grin was mischievous but sexy as hell.

"I doubt you'll ever be good, but Trunk came from locking myself in one when I was trying to win a bet with my brother. I told him I could get out of our grandmother's travel trunk and told him to lock me in. Neither of us knew the thing wasn't locked before because the key was missing," Trunk told them.

The truth was he was hiding in the trunk with his brother to get away from their abusive stepfather. The man was pissed because ten-year-old Trunk had screamed to leave their mother alone. His stepfather had ripped off his belt and chased them up to the attic of their old house.

Since his stepfather was piss-eyed drunk, he couldn't catch them and lost interest when he couldn't find them. They didn't exactly get locked in the trunk, but they were locked in the attic for hours.

"Well, I'm just going to imagine my own story about why you're called Trunk." Abbie's eyes dropped to the zipper of his jeans again.

"I'll be outside your room. Nobody gets in here without my say so." Trunk chuckled as he headed out of the room. "Good evening, ladies, Mike."

"I think I'm going to be all right with being shadowed by him," Abbie said as Trunk stepped into the corridor.

"As long as you remember to do what he says." Mike was serious. "He's good at his job."

"I will." Abbie's tone changed, and Trunk could hear a hint of fear in her voice.

They weren't wrong about Abbie being trouble because she hooked him from the first day. She was sassy, sexy, and had a mouth that would make a sailor blush. Her constant sexual innuendos drove him crazy with want for her.

The police tightened up security on Billie, her family, and friends, which made Trunk a permanent fixture in Abbie's life. With each day, it got harder to resist her, but when her real estate business was targeted with Trunk barely getting Billie and Abbie out of the building, he knew he had to stay professional.

Abbie clung to him, and the only reason he released her was that he'd gotten sliced when they climbed through the broken window. He tried to cover his concern for Abbie by acting pissed about his tattoo, but the damage to his tattoo didn't bother him half as much as what could have happened to Abbie and Billie.

The tattoo was special. Trunk and his brother had gotten matching ink to represent their bond and what they had survived. They were able to escape their violent childhood when the police arrested Jerry for killing someone. Their mother packed up, moved them to central Newfoundland, and changed all their last names to her maiden name, Murphy.

Trunk never met his biological father and didn't know his name. His father left when Trunk's mother was barely pregnant with Chris and Trunk was a toddler. Jerry Stamp was the only father Trunk knew.

Jerry was a violent alcoholic who brutally beat Trunk's mother almost daily. Even as a kid, Trunk knew if they didn't get away, it would end in tragedy. The day Jerry was arrested, he'd beaten Trunk's mom so severely she almost didn't survive. Luckily, she recovered, and Trunk hadn't seen the bastard since.

Trunk walked to the gym located on the east side of Keith's property. Keith had purchased several acres of land in Hopedale, Newfoundland, the small town where he grew up. Keith built his house on the property everyone referred to as *The Compound*, and also erected a building which housed a state-of-the-art gym, and offices for both Keith's security business, as well as his construction company.

Keith also ensured all his employees had comfortable quarters to live. On the back of the acreage, he built bunkhouses where the staff could reside. Some of the guys shared a bunkhouse, and others had taken to buying their own homes around Hopedale. Many of them had fallen in love with the small town.

For a few weeks, Trunk's job was to keep Abbie safe, but his resistance to the tempting brunette was beginning to weaken. She made it clear if he was interested, he could have whatever he wanted, but Trunk had a feeling one night with Abbie would never be enough for him. It was why he avoided physical contact with her as much as possible.

Jess O'Connor was Keith's cousin and a blackbelt in Karate, as was her father, Kurt. It was a family sport for the O'Connors, and as far as Trunk knew, Keith's six brothers and four cousins were involved with the martial art to some degree.

Kurt had opened a small dojo at the local community center for kids in Hopedale and the surrounding communities. Trunk was no slouch, but he knew the girl could take him down without blinking an eye. Jess was the best one to prepare Abbie, Billie, and Dana if they needed to defend themselves. Trunk was there to help, but he enjoyed Abbie's aversion to the whole lesson.

"Ugh," Billie huffed in frustration as she slipped on the mat again.

"Come on, girl," Jess urged.

"I used to like you." Billie groaned as Jess helped her to her feet.

"Just be glad Dad isn't your instructor." Jess chuckled.

Kurt was a badass who could kill a person with two fingers. He'd practiced Karate since he was a kid and even trained in Japan for a short time, as did Keith's father, Sean. Trunk respected the hell out of both men.

"You're bad enough." Billie glared at Jess.

"Abbie, are you ready?" Jess asked.

Abbie sat off to the side of the room as if she hoped they would forget about her. She didn't seem to want to attempt anything Jess taught Billie. Dana looked scared but more involved in the lessons.

"I don't see why we need this." Abbie stood up. "I mean, I'm a lover, not a fighter, and I've got the wall here following me." Abbie hitched her thumb over her shoulder in Trunk's direction.

He had to make Abbie understand what could happen without warning. When she turned her back to him, he wrapped his arm around her neck but immediately regretted it. Her flowery scent filled his senses, and his cock hardened instantly.

"What the fuck?" Abbie struggled against his hold.

"How are you gonna get out of that?" Jess teased.

"Ben, for fuck's sake. Let go," Abbie snapped.

"Do you think an attacker would let you go because you cursed on him?" Trunk growled when her ass brushed against his dick.

He sighed with relief when she stopped struggling and seemed to admit defeat. Dana and Billie smirked from the other side of the room when Abbie went limp in his hold. They knew as well as he did that Abbie hated to be wrong.

"Just sing," Jess told Abbie.

"What?" Abbie tried to throw her arms up in the air, but Trunk kept her firmly against his body.

"Haven't you ever seen *Miss Congeniality*?" Dana chuckled.

"Trunk, come here." Jess motioned for Trunk to step next to her.

He released Abbie and jumped back when she swung her fist at him. She didn't connect, and he laughed when she called him a fucker under her breath. When Trunk locked eyes with her, he saw something he wished he hadn't. Desire.

"Okay, girlies. *Sing* is an acronym. It stands for solar plexus, instep, nose." Jess used Trunk to point out each of the body parts. "And every man's favorite, groin."

Jess gave her hand a slight flick, causing Trunk to cover his jewels. Jess wouldn't hurt him on purpose, at least he hoped she wouldn't, but he wasn't taking a chance.

"Watch it, little girl." Trunk warned with narrowed eyes.

"Watch while I demonstrate on this guy." Jess smirked.

Trunk backed away and held up his hands. There was no way

he was letting Jess beat the shit out of him. He wasn't afraid of her, but he'd seen her bring down some of the guys he worked with while they trained.

"I'm not actually going to hit you. You're such a pussy." Jess rolled her eyes.

Trunk decided he'd make the lesson more entertaining, and as Jess gradually showed each step with an explanation, he exaggerated the movements as if Jess connected with him. Dana laughed, but Abbie looked as if she was hoping Jess would knock him down.

"Do you want to try?" Jess asked the women.

"I'll give it a try." Abbie stalked toward Trunk with a wicked grin on her beautiful face.

Trunk couldn't get too close to her, because it would be like a form of torture to have her pressed against his body. Still, he wanted Abbie, Dana, and Billie to be prepared, which was why he wrapped his large arm around Abbie's neck.

"If you can knock me down, I'll play strip poker with you," Trunk whispered against her ear.

He hoped the comment would encourage Abbie to put everything she had into the lesson. She'd been trying to talk him into the intimate game since the first night he'd been alone with her. Dana had returned to her own home with security, and Trunk was assigned to Abbie exclusively.

Abbie tensed when he pulled her hard against his body. By the way her jaw clenched and the small sigh that escaped from her lips, he could tell she was affected from their close proximity. She stood still for a moment, and he felt her pulse increase.

"What's wrong, Abs?" Trunk murmured,

Before he had a chance to say another word, Abbie struck him in the stomach with her elbow, and all the air whooshed out of his lungs. He hadn't recovered from the surprise blow when she slammed her foot down on top of his.

"Fuck," Trunk cursed and barely escaped an elbow to the face.

Trunk quickly anticipated the next move and grabbed Abbie's fist before it connected with his balls. He lifted his eyes to see a sly grin on her full lips. She knew exactly what she was doing.

Trunk tugged her toward him and hooked his leg behind Abbie's knee, knocking her off her feet. Abbie fell flat on her back with a grunt. Before she could react, Trunk straddled her hips and held both of her hands above her head.

"Get off me, you big ass." Abbie struggled under him, and his cock jerked.

"You're a real tiger, aren't you?" Trunk smirked.

He started to get up off her because the way she squirmed under him was as arousing as fuck. When he released her hands, Abbie grabbed for his crotch, but Trunk jumped up before she had a chance to find out how hard he was.

Abbie lay on the floor with provocation written all over her face. He could see the pulse in her neck pounding erratically confirming that she wanted him as much as he did her. That couldn't happen while he was assigned to protect her.

"How was that?" Abbie sounded breathless as she propped herself up on her elbows.

The position pushed her ample breasts out, and her nipples poked against the fabric of her T-shirt. His mouth watered at the thought of wrapping his lips around those hard buds and sucking them into his mouth.

Trunk tried hard to shake the image from his brain, and his cock throbbed painfully. He had to get away before the girls noticed his arousal. His engorged cock wasn't easy to hide in his jeans.

"Not bad." Jess laughed. "Anyone else want to give it a go?"

"Not fucking likely. I'll send Smash in. You can beat the shit out of his danglers." Trunk grumbled and left the room.

When he stepped outside, he closed the door and leaned against the wall. After a couple of deep breaths, he made his way to the office to send Gabe 'Smash' Hodder to help out. Smash was the other computer analyst employed by Newfoundland Security Services.

It was tough for Trunk to fight Abbie's allure, and touching her made it painful. He'd never felt such an intense attraction to anyone in his life. He always believed everyone had someone in the world meant for them. As much as he struggled with it, Trunk knew Abbie was his.

Chapter 2

Abbie Martin sat on the couch and glared at Trunk. He'd been driving her hormones in overdrive for weeks, and she was ready to explode. For some reason, he kept his distance, and she'd practically given up on him.

Her one piece of happiness at the moment was the knowledge Billie didn't have to worry anymore. The celebration was bittersweet because they'd lost a dear friend during the ordeal. All because of the sick bastards who thought selling women and children was okay. Abbie shuddered as thoughts of what could've happened flashed through her head.

Billie was fearless, putting herself in harm's way to bring down the asshole who murdered poor Peggy. Abbie didn't think she could do it because the whole situation terrified her. The sofa dipped next to her, and she turned.

Sandy O'Connor sat next to her with a gigantic smile on her face. Why wouldn't she smile? Sandy married Ian O'Connor a year earlier and the sexy doctor adored her. With Mike secretly planning to propose the following week, it meant five of the O'Connor

Brothers were now off the market. Not that Abbie had any interest in any of them, but most woman with a pulse would find the men attractive.

She liked Sandy mostly because she was loud and obnoxious, just like Abbie. Sandy also enjoyed teasing the men she worked with incessantly. It was hard to believe she was one of the best computer analysts in the country. Abbie had even heard people say she was the Penelope Garcia of Newfoundland.

"Trunk still not giving it up?" Sandy whispered as she handed Abbie a glass of wine.

"I don't get it. I know he's interested, but he keeps me at arm's length. It's so fucking frustrating." Abbie sighed.

Abbie and Sandy had become friends over the last few weeks. Since she knew Trunk well, Abbie asked Sandy for advice on what to do. Dana and Billie told her to move on, but she couldn't. She felt deeply connected to Trunk, which was the biggest problem.

"I asked him what his problem was, and he told me to mind my own business." Sandy shrugged. "He knows I never do that."

Abbie almost spit her wine across the floor when she burst into a fit of laughter. Leave it to Sandy to help her put aside all the bad stuff and make her remember how great it felt to laugh. So much tension filled their lives over the last few weeks, she couldn't go back to the easy-going person she once was.

She did have something to feel happy about. They found another office to relocate her real estate company until she could rebuild her old office. She was lucky Billie insisted on buying fireproof file cabinets and ensured they back up every evening before they left the office. Abbie would be screwed otherwise.

"I should just give up and join one of those dating sites," Abbie scoffed.

"Sweet Jesus. You're desperate." Sandy gasped.

"You're such a bitch." Abbie slapped Sandy's arm.

"You're only figuring that out now. I'm proud to be a bitch. I'm actually the queen of bitches. I've ordered a crown." Sandy grinned.

"I wouldn't be surprised if you did." Abbie finished the wine in her glass.

It was getting late, so she decided to make her way home. Abbie moved around Mike's parents' home, saying goodbye to everyone. Sean and Kathleen were terrific people, and she was happy Billie found a family who cared about her as much as her own, not to mention a man who loved her more than life itself. Abbie figured she'd never find that. She still had her parents and her friends, but that didn't keep her warm at night.

Abbie avoided Trunk on the way to the front door. With so many people in the house, it wasn't hard to miss one person. Trunk's gaze burned into her as she sauntered by him, swaying her hips more seductively than she usually did. When she pulled open the front door, she turned and gave him one last look.

She thought she could escape without Mike's grandmother giving her a container of food that could feed four people. Betty O'Connor, or Nanny Betty, caught Abbie before she made it outside. The eighty-something-year-old seemed to think it was her job to feed everyone.

"Ducky, doncha leave witout dis," Nanny Betty said, shoving the reusable container into Abbie's hands.

"Thank you, Nan." Abbie smiled.

Abbie learned from the first moment she met Nanny Betty that nobody called her Mrs. O'Connor. They were only permitted to refer to her as Betty or Nan. Since it didn't seem respectful to call someone her age by her first name, Abbie decided to call her Nan like mostly everyone.

Abbie pulled into her driveway about thirty minutes later and turned off her car. She'd stopped at the grocery store, not because she needed anything, but because she didn't want to go home. For the first time in weeks, she'd be home alone, and she didn't know how she felt about it. Without Trunk or any of the men who worked for Keith, she was uneasy with the thought of being by herself.

After a deep sigh, Abbie grabbed her things and made her way up the steps to her house. It was dark, but the streetlights gave enough illumination for her to see the keyhole to her front door.

With a twist of the key, she unlocked the door and opened it. She was about to step inside when an arm wrapped around her.

Abbie froze as she was pushed into the house, and the door slammed behind them. Panic started to bubble up from the pit of her stomach, but she calmed herself and tried to remember what Jess taught her. There was just one problem, her arms were pinned to her sides, and her feet weren't touching the floor. She had to use her head.

Abbie dropped her head forward and was about to slam it back into the guy's face, but she stopped. A whiff of *Polo Red Intense* by Ralph Lauren tickled her nose. It was expensive cologne, and over the last few weeks, the scent played havoc with her hormones. There was just one person she knew who used it.

"Ben, you asshole. Put me down." Abbie squirmed in his arms.

"Why did you say goodbye to everyone but me?" He growled in her ear.

Trunk let her slide down his body until her feet were back on the floor, but he didn't release her. He kept his arms wrapped tightly around her and she could feel every hard muscle pressed against her back.

"I didn't feel like it." Abbie tried to pull from his grasp.

"You were trying to hurt me, Abs. Be honest." Trunk's raspy voice tickled her ear.

"I didn't think cold-hearted pricks could be hurt," Abbie returned.

She was pissed with herself more than him. Her body betrayed her when his lips lightly brushed behind her ear. A shiver of desire raced through her, and goosebumps formed on her skin as her core tingled.

"You think I can't be hurt? Abs, I hurt every day I couldn't be with you like I wanted. I needed to stay focused until we neutralized the danger." His nose skimmed the side of her neck.

"Ben, you're driving me nuts." Abbie sighed and allowed her body to press back against him.

"Good, because you've been making me crazy with wanting you since the first time you undressed me with your eyes at the hospital." Trunk spun her around and backed her against the wall.

"I did not," Abbie griped.

"Yes, Abs. You did," Trunk's deep voice rumbled.

Abbie tipped her head back and gazed into Trunk's deep chocolate-brown eyes. She could get lost in them if she allowed herself, and having his mouth a breath away from hers was making it hard to think.

"What are you doing here?" Abbie asked.

"You're not in danger anymore, so I can show you what you do to me." Trunk ran his index finger down the side of her neck.

"You think you can just come here, and I'll fall into bed with you?" Abbie tried to sound annoyed, but it was impossible when his erection pressed against her and his scent surrounded her.

"Abs, if you don't want this, tell me now because if you don't want me, I'll turn around and walk out that door." Trunk rested his forehead against hers.

"I can't think when you're so close." Abbie's words came out breathy and desperate.

His large hands cupped her ass, which made it even tougher to think about anything but ripping off both their clothes. He teased her with soft kisses across her cheeks and down to the corner of her mouth. Abbie wanted him. She hadn't been with anyone in over a year, and she was tired of helping herself.

"I want you," Abbie murmured as she grabbed the sides of his head and slammed her lips against his.

Trunk didn't need any coaching. He plunged his tongue inside her mouth, and it tasted like chocolate. Between his taste and his scent, Abbie knew she was about to have one of the best desserts of her life.

She fumbled with her blouse and jeans as she kicked off her shoes. Their lips separated long enough for Trunk to tug his shirt over his head. It took less than a second, and his mouth was on hers again.

Abbie was down to her panties and bra when Trunk picked her up. She wrapped her legs around his waist, and he braced her back against the wall. When he pulled his lips from hers, his eyes dropped to her chest.

He pulled the cup of her bra down, exposing her breast, and he lowered his head. Trunk tugged and teased her sensitive nipple with his teeth as his wet tongue circled her areola after every gentle nip. Abbie's head dropped back while his hot mouth sent shockwaves of need through her body.

"Oh, yeah." Abbie panted and ground her throbbing pussy against him.

It had been so long since someone touched her intimately, and it felt like heaven to have his strong caress over her body. Trunk's hands weren't soft, and his rough palms made his touch even more pleasurable.

"I want to fuck you right here, Abs." Trunk growled when she sucked his earlobe into her mouth.

"I won't argue. Fuck me on the roof if you like." Abbie squirmed against his erection.

"We'll put that on the list." Trunk chuckled.

She heard the jingle of his belt buckle and then his zipper. Before his pants dropped, he fumbled in his pocket, and when he lifted his hand, he held a foil package. Abbie grinned because no matter how much she wanted the big gorgeous guy, she couldn't be careless.

"Always prepared, just like a real boy scout." Abbie smirked.

"I'm no boy scout. Abs, this first time is going to be hard and fast. I've been in agony for weeks, but we've got all night, and trust me, you'll be exhausted by the time I'm done." Trunk gently bit her lip.

After another breath-stealing kiss, Trunk lowered her so she could stand up. He dropped his jeans and underwear, showing her what she'd been fantasizing about for weeks. Abbie licked her lips as she watched him slip the condom over his thick cock.

Trunk was hard, but it was the first time she'd ever seen a man who was circumcised up close. He was average in length, but thick, and the purple head glistened with moisture.

"Are you ready, Abs?" Trunk lifted her into his arms again.

"Why don't you check and see?" Abbie teased.

Trunk slipped his hand under her ass, and she heard the unmistakable ripping sound of her sheer panties. She groaned as his finger slid between her wet folds once and skimmed lightly against her opening.

"Oh, you're ready," Trunk groaned.

"Fuck," Abbie gasped.

"Whatever you want, baby." Trunk lifted his finger and wiped the moisture across her lower lip. "Don't wipe that off."

Trunk pressed her against the wall and reached between them. He grabbed his cock, and Abbie held her breath as he positioned the head at her opening, but before he pushed inside, his eyes locked with hers

"I can't fucking wait to bury myself inside you, Abs." Trunk growled and thrust into her.

"Yes," Abbie gasped with pleasure.

Trunk gradually pulled out a little then slammed back inside her as his tongue glided across her lower lip.

"There's nothing as hot as tasting a woman's juice on her own lips while you're inside her." Trunk sucked her lip into his mouth.

"Would you feel that way if it was your juice on my lips?" Abbie flicked her tongue out and touched his.

"That's even hotter," Trunk said with a deep growl.

He pushed deeper as he grabbed her ass, and one finger ran up and down the crack. The more he pounded into her, the harder he squeezed her bottom, and his finger moved closer to her hole.

Abbie had lots of experience, not that she was a slut, but she'd always loved sex. She wasn't squeamish about trying new things, and although she never tried anal, she wasn't opposed to being fingered there. As if he read her mind, Trunk's thick finger slipped inside.

"Oh, God." Abbie gripped Trunk's shoulders.

"Like that, do you, Abs?," Trunk growled into her ear.

"Fuck, yes." Abbie thrust her hips forward and then back.

"Nice, because that ass of yours needs some good fucking too." Trunk covered her mouth with his before she had a chance to respond.

He slammed his cock into her hard and fast as his finger slipped deeper inside her ass. Abbie groaned with pleasure as she felt an orgasm began to build. She'd never come without stimulation to her clitoris, but when Trunk rammed into her with one hard thrust, her whole body trembled. The pleasure slammed through her, and her pussy squeezed around his cock.

"Ben, fuck," Abbie shouted and dug her nails into the back of his neck.

"That's it, baby. Squeeze my cock with that hot little pussy." Trunk growled into her ear.

He slammed into her once more and let out a loud groan. Trunk buried his face in the crook of her neck as his body convulsed. All his muscles contracted as his release spilled inside her.

When they both stopped shaking, the only sound in the hallway was their heavy panting as they tried to catch their breath.

Abbie could feel his cock jerk inside her, and she sighed. When Trunk lifted his head, and he stared into her eyes.

"You think you can put me down so we can go to the bedroom?" Abbie smirked.

"As soon as I can get my legs to work again, you bet." Trunk chuckled, but he did release her so she could put her feet on the floor.

"I'll meet you there. My legs are fine." Abbie grinned as she backed away from him.

"Every inch of you is fine, baby." Trunk kicked off his boots and stepped out of his jeans.

He stood in front of her, naked and beautiful, even with a used condom hanging from his semi-erection. He still looked perfect to her. Trunk deliberately stalked toward her and when he kicked his things to the side, Abbie turned and ran into the room.

She almost made it to the bed, but Trunk grabbed her around the waist. Instead of bringing her to the bed, he turned and headed toward the bathroom. He stepped into her large shower and tugged her in with him.

"Are you trying to tell me I need a wash?" Abbie laughed.

"No, but I've been jacking off to doing you like this for weeks." Trunk growled as he spun her around and pulled her body back against his.

With that, he showed her exactly what he meant, and she had to admit, it was incredible.

Chapter 3

"I need to eat," Abbie panted after she and Trunk made love again.

Trunk was surprised Abbie hadn't tossed him out on his ass when he arrived the previous evening. After almost eight hours in her bedroom, and making love four times, watching her saunter across the room naked was arousing him yet again.

"I don't know, but if I don't eat something, I won't be doing that again." Abbie wiggled her finger toward where his cock lay on his stomach.

"I'll make you a three-course meal because we have to do that again," Trunk jumped out of bed and left the bedroom

"You can't be wandering around my kitchen naked," she shouted as she ran behind him.

"My clothes are in the foyer, remember?" Trunk wiggled his eyebrows as he picked up his boxer briefs.

Luckily, he'd had the presence of mind after their shower sex, to place the containers of food in her fridge. Keith's grandmother would kick their asses if they'd let the leftovers spoil. After he picked up the discarded clothes and pulled on his jeans, he made his way to the kitchen.

For the first time since he met her, Trunk could relax and enjoy her company. While they ate, they discussed her business and what they wanted for the future. When the conversation turned to family, Trunk tensed.

"My mother lives in Corner Brook and works for a doctor as a receptionist. She says when she retires, she's moving to St. John's to be closer to her boys," Trunk told Abbie.

"Your brother lives in St. John's?" Abbie seemed surprised.

"No, he's in Nova Scotia," Trunk replied.

"I'm guessing he's moving back here when your mother retires." Abbie smirked.

"If you ask her, yes. If you ask Chris, no." Trunk stood up.

"What about your dad?" Abbie asked as she sipped on a glass of water.

"He's been out of my life for a long time," Trunk explained as he left the table to place the plates in the sink.

"I'm guessing that means you don't want to talk about him." Abbie moved behind him and wrapped her arms around his waist.

"You're very smart, do you know that?" Trunk turned around and pulled her into his arms.

"I know." Abbie winked.

They spent almost a full day together and were headed into the second night. Abbie talked about her parents and their concerns while she was in danger. She seemed to idolize her father, and Trunk felt a twinge of jealousy deep down in his gut. Not because of her admiration for her dad, but because he couldn't relate to having a father he could look up to.

"Do you have siblings?" Trunk asked.

Abbie stiffened for a moment, and he suddenly felt horrible for asking the question. When she snuggled tighter into his side, he wondered if he'd struck a nerve. He never heard her refer to a brother or sister, but it didn't mean she didn't have any.

"I had a sister," Abbie whispered.

"Had?" Trunk ran his hand up and down her back.

"She died," Abbie murmured.

"I'm sorry." Trunk kissed her forehead.

"It was a long time ago. I was eleven when Laurie died." Abbie swirled her finger around his chest.

"Can I ask what happened?," he asked.

"We were outside with some friends, and a man hit her with his car." Abbie lifted her head and rested her chin on his chest.

"That's horrible." Trunk ran his knuckle down her cheek.

"It was. She saved Dana and me from being hit as well. She pushed us out of the way when the guy swerved toward us. He was drunk and tried to run off afterward, but some neighbors grabbed him," Abbie went on.

"Do you know who hit her?" Trunk asked.

"Who cares? I moved on, and I would rather not think about any of it while I have a hot stud next to me." Abbie dropped soft kisses across his chest.

Trunk's mind swirled with terrible thoughts. It wasn't possible his stepfather killed Abbie's sister, was it? St. John's was a big city, and he'd heard tons of stories about drunk drivers hurting or killing people.

"What's wrong?" Abbie stopped and met his eyes.

"Nothing." Trunk forced a smile.

"Don't do that." Abbie cupped his cheek.

"Do what?" Trunk's heart drummed in his chest.

"Lie. You're tense all of a sudden," she whispered.

Abbie could obviously read him better than he thought. He tried his best to force down the sickening feeling churning through his stomach until he could confirm his fear.

"I think you finally wore me out, Abs." Trunk pulled her tightly into his embrace as he kissed the top of her head.

"Maybe we should get some sleep then." Abbie yawned.

39

Trunk felt torn between wanting to hold the woman he'd fallen in love with, and finding out if what he suspected was true. He prayed he was wrong because he and Abbie couldn't have a future if his stepfather killed her sister.

Abbie drifted off to sleep, and Trunk slipped out of bed. He hated to leave without a word, but he couldn't sleep until he knew the truth.

By the time he made it back to Hopedale, every muscle in his body was tighter than a drum and his jaw hurt from clenching his teeth together. It was a little before five in the morning, and he knew neither Sandy nor Smash were awake.

He drove up to the security gate leading to *The Compound*. Trunk was living in a bunkhouse at the back of Keith's property until his house was finished. Billie helped him find a home, but it needed work before he could move in. He hired Keith's construction company to finish it so he could move in as soon as possible.

He stopped his truck outside of Keith's two-story farmhouse, but it was obvious nobody was awake. Keith and his wife were practically newlyweds, and even if they were up, they were probably in the middle of enjoying each other. Plus, they were expecting their first baby so Emily needed all the sleep she could get.

Next, Trunk headed to the bunkhouse to see if Smash was awake, but before he got to the small cottages, he remembered Smash was out of town for the weekend.

"Fuck." Trunk growled and slammed his hands against the steering wheel.

A workout, shower, and meal killed a little over two hours. Trunk hoped Sandy was up by the time he'd finished eating. He made his way out of *The Compound* and headed straight to Sandy's and Ian's house.

Trunk hoped Sandy's and Ian's three-year-old and one-year-old were early risers. The two older girls would be sleeping in since they were in school all week. At least with the younger kids, he had a chance of Sandy not punching him for waking them up.

Trunk stepped up on the front porch and rang the doorbell. It didn't take long before he heard someone stomping to the front door. Trunk bit back a snicker when Sandy appeared in the doorway with her dark curly hair in disarray and three-year-old Grace on her hip.

"What the fu…" Sandy stopped and looked at the pretty little girl smiling at Trunk. "Why are you here at seven in the morning on a Saturday?"

"I need you to check something for me," Trunk said as Grace leaped into his arms.

"Hi, Trunk." Grace flung her arms around his neck.

"Hi, Gracie. Are you driving Mommy crazy again?" Trunk chuckled as he followed Sandy to the kitchen.

"I wanted juice." Grace pointed to a puddle of orange juice on the kitchen floor.

"Yes, she was thirsty and decided she would get it herself because she thinks she can pour juice from a container that's heavier than her," Sandy complained as she mopped the floor.

"I spilled the juice." Grace stuck out her lower lip, and Trunk wondered how anyone could stay mad at the little girl.

"Don't do that face, Gracie. Mommy needs to stay mad." Sandy pointed at her daughter.

"I'm sorry, Mommy." Grace dropped her head and covered her face with her hands.

"I swear that child should be an actress." Sandy sighed as she took Grace into her arms and hugged her.

Trunk chuckled as he took over the mopping while Sandy settled Grace in bed with her father. When she returned, she'd pulled her hair into a messy ponytail.

"I thought you'd smartened up and went to see Abbie yesterday." Sandy propped her fists on her hips.

"I need you to check something for me." Trunk didn't want to talk about Abbie.

"Okay, so we're going to avoid that statement. What do you want?" Sandy poured three cups of coffee and handed one to Trunk.

"I want you to do a digital search on Jerry Stamp. I need to know the name of the girl he killed," Trunk said as he followed Sandy to her bedroom.

Sandy worked from home most days, and her primary system was in her bedroom. Working for Keith was her main job, but she also worked part-time with the Newfoundland Police Department. Sandy was brilliant, not to mention the best computer analyst he'd ever met.

"Why am I looking up your stepdad?" Sandy asked as they entered the bedroom.

Ian sat in the middle of the large bed with Grace on one side and little Alexander on the other. Ian and Sandy were a blended family with Ian's two girls, Lily and Grace and Sandy's daughter Evie. They had Alexander shortly after they were married.

"Hey, Trunk." Ian nodded.

"Can you just check for me?" Trunk asked as he gave Ian a quick wave.

"No, I want to know why." Sandy sat in her chair and crossed her arms.

"Sandy," Trunk said with a deep rumble in his voice.

"Trunk, you should know better than to ask her anything without an explanation." Ian chuckled.

Trunk had known Sandy for a long time, and she would never do as he asked without justification. It wasn't like she didn't know about his past. Even if he hadn't told her, she would have found out anyway. It always amazed him how much she could find through her computer.

"Don't say a word. To anyone." Trunk met Sandy's eyes.

"I promise." She nodded.

"Abbie's sister was killed by a drunk driver," Trunk said quietly.

Sandy stared at him for a moment, then, without a word, began to turn on her computers. After each of her screens lit up, Sandy's fingers danced over the keyboard and Trunk saw things pop up on each screen.

"I mean, the chances of your stepdad's victim being Abbie's sister are slim to none," Sandy murmured.

"You have to factor in my shitty luck," Trunk returned.

"Das a bad word." Grace tugged on Trunk's jacket.

"She has ears like a bat," Sandy told him without stopping her constant clicking.

"I'm sorry, Gracie." Trunk crouched to talk to Sandy's daughter.

"It's okay, but don't let Nanny Kathleen hear you. She puts pepper on your tongue," Grace whispered as she cupped one of her tiny hands around her mouth.

"I'll remember that." Trunk chuckled as she ran and jumped up on the bed.

"Okay, here it is." Sandy pointed to the screen

Trunk stood up slowly as he stared at the name on the screen. All the air whooshed out of him at the sight of the black characters printed across the white background. It wasn't just the name of the girl Jerry killed that had him sick to his stomach, it was the names of the two kids injured by the crash.

"He killed Abbie's sister," Trunk whispered mostly to himself.

"Trunk, it's not like this is your fault." Sandy touched his arm.

"Don't mention a word of this to anyone. Got it?" Trunk spun around and stomped out of the room.

A relationship with Abbie wasn't in his future and Trunk had to push her away before she found out the truth. Now that he had kissed her, touched her, and knew the pleasure of making love to her, it would be hell, but he didn't have a choice.

"Doesn't matter. If she knew, she'd hate me," Trunk mumbled to himself as he jumped in his vehicle.

Sandy would tell Keith and Bull because she didn't keep anything from those two. Bull was kind of in the same predicament as Trunk. Bull was in love with Keith's cousin Kristy, but because of some family shit, he kept the feisty woman at a distance. Kristy wasn't making it easy for the man.

His eyes filled with tears as he drove to the bunkhouse. Trunk had found happiness with Abbie, but as usual, things didn't go the way he wanted. Life with Abbie wasn't in his future, and the sooner he came to terms with that, the better off he would be.

"I'm so sorry, Abs, but this is for the best. You'll be better off with someone else. At least I got to be with you once, and I'll remember that for as long as I live." Trunk sighed.

Chapter 4

Abbie gave up on ever getting an explanation for why Trunk disappeared out of her bed. He'd dodged her calls, ignored her texts, and when she did talk to him, he simply said it was fun, but it couldn't last.

By the time she pushed him out of her heart, five years had passed. It was why she sat across the table at *Maison De Vaisselle* having another boring date with Chad Grady. He worked for a real estate developer and she met him at a Conference a week earlier.

Chad was a few inches taller than her five-feet and seven-inches. He didn't have all the sexy muscles Trunk did, but Chad had a decent body. Chad's light-brown hair was thinning, but he kept it neat and she had a feeling he was doing something to thicken his hair. His gray, almond-shaped eyes seemed too far apart but she wasn't the type of woman who went strictly for looks.

Although she had a lot in common with him, Abbie found herself bored with their conversations. Chad was predictable and didn't seem to be the type to do anything out of his comfort zone.

He'd started hinting at taking their relationship to the next level, and she knew what that meant.

Abbie wasn't sexually attracted to the man. He'd kissed her a few times, but it didn't even ignite any kind of spark. The problem was if she didn't try with someone else, she would never get over Trunk.

"What do you think about that?" Chad asked.

Abbie had no idea what he was asking because she'd stopped listening to his mind-numbing dribble ten minutes earlier. Was this how low she'd sunk, being with a man because she didn't want to die alone? She just hadn't found anyone who flicked that switch for her, and she doubted she ever would.

"Sorry, I was thinking about something. What do I think about what?" Abbie forced a smile.

"What do you think about going away with me next weekend?" Chad grinned and Abbie's stomach lurched.

She didn't want to go, but how was she going to get out of it? She'd told everyone how great Chad was and how happy she was with him, so wouldn't the next step be to go away for a romantic weekend with him?

"I'll have to check my schedule," Abbie lied.

"Come on. We could spend time by the lake, just the two of us. I'm ready for that step, Abbie." Chad reached across the table and held her hand in his.

He was a nice guy, and any woman would be lucky to be with him. She had to move on. Abbie hadn't been intimate with anyone since Trunk, and that wasn't like her. She used to enjoy dating and sex.

"You know what? It sounds wonderful." Abbie smiled. "You set it up and let me know the details."

"We'll have an amazing time, Abbie." Chad kissed her hand and then released it.

When the day arrived for her and Chad to go away, Abbie felt an overwhelming sense of dread. Of course, she didn't tell anyone because they would try to talk her out of spending the weekend with him. Billie and Dana still believed Abbie should be with Trunk, thanks to Mike's aunt.

Cora Nightingale was known to many people as Cora the Cupid because she supposedly had a gift for matchmaking. According to Nanny Betty and Billie, the woman was never wrong. Abbie thought it was a load of crap.

"What time do you leave?" Billie asked as they were locking up the office.

"He's picking me up at six," Abbie told her friend.

"Are you nervous?" Billie smirked.

"What am I? The virgin bride?" Abbie scoffed.

"It has been a while, Abbie," Billie reminded her.

"I'm well aware of how long it's been." Abbie locked the door and walked Billie to her car.

"Well, call me when you get there, and we'll talk when you get back." Billie hugged Abbie.

"I will. Hug Maggie for me," Abbie told her.

Billie and Mike had a baby girl almost three years earlier, and she was the most beautiful child Abbie had ever seen. Of course, it seemed as if all the O'Connors were popping out kids like rabbits. Not that Abbie begrudged them having kids. She'd always wanted some herself, but she was getting to the age where it didn't look promising.

The ride to Chad's cabin was not too long, and true to his word, the place was like paradise. The bungalow was in a small town called Calvert and right next to a lake. The view of the hills in the distance was amazing, and she felt a sense of peace as she gazed out at the scenery.

"Do you want to bring in your bags?" Chad asked as he picked up his own suitcase.

Abbie was an independent woman, but she'd never met a man who didn't offer to carry her bags. Abbie shrugged as she grabbed her overnight bag and tossed the strap over her shoulder.

She followed Chad inside and gasped. The place was like something out of a magazine. Lush carpet and pristine white furniture adorned the living room. The kitchen had dark oak cupboards and black appliances that looked new. It was a kitchen she'd imagined in her own house one day.

"The bedrooms are in here." Chad motioned to the two sets of double doors at the end of a short hallway.

"This is the guest room, and this one is the master." Chad pointed to each door. "We'll be staying in the master, of course."

The smirk on his face nauseated her. Abbie had to push down the overwhelming feeling to turn and run out the door. She had to get it over with, plus, she was also out in the middle of nowhere. She couldn't call anyone to come get her because they'd know she wasn't happy with Chad.

"It's lovely." Abbie smiled as Chad opened the door.

A large, king-sized bed stood in the center of the room with the foot facing a beautiful propane fireplace. The plush carpet was soft under her feet as she entered the room, and it was as if she was sinking into it.

As a real estate agent, she'd seen some pretty expensive furniture. The bed was an *Astoria Grand Prange* sleigh bed. The head and footboards had a leather inset surrounded by dark cherry wood. Two nightstands stood on either side of the bed that matched the oversized dresser against the far wall.

"I wanted the best furniture in the place. Don't want anything that's going to fall apart in a year." Chad moved toward her.

"Good investment too." Abbie tried not to back away as he rested his hands on her hips.

"I'm so glad we're here together. We make so much sense as a couple." Chad leaned in and brushed his lips across hers.

He wasn't a terrible kisser, in fact, he was pretty good. The problem was it felt awkward because she wasn't attracted to him. Abbie hated to make him feel insecure about himself, so she slipped her arms around his neck and smiled when he gazed into her eyes.

"You feel the chemistry, too, don't you?" Chad's eyes were heavy with desire.

"Of course," Abbie lied.

"It's going to be great." Chad stepped closer and proceeded to cover her mouth with his.

Abbie lay in the bed twenty minutes later, trying to remember the last time she had such uncomfortable sex. Chad enjoyed it, and as soon as he finished, he passed out next to her. Abbie hadn't faked an orgasm in a long time, but he didn't even seem to care if she had one or not.

Was this her life? Dull sex with someone she kind of liked in a friendship capacity? Maybe it wasn't as bad as she thought. The first time with someone new was a learning experience. A couple had to get to know each other.

Her night with Trunk flashed in her mind, and she remembered they didn't need to learn about each other. He knew how to bring her to heights of pleasure she'd never experienced in her life. Considering where she was at that moment, it was never going to happen again.

Abbie turned on her side away from Chad and tucked her hand under her cheek. Would she ever get over Trunk, or was she doomed to spend the rest of her life in love with someone she would never have?

Chapter 5

Trunk sat in Keith's living room, with his co-workers. Keith asked all the staff to come in for an important meeting. Trunk hoped it wasn't bad news because the truth was, he loved his job and didn't want to start another career.

Trunk sat on the couch next to Brent 'Crash' Adams and Hunter 'Crunch' Crawford. On the couch across the room was Bruce 'Hulk' Steel, Caden 'Rex' Dixon, Lane 'Shadow' West, and Adrian 'Rock' Hudson. Near the window was Ethan 'Ace' Norris and Joel 'Cannon' Wiseman. Smash and Sandy were in each of the armchairs.

"Do you know what all this is about?" Crash asked Trunk.

"Not a clue." Trunk shrugged.

"Are we going to have to look for new jobs?" Cannon asked the question they were all thinking.

"No, you don't need to look for jobs." Sandy rolled her eyes.

"Do you know what this is about?" Cannon asked.

"All will be revealed, young Cannon." Sandy smirked.

"You're no help," Cannon complained.

A short while later, Bull and Keith dropped two boxes on the floor in the living room and shuffled through some papers. Bull handed small plastic cards to each person. When Trunk received his, he realized it was an identification tag.

"Okay, guys," Bull began.

"I'm a girl," Sandy interrupted.

"For fuck's sake. Okay, guys and Sandy." Bull rolled his eyes. "Keith and I have done some revamping of the company. We're going to need to hire a few more people, and we're in the process of looking for qualified individuals who will fit with us."

"The first of the changes is a big one. The company has a new name. *Newfoundland Elite Security* or *NES* for short. The provincial government has contracted *NES* for all security they need for officials. It's why we had to replace all your ID cards. You'll see the provincial crest as well as our new company logo in the bottom corners," Keith explained.

"You guys and Sandy are the heart and soul of this company, and we wouldn't have the wonderful reputation we do without you," Bull interjected.

"All of you are so much more to us than employees. You're family. It's why we've decided to introduce profit sharing with all the staff." Keith smiled.

When the excitement of the news subsided, Keith and Bull went into detail of how everything would work. It all seemed overly complicated to Trunk, but he was just glad he wasn't losing his job. The two things he did know was, all the changes were taking place immediately, and he'd be making more money. That was fine with him.

Trunk glanced at his watch and was relieved when Keith announced the meeting was over. He was happy about the news but he didn't want to be late for his date with a very important lady.

"Everything sounds great, Rusty," Trunk said, using Keith's nickname. "But I have to run. I've got to take Mom on her weekly shopping trip."

"Good luck with that." Bull laughed.

"I look forward to it every week." Trunk grinned.

"Tell her we said hi," Keith said.

Trunk pulled his SUV into a parking spot next to his mother's apartment building. He was there to take her grocery shopping and run errands. Since she moved back to St. John's, it was his weekly schedule, and he was happy to do it.

He couldn't blame her for wanting to leave St. John's all those years ago. It was the best thing she could have done for Trunk and Chris. She lived through hell with a man who used her as a punching bag, and when she was able to escape him, she'd needed a complete change of scenery.

Trunk vividly remembered the beatings and his mother's screams. Chris didn't see as much of the violence because Trunk tried to keep his younger brother away from it as much as possible. The move had been easier on Chris but for Trunk, it was more difficult, and he spent a lot of time alone.

Chris completed the firefighter's training and moved to Halifax with his girlfriend, but things were falling apart for his brother over the last few months. Chris was struggling with the split, but he wasn't keeping it bottled up inside. When he needed to vent, he'd call their mother or Trunk.

Trunk walked into the senior apartment complex, and as usual, the people in the lobby stared at him. It didn't make him uncomfortable because he was used to it. Folks tended to stare when he walked by. Maybe because of his six-feet, and three-inches height, or possibly because of his bald head and beard, but chances were it was his tattoos.

Many of the seniors in his mother's apartment building wouldn't get on the elevator with him. He understood their aversion and didn't let it bother him. No matter how friendly Trunk was with some people, they perceived him as if he was some sort of criminal.

Trunk stepped onto the elevator with an older lady who glanced up at him. She appeared more curious than frightened of him. She sized him up from head to toe and didn't even try to hide her scrutiny of him. When she lifted her eyes to meet his, Trunk smiled.

"You don't live here," she said.

"No, ma'am. I'm here to visit my mother," Trunk replied.

The lady stared at him for a minute before she turned without another word. When the elevator doors opened, she glanced back at Trunk.

"You're a good boy." She nodded and stepped off the elevator.

"Thank you. I try." Trunk smiled.

"Don't get any more tattoos. Makes you look like a hoodlum." She shook her finger and then scurried out of sight.

Trunk chuckled in amusement as the doors closed. The lady reminded him of Keith's grandmother. Nanny Betty was a tiny woman, but she could make the biggest man bend to her will with just one look. She'd recently remarried, and the senior couple had just returned from their honeymoon.

Trunk's mother had become close to the O'Connors since she'd returned to St. John's. They included her in all the family get-togethers, and she'd become great friends with Keith's parents. He liked that her circle of friends started to grow when they moved to Corner Brook, but he'd noticed she was much more social since she returned. It made him happy to see it.

"Mom, I'm here," Trunk called out as he walked into the apartment.

Her soft voice floated out from the living room, but she wasn't responding to him. He didn't hear anyone else and assumed she was on the telephone. That meant two things, she didn't hear him, and they wouldn't be leaving right away. When Fatima Murphy was on a call, it was never less than an hour.

He waved to her as he stepped into the kitchen to grab himself a coffee. She always had a small pot ready for him when he came to chauffeur her around. There would always be a cookie next to the pot as well.

Trunk gazed out of the small window over the sink as he sipped the hot beverage and ate the sweet treat. A house across from the building looked a lot like the houses in Abbie's neighborhood. A knot formed in the pit of his stomach, as it always did when he thought about her.

More than six years had passed since he and Abbie had their one incredible night. She'd called him for weeks afterward, and it took all his strength not to run back to her. It wasn't easy, but from what he'd seen and heard, Abbie had moved on.

It killed him every single time he saw her and her man together, but it was for the best. Although it was hard to believe things would last with Chad. The guy wasn't her type. Chad always looked as if he stepped out of an issue of *GQ* magazine but something about him rubbed Trunk the wrong way.

A few months earlier, Billie introduced Trunk and Chad when Abbie dropped by the local pub in Hopedale. It was the first time he felt uncomfortable at *Jack's Place*. He knew Billie was trying to get a reaction, but Trunk forced a smile and shook the guy's hand. Trunk did get some satisfaction in the fact that Chad seemed intimidated.

That night, it was surprising he didn't crack half his teeth from clenching them. Every time Chad touched, kissed, or danced with Abbie, Trunk had to remind himself she wasn't his. It didn't stop the agony he felt seeing her with another man.

"Ben, your brother says hi." His mother's voice brought him out of his depressing thoughts.

Trunk entered the living room and dropped down on the couch. He propped his feet on the coffee table and held out his hand. As his mother placed the phone in his hand, she glared at him.

"What?" Trunk stared at his mother in confusion.

"Could you get your feet off my coffee table and stop falling on the couch like a big lump?" His mother stood up.

"Sorry, Mom." Trunk sighed as he pulled his feet off the table.

"Trouble as usual." Chris chuckled.

"Always. How are you doing?" Trunk asked.

"Hanging in there. I'm coming home at the end of the month," Chris told him.

"That's great. You need a break." Trunk was glad he would get the chance to spend time with his brother.

"It's for good, Ben. I can't stay here anymore. She's dating a guy on the alternate shift." Chris' voice cracked.

"One of the firefighters?" Trunk was stunned.

"Yeah, he's a dick and keeps making snide comments like, I wasn't man enough for her," Chris said.

Trunk could hear the irritation in his brother's voice. Chris and his ex had been together for years, and it seemed as if marriage was the next step. The last thing Trunk expected to hear was that she cheated on Chris.

"You need me to come up and beat his ass?" Trunk said partly joking.

"I can do that myself, but he's not worth it," Chris responded.

"It'll be great to have you home," Trunk admitted.

He missed his brother, but Chris needed to go on his own path. Trunk could use the extra family around to take his mother on her endless errands. The woman did more in a day then most people did in a week. Most of the time, she'd walk or get the bus, but since there was still a lot of snow around, he didn't want her walking and possibly slipping on ice.

"I have an extra room if you need a place to stay," Trunk told him.

"I was going to stay with Mom until I got a place, but I think it would be better to stay with you," Chris said.

"Yeah, can't bring women here." Trunk laughed.

"I'm afraid I won't be doing that for a while." Chris snorted.

"You'll get there," Trunk told his brother.

It was ironic that Trunk was encouraging his brother to move on when he couldn't do it himself. There was no doubt in his mind Chris would find someone else. His brother was a great guy.

An hour later, Trunk stopped at the third supermarket. His mother had a system for grocery shopping, and although it made sense to her, it annoyed Trunk. She'd go through every flyer she could find and make a list of what places she had to go for each list.

"Wait here. I have to pick up one thing here," she said as she hopped out of the car.

She might say one thing, but she tended to linger in grocery stores. Trunk was tired of waiting in the truck and decided he'd walk through the supermarket to stretch his legs.

Trunk rolled his eyes as his mother tossed another item in the basket that wasn't on her list. She strolled up and down each aisle, scanning the shelves for sales. The funny thing was, Trunk would end up with a bag of the groceries she picked up. She would never allow him to go home without something she'd bought that day.

"Ben, hand me two cans of those tomatoes up there." She pointed to a large can on the top shelf.

Trunk reached up but stopped when he heard his mother gasp. When he turned to see what was wrong, she'd gone ghostly white. Trunk immediately had his arm around her, but before he could ask her anything, another voice made his blood run cold.

"Aren't you a sight for sore eyes." The man smirked.

Trunk hadn't seen him since that terrible night, but he'd know Jerry's face anywhere. It didn't matter that he was sixty years old now and holding a cane, Jerry still had the glare that used to make Trunk tremble. Trunk instinctively pulled his mother closer to him.

"Jer... Jerry," his mother stammered.

"You're looking good, Fatima." Jerry smiled, but it seemed more sinister than friendly.

"What are you doing here?" Trunk's mother straightened her shoulders.

"I live around here. Isn't this guy awfully young for you?" Jerry glared at Trunk.

"Back off," Trunk snapped.

"Ben, don't." His mother laid her hand on his arm.

"Ben? Not whiney little Benji?" Jerry laughed.

"Why don't you keep walking?" Trunk guided his mother around the cart.

"Not even a hug for your old man?" Jerry blocked their escape.

Trunk stepped in front of his mom and glared down at the man who terrorized him as a kid. Jerry didn't seem so intimidating when Trunk towered over him, but it took every bit of restraint not to give Jerry a taste of what he deserved.

"I suggest you be on your way. I'm not the kid you used as a punching bag." Trunk hardly recognized his own voice, and he didn't like the way it sounded.

"Fatima, are you going to let him talk to his father like that?" Jerry asked Trunk's mother.

"Father? You don't deserve that title. As I said, I suggest you be on your way, Jerry," Trunk snapped.

"Still as disrespectful as ever. I guess the discipline stopped when I moved away." Jerry narrowed his eyes.

"Moved away?" Trunk scoffed. "You went to prison for killing a young girl and almost killing two others. Not to mention leaving your wife on the bathroom floor barely alive."

"Why was I out driving that day? Who was I looking for?" Jerry sneered.

"I'm not going to waste our time with the likes of you. Let's go, Mom." Trunk grabbed the end of the cart and guided his mother around Jerry.

She didn't say a word as they made their way to the cashier, and the silence was deafening on the drive back to her apartment. He'd placed the last bag on her couch when she spoke.

"It wasn't your fault, Ben," she whispered.

Trunk turned to see tears running down her cheeks. It broke his heart, and he pulled her into his arms. As his eyes closed, the memory of the day that haunted him came flooding back. Trunk always felt guilty for what happened.

Twenty-six years ago…

Benji and Christopher played catch in the backyard. At eleven, Benji was a year older than his brother. Christopher was trying out for a local little league team and asked Benji to help him practice.

Thankfully, they could relax for the day because their stepfather was supposed to work late. As a taxi driver, Jerry picked his own hours, and Friday, he usually worked late to make extra money, not that Benji's mother saw any of it. It was always Benji's favorite day of the week.

Benji didn't care as long as the man wasn't home. If Jerry was, it meant drinking, and one or all of them would become targets for his fists. Benji hated his stepfather and tried to prevent him from hurting his mother.

The last time Benji stood up to the man, he and Christopher had to hide in the attic. An old travel trunk became his safety from Jerry's thick belt. When Jerry stumbled out of the attic, Benji and Christopher discovered they were locked up in the dusty room. They were there a long time before his mother found them. She'd been frantic because Jerry told her they had run off and hadn't come home. She realized that he'd locked them in the attic and came to find them after Jerry passed out.

Benji knew Jerry wasn't his real dad, but Christopher didn't, and since their birth father was never around, Jerry became Dad. As much as Benji hated the man, he didn't want Christopher to know their father had run off.

"Do you think I'll make it on the team?" Christopher asked as he tossed the ball for the hundredth time.

"It's little league. Everyone makes it." Benji laughed as he tossed the ball back to his brother.

Christopher caught it and threw it back, but he tripped over a rock, and the ball flew over Benji's head. The sound of glass breaking caused him to turn around, and his eyes widened in horror. They could hear Jerry's voice through the broken window. Jerry must not have left for work, and that meant Christopher was in huge trouble. Benji ran up next to Christopher.

"I threw the ball, Christopher," Benji whispered and helped his brother to his feet.

"But…" Christopher tried to argue, but Benji stopped him.

"No, I can deal with the belt. Just tell him I threw the ball." Benji glanced toward the back door when it opened.

"Which one of you little bastards broke that?" Jerry stumbled down the steps.

He was drunk, which meant he'd be in no hurry to leave. He sneered as he walked toward Benji and Christopher. Without thinking, Benji pushed his brother behind him and faced the man he hated.

"I did," Benji shouted.

"You're paying for that." Jerry pulled off his belt as he staggered toward Benji.

"Get inside," Benji told his brother.

"No." Christopher's voice trembled.

"Get the fuck inside," Jerry shouted at Christopher.

Benji watched his brother run into the house and then turned to face Jerry. He knew the beating would hurt, but there was no way he'd let Christopher get beaten for an accident, but if Jerry wanted to hit him again, he would have to catch him.

"Turn around," Jerry snapped.

"No," Benji replied defiantly.

Jerry's face turned red, and he narrowed his eyes. He took two more steps toward Benji and reached for him. Benji turned and ran toward the broken fence at the back of the yard. He didn't know if he could get through the broken panel before Jerry reached him, but he would try.

"Get back here, you little fucker," Jerry shouted as Benji ran through the field behind the yard and out to the main road.

Benji glanced up and down as he tried to figure out where he could go. They had no other family, but he'd met a police officer at the store a few weeks earlier, and the man told Benji if he ever needed to talk, he could call him. The officer was related to the owner of the shop, so he knew he'd be able to contact him.

Benji was out of breath by the time he made it to the shop two blocks from his house. He'd heard Jerry's car rumble as he'd ran up the street doing his best to stay out of view. It wasn't hard to hear the car because it didn't have a muffler. When he heard it turn the corner, Benji crouched behind a truck.

The car took another turn onto a side street, and Benji made a run for the entrance to the convenience store. His hand was on the handle when he heard screeching tires and screaming.

Benji ran up to the corner and as he peeked around the house, he saw Jerry stagger away from the vehicle. The car had run into a house, and it looked like someone was laying on the hood. Benji gasped when he realized Jerry hit someone with his car.

"That bastard is drunk, grab him," a man shouted.

Benji backed away from the corner as two men grabbed his stepdad and knocked him to the ground. Benji swallowed hard as he sprinted back to his house. When Jerry got home, Benji knew he'd be in for the beating of his life.

Present day…

Trunk shook his head to clear the memory. His mother sobbed in his arms, and he needed to be strong for her the same way he'd been back then. The same way she'd been when she packed them up and started over in Corner Brook.

"I didn't think seeing him again would make me feel like this." She pulled back and wiped her hands across her cheeks.

"Mom, he's a piece of shit who doesn't deserve your tears." Trunk held her shoulders.

"He's your father, Ben," she chastised.

"No, he's not, Mom. He may have married you, and we had his name for a time, but I never considered him my father," Trunk admitted.

"He had a rough child…" she began, but Trunk stopped her.

"Mom, I love you, but you've got to stop making excuses for his violence. He beat you. Daily. He beat Chris and me if we so much as breathed the wrong way. The best thing that ever happened to us was the day they tossed that piece of trash in jail," Trunk said.

"It wasn't the best thing for that little girl he killed." She sighed.

Trunk didn't say another word. He pulled his mother in for another hug and swallowed the lump in his throat. She was right because it wasn't fair that Abbie should lose her sister. All because Trunk ran off to avoid a beating.

"How about we forget about all this, and I take you to *Jack's Place* for supper?" Trunk kissed the top of his mother's head.

Jack's Place was not just a pub. It was a combo diner as well. Keith's uncle Kurt and his wife, Alice, owned the establishment. It was a family place with great food and an incredible view.

"That sounds wonderful," his mother said softly.

Trunk helped her put away the items she bought, and then they made their way to Hopedale. His mother decided to spend the night at his house since she was still shaky from coming face-to-face with Jerry. Trunk was glad because he didn't want her to be alone after that encounter.

Trunk began to regret taking his mother to the tiny town where he'd chosen to live. Every time she entered his house, she would comment on what a lovely place he had, and all it needed was a woman's touch. She was less than subtle about how old he was getting and how he needed to find someone to make him happy.

"You aren't getting any younger, Ben," she reminded him.

"I know, Mom." Trunk sighed.

"You need to find a nice girl and settle down," she insisted.

Trunk didn't believe it was in his future, and he'd made peace with the fact he'd be a bachelor for the rest of his life. Of course, he'd had a couple of one-night stands since Abbie, but the women knew where they stood, and he wasn't looking for anything serious.

It was hard for him to imagine being with anyone forever. He'd seen it with Abbie, but when he found out the truth, that dream disappeared. He tried everything to get over his feelings for her and even begged Keith at one point to send him to another province so he wouldn't have to see her with Chad.

He'd never find anyone who ever meant as much to him as Abbie did, and that was his cross to bear. He loved her enough to let her find happiness with someone who could make her happy.

Chapter 6

Abbie sat across the table from Chad as he continued to brag about the large commission he'd gotten for the sale of a mansion. A commission that should have been hers because she was the licensed real estate agent.

It pissed her off that Chad didn't tell her one of his friends wanted to sell. One of his wealthy friends whose house was worth more money than she'd make in ten years. The commission would have kept her agency in the black for months, but here he was excited over his windfall. He'd even completed the sale from her laptop while he was at her house for supper.

She shouldn't begrudge him the luck, but if he cared about her, wouldn't he have given her the sale? He was getting a rather large paycheck from *Donovan's Commercial Development Corporation.* He always reminded her of how much money he made.

"So, he told me his friend was putting a house on the market too. It's a huge place, and the commission will be more than this one," Chad went on.

"Chad, can we talk about something else?" Abbie sighed.

"I'm sorry. I thought you'd be happy for me," Chad said as the waiter poured them another glass of water.

"I am, but I'd rather not talk about work." Abbie pushed the food around on her plate.

"Don't worry, darling. When we get married, you won't need to be concerned with your little agency," Chad said with a raised eyebrow.

"I'm sorry. What?" Abbie almost choked.

"You don't think you'll have to work after we're married, do you?" He seemed sickened by the idea.

"First of all, we aren't even engaged, and second of all, it doesn't matter if I'm married. I'm not closing my agency." Abbie tried to remain calm.

"Why would you work? I'll have enough money to support you." Chad glanced over her shoulder and waved to the waiter.

Abbie took several deep breaths before she responded. The truth was she wanted to tell him to go fuck himself, or punch him in the nose. Since she couldn't do that in the middle of a fancy restaurant, she opted to calm herself before she spoke.

"Chad, I'm an independent woman, and I'm not going to sit home like a good little wife. It's not the way I was raised, and it's not what I want." Abbie folded her hands on the table.

"Isn't what I want important?" Chad covered her hands with his.

It wasn't the first time since she'd started dating him that Abbie got an uneasy feeling from him. The truth was she was staying with him because she didn't want to be alone. Abbie also enjoyed the way Trunk reacted when he saw her with Chad. It was childish, but she wanted him to feel the pain she felt.

"No," Abbie replied.

"I won't have a wife of mine working," Chad returned.

He narrowed his eyes, and his lip curled up. His attempt at intimidation made him look more like he was constipated. Abbie couldn't hold it in any longer, and she burst into hysterical laughter.

"You're out of your fucking mind," Abbie scoffed as she pulled her hands from his.

"Please watch your language. It's not ladylike, and we're in public. There could be future clients here," Chad snapped.

"After more than a year together, you don't get me, do you?" Abbie shook her head as she stood up and pulled on her coat.

"Where are you going?" Chad demanded.

"Home. Goodbye, Chad." Abbie hoisted her purse onto her shoulder.

"I don't know what's wrong with you tonight. It must be a PMS thing, but you should go home and sleep off your mood. We'll discuss this tomorrow." Chad went back to his meal.

She would have laughed again, but it was hard when her blood felt as if it were boiling. She would never cause a scene in a place with so many people, and Chad was right about one thing, there could be future clients in the restaurant. Abbie knew a potential business contact could be anywhere. The last thing she needed was to cause an uproar around people who would recognize her from her ads.

Abbie used every ounce of restraint she had to not tip Chad over in his chair. She pulled a hundred-dollar bill out of her purse and leaned over the table until she was eye level with Chad.

"This is for my supper. I'm going to say this to you as calmly as I can, because right now, I'm about a hair away from breaking your nose. Don't call me. Don't come to my house. Don't email me. Don't text me. We. Are. Done. Why don't you go to the nineteen fifties and try to find a little woman for yourself? I'm certainly not her." Abbie tossed the hundred on top of his steak and turned away.

"It's not over yet," he called after her.

Abbie walked out with her head held high and felt like the weight of the world was off her shoulders. She'd spent far too many months trying to convince herself she and Chad would be happy together. She couldn't shed a tear over the end of the relationship because the truth was, she knew it wasn't going anywhere.

She pulled her keys and phone out of her purse on the way to her car. Abbie needed to talk to someone, and Billie was usually the ear she would bend at a time like this. She'd end up spending the night at Billie's place and drink way too much wine while she celebrated the end of her and Chad. The last thing she wanted was to go home alone. Abbie hated being by herself since the night Trunk walked out and left her.

She would never admit it, but that night meant more to her than she could ever say. It wasn't just the sex. It was the connection they made, laughing and sharing stories. He was the first man she ever told about the day Laurie died. She'd slept better that night than she had before or since.

"I was just a fuck to him, and I've got to keep reminding myself of that," Abbie muttered as she unlocked her car.

When she pulled open the door, an arm slipped around her neck. At first, she thought it might be Trunk, and her heart started to pound in her chest. That was until she got the scent of beer and body odor.

"This is payback," an unfamiliar male voice rasped in her ear.

Before she had a chance to respond, something sharp rammed into her side, and she gasped. Seconds later, he knocked her to the ground with such force her head bounced off the pavement.

Abbie tried to scream, but she couldn't get any air. When she tried to inhale, it was as if her lungs weren't working. Her mouth filled with blood as Abbie gasped for air. She felt like she was drowning, but before darkness engulfed her, she watched her car drive away.

"Help me, Ben," Abbie tried to shout but everything went black.

Chapter 7

Why did he bring his mother to a place where all the women were working together to get him to settle down? His mother was bad enough, but when she was in the company of Keith's mother, aunts, grandmother, and the rest of the women in the O'Connor family, it was like being swarmed.

To top it off, Keith's quirky Aunt Cora had him in her sights. They called her Cora the Cupid because she was supposed to have a gift for matchmaking. Trunk seemed to be her current target, and she believed Abbie was his destiny.

"As soon as that girl comes to her senses and realizes that stuck-up man isn't right for her, the sooner Ben can be with her," Cora said as she sipped her tea.

"I don't like that guy. He's such a pig, and he gives me the creeps," Billie interjected.

Trunk glanced at Mike, hoping for some backup, but the asshole shrugged as he wrapped his arm around Billie. While the women went on about how wrong Chad was for Abbie, Trunk had the urge to agree, but it would give the women more ammunition. Any fool could tell Chad was not the guy for Abbie, but neither was Trunk.

No matter how much he loved her, there was no way they could be together. His mother hadn't made the connection with Abbie's last name, and he thought about telling her, but it would bring back bad memories.

Twenty-six years ago…

Benji ran into the house and frantically searched for his mother and brother. They needed to know what Jerry did before he returned home. Benji knew his stepfather would be furious and that anger would be taken out on them.

"Mom, Christopher?" Benji shouted.

When he didn't get an answer, he ran upstairs to the bedroom, bellowing even louder. He was about to run next door when he heard Christopher crying in the bathroom.

Benji pushed open the door and found Christopher with tears streaming down his cheeks. When he turned to the bathtub, he saw his mother's motionless body on the floor. Her face was bruised and bloody while her clothes were torn and barely covered her naked body.

"I think she's dead." Christopher sobbed.

"No, she's not," Benji yelled and ran out of the bathroom.

They didn't have a phone, and the only person he trusted was the lady next door. She and her husband often took Christopher and Benji inside when Jerry was on a rampage.

"Mrs. Maher, Mrs. Maher." Benji pounded on his neighbor's door.

"Heavens, Benji. What's wrong?" The older woman pulled him into her arms.

"It's Mom. She's hurt really bad." Benji tried to keep the tears from falling, but it was no use.

"Ambrose, come quick," she called behind her.

"What is it?" Ambrose asked.

"Go next door and see what that monster has done now." She pulled Benji into the house. "Where's your brother?"

"He's with Mom. Please help her," Benji begged Ambrose.

"You go inside with Bridget and don't open that door for anyone but me," he told them. "Call the police, honey."

With those words, Ambrose ran to Benji's house. It seemed to take forever for him to return with Christopher, but he did and then left again. Benji sat on the sofa next to his brother in silence while Bridget talked to the police.

Benji waited for someone to tell him their mother was dead. He didn't want to upset his brother, but he believed this time Jerry killed her. He was scared of what would happen to him and his brother.

"Benji, Christopher, this is Constable Simms." Bridget sat next to them.

"You can call me Paul." The man crouched in front of them.

Christopher pulled his legs up and wrapped his arms around them, but Benji sat up straight and looked the friendly officer in the eyes. He had to be brave for his brother.

"You're Benji, right?" Paul asked.

Benji nodded as Paul shook his hand like grownups did. The officer glanced at Christopher and then back at Benji.

"Would you mind if I ask both of you some questions?" Paul asked.

"You can ask me," Benji told him.

"That's good, but before we start, I wanted to let you know something," he said.

"You don't need to tell us. Our mom is dead," Benji whispered.

"No, she's not, buddy. She's hurt, but she asked me to make sure you both were safe." Paul smiled at Benji.

"She's not dead?" Christopher lifted his head for the first time since the officer arrived.

"No, pal, but I still have some questions." Paul took off his cap and placed it on the floor.

Benji and Christopher nodded.

"Do you know who did this to your mother?" Paul asked.

"It was Dad," Christopher whispered.

"Do you know where he is?" Paul glanced at Bridget.

"I haven't seen him." Bridget shook her head.

"I know where he is," Benji told them.

"You do?" Bridget seemed surprised.

"He was looking for me because I broke a window with a ball." Benji started, but Christopher stopped him.

"Benji didn't break the window, I did, but he wanted me to say he did it. Dad was mad and took off his belt…" Christopher stopped.

"Did he spank you, Benji?" Paul asked.

"No. I ran away. I was going to the store to find the policeman I saw there before. He said if I needed help to let the guy at the store know. They're brothers." Benji sat up straight.

"I know them. The Parkers own that store, and I work with Conrad." Paul nodded.

"He was nice." Benji dropped his head.

"Both he and I have sons about your age," Paul told him.

Benji wanted to ask if he used a belt on his son, but he had a feeling Jerry was the only one who did it. He'd asked one of his friends at school about being hit, and after the boy gave him a weird look, Benji knew his life was different.

"You said you knew where your dad was," Paul pushed.

"He was in his car, and he was drunk again. I think he hit someone..." Benji's words stopped when another police officer ran into the room.

"We got him. A unit arrested him on Gilbert Street. He hit some kids with his car," the officer told Paul.

Paul didn't say anything as he pulled the police officer aside, and they spoke quietly. Bridget pulled Christopher onto her lap and Benji into her side. It made Benji feel better to know that Jerry had been arrested and his mother was okay, but he was still afraid of what would happen to him and his brother.

When Ambrose entered the room a while later, he said something to Paul. Benji had no idea where they were going to go, but there was no way they were splitting up him and Christopher.

"It's okay, boys. Everything will be okay." Bridget hugged them.

Paul and Ambrose walked toward the sofa. Ambrose sat down next to Benji and Paul sat on the coffee table.

"How would you boys like to stay with your friends here for a few days?" Paul asked.

"What about Mom?" Christopher's voice cracked.

"Your mom will be in the hospital for a while, but she told Mr. Maher you could stay with them until she's home." Paul smiled.

"What about Dad?" Benji didn't care, but he also didn't want his stepfather to come back and take them away from the Mahers.

"He won't hurt you or your mom again." Ambrose sounded angry but it didn't scare Benji.

"Is he dead?" Benji gasped.

"No, buddy. He's going to jail. He hurt your mom, and he hit some little girls with his car," Paul said.

"I hope I never see him again," Benji murmured to himself.

Present day...

"Trunk, are you okay?" Mike seemed to be the only one who noticed Trunk had drifted off into his painful memories again.

"What? Oh. Yeah. Just off in my own world." Trunk forced a smile.

"Do you need anything?" Sandy asked.

Sandy, Keith, and Ian knew about Abbie's sister and who killed her. He could trust them, which was why he didn't worry about his secret slipping to Abbie or anyone else.

"Ya needs Abbie, dats wat ya needs," Nanny Betty said in her Irish-Newfoundland accent.

Alice had placed a large table at the back of the diner half of *Jack's Place*, and it was where the family would sit. The table seemed to grow every year. The O'Connors didn't care if someone was family or not, because they welcomed everyone with open arms.

"Nan, that's enough." Keith met Trunk's eyes.

"She's not wrong," Trunk's mother said.

"I'm never wrong," Cora reminded everyone.

"How long more does Pam have to go before the twins are born?" Trunk asked Cora.

Cora's daughter, Pam, got married in the early part of March. She and her husband wanted to be married before she delivered in May, but nobody knew she was having twins until they announced it on her wedding day. The last time he'd seen her, she looked ready to pop.

"I thought she would go early, but the babies are still inside, and she has three weeks to go." Cora smiled.

"Nice distraction, Ben." Billie smirked.

Most of the women in Keith's family refused to call any of the guys who worked for *NES* by their nicknames. Sandy was the only one who did, but that was probably because she'd worked with them for so long. Sandy also had another nickname for Trunk and

Bull when they pissed her off. She referred to them as Chrome Dome because Bull was bald, and Trunk had started shaving his head over the last couple of years.

"You didn't think that worked, did you?" Cora chuckled. "I just love talking about my grandbabies."

None of them would let it go. As much as Trunk hated the thought of Abbie with that stuck-up ass-wipe, it was better for her. Trunk would have to get used to the gut-wrenching pain knowing she was not his.

Billie was interrupted by the soft music coming from her phone. She hopped up from the table to answer, because with all the chatter at the table, she'd never hear whoever was on the other end of the call. Trunk didn't think anything odd since she was a real estate agent, and he'd seen Abbie get calls at all hours of the day and night.

Trunk relaxed as he listened to the din of the conversation of the people he'd grown to love. They discussed their plans for the summer and throwing sweet sixteen parties for Sandy and Ian's two oldest girls.

"I can't believe they're both going to be sixteen this year." Kathleen shook her head.

"I asked if they wanted two separate parties because Evie's birthday is in July, and Lily's isn't until September, but they split the

difference and want to have a big party on Ian's birthday in August."
Sandy shrugged.

"So, they want to make their father miserable on his birthday
by flaunting the fact they aren't little girls anymore. Happy Birthday,
Ian." Keith chuckled.

"Sounds about right," Sandy returned.

Trunk glanced toward Billie and noticed her face had gone
pasty white. Her eyes were wide, and she was waving her hands
anxiously. It wasn't like her, which meant something was wrong.

"Mike." Trunk tapped his friend on the shoulder and pointed
toward Billie.

In seconds Trunk, Keith, and Mike surrounded the frantic
woman as she ended the call. She dropped her phone on the counter
and immediately fell into Mike's arms, sobbing hysterically. They
couldn't understand what she was saying, but Trunk tensed when he
heard Abbie's name.

"Baby, you've got to calm down and tell us what happened."
Mike kissed her forehead.

"Abbie... she... she's in the hospital... she was... she's
hurt... someone stabbed her," Billie cried.

"What?" Trunk's body stiffened, and his heart thundered in
his chest.

"Explain on the way." Mike wrapped his arm around his wife as Keith hurried to the table to fill everyone in.

"I'll get Mom to take Fatima back to my parents' place," Keith said.

"I'll drive," Trunk said as he stalked ahead of Mike and Billie.

Trunk was back in the same place where he first met Abbie. This time, they were waiting in a room for news on whether Abbie would make it out of surgery. It hurt to know she was with another man, but at least she was still alive. If she didn't make it through this surgery, Trunk would not survive the pain.

He listened while the police explained everything they knew to Abbie's parents. His blood ran cold when they said someone attacked her from behind. Whoever hurt her stole her car, her phone, all the jewelry she wore, and they left her in the middle of the parking lot to die.

The more Trunk discovered about the attack, the more enraged he became. He prayed the police found the bastard who hurt her before he did. If he got to the prick first, the guy wouldn't make it to prison.

"We can't lose her. I won't survive losing another child." Abbie's mother sobbed.

Trunk met Claire and Darren Martin when he was Abbie's security. Darren wasn't a big man, but he'd definitely kill someone who hurt his daughter. Trunk would help the man when they found out who did this to Abbie.

"Are you okay, Ben?" Billie whispered next to him.

"I'm fine," Trunk lied. "Are you okay?"

"I know how you feel about her, and I'll be fine when they let us know how she is." Billie's voice cracked.

Trunk swallowed hard as a tear ran down her cheek. He wrapped his arm around her shoulder and gave her a comforting hug. It took everything he had to keep his fear hidden so he wouldn't upset Abbie's family and friends.

"She'll be fine. She's as tough as nails." Trunk hoped he sounded more confident than he felt.

The truth was, he was scared to death. From what he'd overheard, Abbie lost a lot of blood, the knife had nicked her lung, and when she hit the ground, she cracked her head on the pavement.

"Has anyone called to see what's taking Chad so long?" Dana asked.

Dana was the one who called Billie and was with Abbie's parents when Trunk arrived at the hospital. As a nurse, Dana knew more than anyone how critical Abbie's condition was. She seemed to be doing her best to keep everyone updated, but Trunk could see the concern in her eyes.

"Leave that SOB where he is. The last person I want here is that conceited piece of shit." Darren snapped.

"Darren, he's her boyfriend." Claire sighed.

"Then why the fuck was he not with her? That prick let her walk to the car alone." Darren's voice echoed in the small waiting room.

"What do you mean?" Trunk found it hard to get his head around the idea of Chad not walking Abbie to her car at night.

"Abbie told us they were having supper at that overpriced pretentious restaurant where all the snobs go. The place on Water Street," Darren told them.

"You mean, *Maison De Vaisselle*?" Billie asked.

"Yes," Darren replied.

"I don't get the name, it's French, but in English, it means house of dishes." Dana shook her head.

"Should be called the house of overpriced food," Darren scoffed.

"Does he know what happened?" Mike asked.

"He called us to let us know she was attacked and was in the ambulance on the way to the hospital. We haven't seen or heard from him since, and that was over two hours ago." Claire sniffed.

"He's a selfish bastard, and I wish she would throw him to the curb. Tattoo boy would be better for her than that idiot." Darren motioned toward Trunk.

"She'd be with tattoo boy if he would get his head out of his ass," Dana whispered.

"Don't start." Trunk muttered.

"Then tell me why you left that night." Dana narrowed her eyes at him.

"That was a lifetime ago. It was better to stop it before it went too far," Trunk stated with a matter of fact tone.

"How much further could you go? You slept with her." Dana snorted.

"This is not the time or place to discuss any of this," Trunk reminded her.

"You're right." Dana sighed and turned away from him.

Trunk couldn't blame Dana for being pissed with him. He'd treated her friend like a one-night stand, and Abbie was so much more to him. One glance at her, and she'd make his day brighter, but that was all he could ever have with her, and it had to be enough.

It was over four hours before the doctor came to get Abbie's parents. She'd made it through the surgery, but there was some slight swelling where she injured her head. They said they wouldn't know anything about the damage until she regained consciousness.

Billie asked Keith to assign someone to Abbie until the police apprehended Abbie's attacker. Law enforcement seemed to think it was a mugging gone wrong, but Trunk couldn't shake the feeling it was more than that.

"I trust him. He kept our daughter safe before." Claire pointed to Trunk.

"I don't think Trunk is the one to put on this…" Keith began.

"It's Trunk, or it's Trunk. My wife trusts him. If he won't do it then we'll find another company," Darren interrupted.

Keith glanced at Trunk and raised an eyebrow as if asking him if he wanted to do it. It was obvious Trunk avoided Abbie as much as possible, but it would be a form of torture to spend every day with her again. He knew all the men who worked for *NES* were qualified, trustworthy, and would protect Abbie with their lives.

"I'll do it," Trunk said without hesitation.

"Good. I want you by her side until they find this son of a bitch." Darren shook his finger in Trunk's face.

"I'll protect her with my life," Trunk promised.

Darren insisted Keith send the invoice for the services as soon as possible. When Keith assured him Abbie was family, Darren wouldn't hear of it. Abbie's father made it clear that he could afford to pay for his daughter's protection.

"I'll send it." Keith nodded.

"You better." Darren left the waiting room and headed into the intensive care unit where Abbie was recovering.

By four in the morning, Trunk was the only person left with Abbie. At first, the unit said he couldn't stay all night, but when Darren explained the situation and Keith's father arrived to speak with the administration, Trunk was given a comfy chair, and they moved Abbie into a private ICU room. Keith's father being the well-respected Dr. Sean O'Connor had come in handy.

Trunk's stomach was in knots as he watched Abbie's chest rise and fall with the soft whoosh of the ventilator. She was pale, and with so much equipment attached to her, he didn't know how she could be comfortable, especially with the tube down her throat.

"She's doing well," an older nurse told him as she checked Abbie's vitals.

"Her family will be relieved to hear that," Trunk said without looking away from Abbie's face.

"I'm sure it makes you feel better as well." The nurse reminded him of his mother.

"I'm simply here for security." Trunk smiled.

"Honey, no man looks at a woman like that unless she owns his heart." The nurse touched his shoulder.

"I…" Trunk started to speak.

"Talk to her. I believe they hear everything around them."
The nurse walked out, leaving him alone with Abbie.

Trunk turned his attention back to the woman lying motionless in the bed. She did own his heart, but if telling her how he felt while she was unconscious would help her recover, he'd do it.

"You've got to come out of this, Abs. I can't live in a world that you aren't in. We might not be able to be together, but knowing you're out there living your life makes me happy. I'm saying this because I know you won't remember, but I love you more than my own life. I love you so much that I let you go so you can find someone who could make you happy. By the way, you need to keep looking. That piece of shit you're with now hasn't even come here to see you. So, get better so you can dump his ass," Trunk whispered the words into her ear.

Two days of agony followed as they waited for the doctors to decide when to remove the respirator. Before they could do that, they had to wean her off the medication that was keeping her unconscious. Her parents sat on one side of the bed and Trunk on the other as they waited for Abbie to wake up.

"It'll take a little while before you see any signs of her coming out of the sedation," the doctor told them as he checked Abbie's surgical site.

"I thought you would take out the respirator before she woke up." Claire seemed ready to burst into tears at any moment.

"No, she needs to be somewhat alert when we remove it. That way it's easier to see if she can handle breathing on her own," the doctor explained.

Almost thirty minutes later, Abbie began to stir. Her eyes fluttered open, and at first, she seemed panicked. Her father shot to his feet and held Abbie's hand before she pulled all the medical equipment out.

"Shh, Monkey," Darren whispered. "You're fine. This stuff is to help you get better."

Abbie's eyes flicked back and forth between her parents, then her eyes locked on Trunk. He was surprised when she motioned for him to come closer. When he did, Abbie grasped his hand and pointed to the tube in her mouth.

"The doctor is coming in to take it out soon. You need to calm down, Abs," Trunk whispered softly.

Abbie nodded, and her body relaxed, but she kept a tight hold on Trunk's hand. She began to make signs with her hands and got frustrated when they couldn't understand her.

Trunk recognized it as sign language because he'd seen Billie communicate with her niece that way. He never understood what they said, but it was obvious Abbie was trying to communicate with it. Billie, Mike, Abbie, Dana, and Billie's family all knew how to sign. None of it made sense to Trunk, and from the looks on her parents' faces, they didn't understand it either.

"I have no idea what you're saying, Abs. It won't be long, and you'll be able to talk again." Trunk smiled.

There was something odd in the way she gazed up at him. Abbie hadn't looked at him with such affection since their one night together. In the last six-plus years, she gave him two types of looks, detest and hurt. She had to be still groggy from the medication, but he'd enjoy it until she was herself again.

Trunk had a feeling it would change when Chad showed up to see her. The asshole called Claire a couple of times to find out Abbie's condition, but when Claire asked if he was coming to see her, Chad said he got tied up with some business that he couldn't put off. He promised to be by before Abbie woke up, but it looked like that didn't happen.

Before they removed the tube from Abbie's throat, they turned off the respirator. They had to make sure she could breathe on her own before they disconnected her.

A short while later, Abbie gripped Trunk's hand. It was difficult to watch the nurse pull the long tube from Abbie's throat, but even though Abbie gagged, she remained calm. Once the tube was gone, her grip on Trunk's hand eased.

"I'm going to get you to take a couple of breaths on your own while I listen to your lungs," the doctor told her as he placed his stethoscope on Abbie's chest.

The doctor listened intently, and after several minutes, he seemed satisfied with what he heard. When the doctor left, Abbie's parents followed, asking questions about what to do next. It left Trunk alone with Abbie gripping his hand as if she needed it to live.

"It's good to see those beautiful green eyes again." Trunk smiled down at her.

"How did I get here? It must have been some night we had. Why are you bald?" Abbie's voice was raspy, and she stared at him with narrowed eyes.

"Abs, you were stabbed outside the restaurant," Trunk explained, but her question about his shaved head confused him.

Abbie had seen his bald head many times but with the way she was studying him, it seemed as if she was looking at it for the first time. Her eyes darted back and forth as if she was searching for the memory. She winced when she lifted her head, and Trunk explained how she hit it when she fell.

"I don't remember going to a restaurant. The last thing I remember is…" Her words stopped when a commotion started outside her room.

Abbie's eyes widened, but Trunk assured her he'd see what was going on and be back. At first, it didn't seem as if she would release his hand, but when he brought her hand to his lips and kissed it, she let him go.

"What do you mean I can't go inside?" Chad's voice sounded like nails on a chalkboard to Trunk.

"I'm sorry, sir, but Ms. Martin has a restricted list of visitors, and your name is not on it. This is a secure patient and all visitors have to be cleared. It's why when I saw you at the door, I stopped you," the male nurse told Chad.

"I can't see why I wouldn't be on the list. I'm her boyfriend, for Christ's sake. As a matter of fact, we got engaged the night she was mugged," Chad spat.

Trunk stepped next to the nurse and glanced around for Abbie's parents. They seemed to have disappeared, and they might not want Chad to see Abbie. If it were up to Trunk, he'd have tossed the bastard out a window, but if what he said was true, it meant Abbie was engaged.

"What's going on here?" Trunk asked.

"What are you doing here?" Chad sneered.

"He's Ms. Martin's security detail," the nurse explained.

"Why does she need security? She was mugged by some low life who is more than likely out of the province by now," Chad scoffed.

"Her parents don't believe that," Trunk responded.

"She must not have had a chance to tell them we were engaged." Chad glared at Trunk.

"They didn't know since it took you three days to come to see her," Trunk returned.

"I don't need to explain myself to you. I want to see Abbie." Chad tried to go into the room, but before Trunk could stop him, the nurse immediately stopped the irritated man.

"What you want and what you get are two different things. Until Ms. Martin's parents say it's okay, you won't be going through this door." The nurse crossed his massive arms and glared down at Chad.

Trunk wanted to pat the guy on the back, but instead, he mirrored the nurse's stance and glared at Chad. After a few seconds, Chad spun around, mumbling something about heads rolling as he pulled out his phone.

"You can't use your phone in here," the nurse called after Chad.

Trunk almost laughed as the arrogant bastard stomped out of the ICU. Claire and Darren wouldn't be happy with Chad visiting. Especially since Abbie's dad was so furious that the asshole didn't walk Abbie to her car. Then there was the fact that he hadn't taken the time to come see the woman he supposedly cared about.

"I caught him listening at the door. That guy is a huge douche." The nurse shook his head.

"You said it." Trunk chuckled.

"I hope I wasn't out of line." The man turned to face Trunk.

99

"Not at all. Thanks." Trunk held out his hand.

"It's in my blood. I'm former military, but after an IED took part of my foot, I had to change careers," the nurse explained.

"Thank you for your sacrifice." Trunk had great respect for military veterans.

"If you need anything else, I'm here until midnight. Just ask for Justin Bishop." He shook Trunk's hand.

"Thank you, Justin. I'm Ben Murphy, but everyone calls me Trunk," he told Justin.

"Trunk? I guess there's a story there. Everyone usually calls me Bish, so if you're looking, they'll know me by that name too." Justin nodded and returned to the nurse's station.

When he returned to her room, Trunk found Abbie looking at the bandage covering her side. She looked up when he stepped next to the bed and pointed to her stomach.

"Am I gonna have a scar?" Abbie whispered.

"You're alive. I don't care if you have a hundred scars." He smiled.

"I guess it'll be a while before we can take a tumble again." Abbie laid her head back on the pillow and gave him a cocky grin.

Before he could respond, Abbie's parents stepped into the room. From the expressions on their faces, they both were not happy. Claire seemed completely flustered, but Darren looked pissed.

Trunk was about to ask what was wrong, but the problem walked in behind Darren with a huge smile. It made Trunk want to punch Chad in the face because it was one of those looks that said, I won.

It wasn't the fact that Chad had gotten his way that made Trunk uneasy, it was the way Abbie stared at the man. Something wasn't right but before Trunk could voice his concern, Chad turned on the charm.

"I'm so happy to see you." Chad hurried to Abbie's side and reached for her hand.

Abbie pulled away and grabbed for Trunk's arm. Chad didn't seem to notice the reaction and when he leaned down to kiss her, Abbie shoved him hard. She glanced at Trunk but when she turned back to Chad and spoke, she surprised everyone.

"Who the hell are you?" Abbie asked.

Chapter 8

Abbie was confused about why some strange man tried to kiss her as if they knew each other. The guy wasn't her type and looked like the assholes she avoided. Besides, she was head-over-heels for Trunk, and since they had made love, she didn't want to lose him.

"What do you mean? Who am I?" The man seemed hurt.

Abbie glanced at her parents, but they looked puzzled by Abbie's reaction. She turned to Trunk, and he seemed just as concerned. Abbie turned to the preppy snob and shook her head.

"I don't know you," Abbie said.

"Abs, are you sure you don't know him?" Trunk leaned forward.

"Yes, I'm sure. How would I know someone I never met?" Abbie rolled her eyes.

"Abbie, he's your boyfriend." Her mother sat on the foot of the bed and gently touched Abbie's leg.

"Fiancé." The preppy man grinned as if he'd just told her something that would make her happy.

"I'm sorry, what?" Her father roared.

Abbie knew by her father's narrowed eyes he didn't like the man, and she didn't either. He seemed much too smug, and something about the way he looked at her made her uncomfortable.

"I proposed the night at the restaurant, and she said yes," the man said proudly.

"You proposed to my daughter without talking to me first and then let her walk to her car alone at night? You're a fucking asshole." Her father gripped the foot of the bed.

"Chad, you should have talked to us first. That's disrespectful," her mother replied.

"For God's sake, it's the twenty-first century." The man rolled his eyes.

Before Abbie could say a word, her father was around the foot of the bed and fisted the front of Chad's expensive suit. Her dad's face was red, and all she saw was pure rage. Abbie's mouth dropped open because she'd never seen her father act that way before.

"Darren, stop it," her mother ordered.

"You egotistical piece of shit. How dare you talk to me and my wife like that." Her father was pissed, and Abbie turned to Trunk.

Trunk looked furious, but there was something else she couldn't quite put her finger on. Abbie didn't know what the hell was going on, and her side hurt, not to mention her head pounded like a thousand hammers were knocking inside her skull.

"Okay, everyone out. Now." A huge man in scrubs stepped into the room.

"I'm not going anywhere," Chad snapped.

"You can leave this room on your own, or Trunk and I will physically remove you." The nurse narrowed his eyes and glared at Chad.

"Okay. Everyone, stop," Abbie tried to shout, but it was difficult because her throat was still sore from the ventilator.

Everyone turned, and the room was suddenly silent. Abbie's father still had Chad by the jacket and looked as if he could kill the man. Abbie felt sick to her stomach, and everything started to spin around her. She squeezed her eyes shut for a second then opened them again.

"First of all, Dad, let the guy go." Abbie pointed at her father.

"But..." her father began.

"Darren, let him go," her mother said.

Her father released Chad with a small shove and stepped next to her mother. Abbie glanced around the room and tried to will someone to tell her what the hell was going on. When nobody said anything, Abbie turned to Chad.

"Now, I've got no idea who the hell you are and what makes you think I ever agreed to marry you, but you need to go see a doctor about that," Abbie told Chad.

"Abs, you don't know him?" Trunk crouched next to her bed.

"I'm pretty sure I'd remember if I met this guy." Abbie hitched her thumb toward Chad.

"Monkey, what's the last thing you do remember?" her father asked.

Abbie felt the heat rise in her cheeks as she glanced at Trunk. The truth was the last thing she remembered was snuggling next to him after a night of incredible sex.

"Leaving Kathleen and Sean's house." Abbie glanced at Trunk.

"What were you doing there?" her father asked.

"Dad, they caught the guy who was after Billie. We were celebrating." Abbie said.

"Abbie, that was nearly seven years ago," her mother said softly.

Abbie stared at her mother as if the woman had lost her mind. She wasn't sure what everyone was trying to do, but none of it was funny. She waited for someone to crack a smile and tell her it was all a joke, but every face in the room showed nothing but concern. Except for Chad, he looked annoyed.

"Not funny, Mom." Abbie tried not to sound frightened.

"She's not joking, Abs." Trunk held up his cell phone and pointed to the date.

Abbie stared at it as if she was looking at something in another language. If that was right, then why didn't she remember anything since the night she was with Trunk. It also meant she and Trunk were not together. What happened between them?

"Why don't I remember…" Abbie found it hard to get air in her lungs.

The nurse ran next to the bed and pushed Chad out of the way. The man spoke to her calmly, and Abbie tried to focus on him. It was so hard to breathe, and she felt light-headed.

"Find something to focus on and breathe, Abbie," the nurse said.

"Listen to Justin, Abs. Slow your breathing." Trunk held her hand between his, and she focused on his eyes.

"That's right, Abbie. In through your nose and out through your mouth. Slowly," Justin said.

"This is bullshit," Chad grumbled but stepped away quickly when Trunk glared at him over Justin's shoulder.

"Good." Justin seemed to be completely focused on her and ignoring the situation around him.

How could this be true? If it was, she was missing almost seven years of her life. She glanced over Justin's shoulder at Chad and didn't see anything familiar. She didn't understand how she could be engaged to the man when she was so in love with Trunk.

Chad was handsome enough, but he was the type of guy she would wine and dine to get a sale, not date. He looked like many of her clients, and Abbie never mixed her business with dating.

"That's better." Justin smiled as her breathing returned to normal.

"You have to take it easy, Abs." Trunk held her hand.

"I'm going to have to ask everyone to leave. It's almost quiet time anyway, and I'm going to get the doctor to come see if we can figure out what's happening with the memory loss." Justin turned to her parents and Chad.

"I'm not going anywhere." Chad straightened his shoulders.

"Look here, buddy, I may be a nurse here, but I don't have any trouble grabbing you by the neck and dragging you out." Justin's voice was low and lethal.

It reminded her of Trunk when he was in protective mode. Justin was shorter than Trunk but didn't lack muscle, and she could picture him tossing Chad out. Considering what an ass Chad was, it was something she'd love to see.

"You're going to let him talk to me like this, Abbie?" Chad narrowed his eyes at her.

"I'd help him if I could," Abbie snapped.

"How can you not remember me?" Chad tossed his hands in the air.

Abbie didn't know what to say to the man. Of all the things she didn't remember, he was the last thing she was concerned about forgetting. He must be a nice guy if she agreed to marry him, but Abbie didn't know how she could be so involved with him when her heart belonged to Trunk.

"Why does he get to stay?" Chad complained as he pointed at Trunk.

"He's here to keep her safe," her father shouted as he pushed Chad through the door.

"We're going home to get something to eat. We'll be back after supper, and I promise I'll get your father to calm down." Her mother kissed the top of Abbie's head and stepped back.

"I love you, Monkey. I'm sorry I upset you." Her father pressed his lips against her forehead then stepped back. "Keep that piece of trash out of here."

"He won't get inside the door," Justin answered before Trunk could.

Abbie stared at the door as it closed, leaving her alone with Trunk. She couldn't comprehend what happened. He touched her hand, and she turned to gaze up at him.

"What happened between us?" Abbie whispered as she stared at their joined hands.

"It's complicated, Abs." Trunk released her hand and walked to the window.

"Complicated? Complicated? Are you fucking kidding me?" Abbie tried to shout, but her voice cracked.

Trunk didn't turn around, but he dropped his head, and the muscles in his back and shoulders tensed. She needed to know what happened because nothing could be bad enough to make her run into the arms of an arrogant jerk.

"Ben, please." Abbie swallowed the lump forming in her throat.

Trunk turned around and leaned against the window ledge. His dark eyes glistened with tears, and she suddenly wondered if she really wanted to know why they weren't together. He seemed agonized by whatever broke them apart.

"Abs, it just didn't work out," Trunk whispered.

"Bullshit. Tell me the truth," Abbie demanded.

"This isn't the time to talk about this. You need to rest." Trunk smiled.

Trunk had a smile that made her weak in the knees, and with his new look, he was sexier. If that was even possible. She didn't return his smile because she knew he wasn't telling her the truth. She needed to know what happened.

"Stop trying to handle me. Was I just a one-night fuck?" Abbie retorted.

"No, you weren't." Trunk practically jumped from the window to the side of her bed.

He cupped her face, and his touch made her forget her irritation, not to mention it helped ease the nagging pain in her head. The heat from his hands was soothing and relaxing, but she still wanted to know everything.

"Tell me what happened during my missing years to break us apart," Abbie begged.

Trunk gazed into her eyes, and it was obvious he had some sort of internal struggle going on. Did he cheat on her? Did she screw around on him? *No.* There was no way she would ever do that, and he wouldn't either.

"Ben, I need to know," she whispered.

"I can't say no to you." He pulled a chair close to the side of the bed and pulled out his phone.

"You're not supposed to use that in here," she told him.

"Before we talk, I need to make sure someone is here to take over for me," Trunk replied.

Abbie didn't respond. It had to be awful if he believed she would kick him out once she knew the truth. It was tough to think of anything that would turn her against him. She'd fallen for him harder than any man she'd ever met.

"Rusty, I need you to send someone over here to take over for me." Trunk always called Keith by his nickname.

All the men who worked with Trunk and Keith never used their given names. She didn't know why, but it usually had something to do with something they did or how they looked. Keith was Rusty because of his auburn hair.

"She doesn't remember anything since the night we were together. I need to tell her what happened and why I left that night." Trunk met her eyes as he explained things to Keith.

"That night?" Abbie narrowed her eyes.

"I will. Thanks, Rusty." Trunk tucked his phone back into his back pocket and dropped his head.

"You left after we spent practically two days in bed together?" Abbie tried not to sound crushed, but her heart hurt.

"Yes." Trunk wouldn't look at her.

"Ben," Abbie shouted as much as she could.

"I left because I didn't want you hating me." Trunk lifted his head and met her eyes.

"You thought fucking me and then leaving would make me happy? Are you kidding?" Abbie's head was pounding, but she fought it.

"Abs, this is worse." Trunk linked his fingers and rested them on the top of his head.

"Is this the reason you started shaving your head?" Abbie asked.

"No, that started because my hair was thinning." Trunk chuckled.

"Ben, tell me," Abbie begged.

"Do you remember telling me about your sister?" Trunk asked.

"Yes, but what does that have to do with anything?" Abbie pressed her fingers against her temples.

"Abs, you're in pain. Why don't we talk about this later?" Trunk stood up and headed to the door.

"For Christ's sake, will you just tell me? All this running around the subject is making my head want to explode," Abbie snapped.

"Why do you have to be so fucking stubborn?" Trunk sighed.

Trunk stopped, and for several seconds, he stood with his back to her. Why was this so hard for him? He didn't even know her sister. What could her sister's death have to do with her and Trunk?

Chapter 9

Trunk's gut felt as if it was flipping inside. How could he tell the woman who owned his heart her sister was dead because of his stepfather? It made him sick to think about how she would look at him when she found out. The problem was Abbie wasn't going to let it go.

"Up until I was eleven, I lived on Atlantic Avenue here in St. John's," Trunk began.

Since the street was two blocks from where Abbie grew up, he figured she would know the address. Most of the people in that area of town shopped in the same stores and went to the same schools.

"That's not far from where I grew up." Abbie tilted her head. "But you knew that, didn't you?"

"I did," Trunk admitted.

"But you moved to Corner Brook when you were a kid. I remember you telling me that." Abbie winced when she changed position in the bed.

"Abs, please just get some rest, we'll talk about this when you're up to it." Trunk hated to see her in pain.

"You're pissing me off," Abbie grumbled.

"You're so fucking stubborn." Trunk sighed.

Abbie glared at him as he stepped next to the bed and sat in the chair. Before he said another word, his phone vibrated. He pulled it out and saw a message from Hulk.

Hulk was a close friend and going through his own romantic hell. Hulk was in love with a woman who was living in his house, but she thought she was renting from Trunk. Hulk asked him to go along with the ruse because Caroline wouldn't like the fact Hulk moved into a bunkhouse so she, her mother, and two children would have a safe place to live.

Hulk: I was in the city. I'm just outside the ICU. Let me know if you need backup.

Trunk: I will.

"Damn it, Ben. Put the phone away." Abbie huffed.

He did as she asked and lifted his eyes to meet hers. Trunk could tell by the strained expression she was in a lot of pain, but he also knew she wouldn't give in until he told her what she wanted to know.

"At least let Justin give you some pain medication," Trunk suggested.

"You're going to need pain medication if you don't tell me," Abbie replied through gritted teeth.

"Jesus, woman. Why do you have to be so fucking pig-headed?" Trunk shot to his feet.

"Because I want to know why I was tossed away like a piece of trash," Abbie retorted.

"I didn't toss you away. It killed me to walk away from you. I can't tell you how agonizing it was to stay away from you and watch that preppy asshole paw you." Trunk gripped the foot of her bed.

"Then why did you leave?" Abbie demanded.

"My stepfather was the one who killed your sister." Trunk almost choked on the words as they flew out.

Abbie's mouth dropped open, and her eyes grew bigger than he'd ever seen them. For what seemed like an eternity, she stared without a word. It was time to go.

"Goodbye, Abs." Trunk practically ran out of the room.

He made his way to where Hulk was casually propped against the wall, scrolling through something on his phone. As if he sensed something wrong, Hulk looked up and met Trunk's eyes.

"What's up?" Hulk asked.

"You're on duty," Trunk told his friend.

"Okay," Hulk said with a hint of uncertainty.

"Keep her safe and nobody goes in that room unless she wants them there. You got it?" Trunk forced out the words as his throat began to close over from the huge lump forming there.

"I'll protect her the same way you would." Hulk dropped his hand on Trunk's shoulder.

"Thanks, buddy." Trunk couldn't say another word as he stalked out of the hospital to his vehicle.

He blinked back tears as he drove out of the parking lot and made his way back to Hopedale. Trunk needed to be alone, and he wanted to punch something. Thankfully at his house, he could do both.

His mother messaged him as soon as he walked into his house, asking how Abbie was doing. He was glad she didn't call because he couldn't put any words together. Abbie's expression gutted him, and he never wanted to see that look on her beautiful face again.

The one thing that worried him the most was how Abbie would deal with her amnesia. The best thing for him to do was to stay away and let her recover. Once the swelling went down, she would regain her memories and get back to her fiancé again. He'd deal with the pain of watching her marry another man as long as she was alive.

Trunk slammed his fist over and over into the heavy bag. Every bit of pain and anger going into each punch. Sweat poured down his face as he tried to pulverize the black bag hanging from the beam. All he could hear was Guns and Roses' "Welcome to the Jungle" on repeat, blaring through the earbuds.

He'd hoped the music and the intense workout would dull the grief of losing Abbie for good, although it hadn't worked for the last seven years. Trunk also didn't want to think about what Darren and Claire would say once they found out. Abbie would have to tell them why Trunk wasn't her security anymore. It shouldn't bother him. because he didn't know them well, but they were her parents, and for some reason, he felt drawn to them.

After almost an hour, Trunk dropped down on the floormat, panting hard. He ripped the earbuds from his ears and flopped back on the floor with his arm draped over his eyes.

"Glad I'm not that punching bag." A male voice said.

Trunk jumped to his feet at the sudden realization he wasn't alone. His brother chuckled and tossed the towel laying on the chair at Trunk. After he wiped the dripping sweat from his face, he began to remove the wrapping from his hands.

"How did you get in here?" Trunk asked.

"It's nice to see you too, big brother." Chris chuckled.

"Sorry, I thought I locked the door when I came home." Trunk wrapped his brother up in a hug.

"I love you, Ben, but can you shower before you hug me. You're sweaty as fuck." Chris pushed Trunk away.

"That's what happens when you work out. You should try it sometime." Trunk punched his brother in the shoulder as they headed out of the workout room.

"I work out." Chris flexed his massive arms.

His brother was no longer the skinny kid Trunk protected. He was a little shorter than Trunk, but he obviously kept himself in shape. Still, Trunk felt the urge to keep him safe.

"You keep working at it, and one day you might actually have a muscle on that arm." Trunk chuckled as he made his way to his bedroom.

"Fuck you," Chris shouted.

By the time Trunk showered and changed, he found Chris on the couch with a beer in his hand. It wasn't that Trunk didn't drink, but it was rare, and to see Chris with a beer in his hand brought back bad memories of Jerry.

"There's another cold one in your fridge." Chris held up the bottle.

"Nah, I'll stick to water." Trunk grabbed a bottle of water out of the fridge and plopped down next to Chris.

"Still staying away from the bottle?" Chris asked.

"Don't see the point of drinking," Trunk told him.

"I don't drink a lot if that's what you think." Chris nudged Trunk.

"I hope not." Trunk propped his bare feet up on the table.

They sat watching a hockey game in silence. Trunk didn't care who was playing or what was on television. It was something to distract him from thoughts of Abbie.

"So, are you here to stay, or are you going back to Mom's place?" Trunk asked.

"I told her I'd spend the night with her, but then I was moving in here. I wanted to drop off my shit instead of leaving it in the car." Chris pointed to the pile of boxes next to the door.

"I thought you weren't coming until next week?" Trunk asked.

"I needed to get out of there." Chris shrugged.

"How are you doing, by the way?" Trunk asked.

"I'm dealing. I don't want them dead anymore, so there's that." Chris scoffed.

"That's progress." Trunk returned.

"Mom said your girl is in the hospital." Chris sipped his beer.

"She's not my girl. She's a friend of my boss' sister-in-law, and Keith assigned me to her until they find out who attacked her." Trunk's shoulders tensed.

"Mom said some woman told her you and this girl were a couple, or you should be, something like that." Chris shrugged.

"Cora," Trunk grumbled.

"Yeah, this woman is gifted or some sort of shit." Chris chuckled.

"That's a long story and something you don't want to know." Trunk snorted.

After unloading Chris' SUV, Trunk grilled two steaks and steamed some vegetables for supper. Shortly before ten, Chris said he'd be heading to his mother's apartment.

"You've had at least four beers. You aren't driving." Trunk snatched the keys out of Chris' hand.

"I'm fine. I ate, and I'm not drunk." Chris tried to take back the keys.

"You're not driving. Now either get in my truck, and I'll bring you back to Mom's place, or go crawl in the bed in the guest room." Trunk shoved Chris' keys in his pocket.

For a few seconds, Chris stared at Trunk. If his younger brother thought he would give in, then he'd be sadly mistaken. There was no possible way he'd let his brother drive after drinking.

"Fine, take me back to Mom's, but you'll have to get me again tomorrow." Chris huffed.

"I don't have any clients as of today." Trunk pulled on his jacket.

Chris must have sensed Trunk's tension because he simply followed him and hopped in the vehicle. The drive back to St. John's was nice, although the late April wind had an icy chill. Trunk still enjoyed the breeze blowing through the open window.

"It's fucking freezing." Chris zipped up his coat.

"Your blood needs to thicken up a bit," Trunk teased.

"It's April. Shouldn't the snow be gone by now?" Chris motioned to the small snowbanks on the side of the roads.

"It's Newfoundland, not Disneyland. You lived in Nova Scotia. The weather isn't much different," Trunk returned.

By the time they got back to his mother's, Trunk knew a lot more about what happened between Chris and his ex. It turned out she'd cheated on Chris before, but he'd forgiven her and tried to work it out. This time he couldn't. She betrayed him with one of his co-workers.

"I've got some shit to do in the morning, but I'll drop by after lunch to pick you up," Trunk said.

"Sounds good. If plans change, then I'll give you a call." Chris waved as he made his way into the apartment building.

Over the next few days, Trunk tried to keep himself busy, so he wouldn't think about Abbie. It wasn't easy, and at night he was plagued with dreams of her being hurt or telling him how much she hated him.

To top it off, the police had no clue who attacked her. The CCTV cameras on the restaurant didn't get anything because a tree blocked it. They did manage to get a view of Abbie's car speeding out of the lot but not the person driving. Since Abbie was a close friend of the O'Connors, Trunk knew they weren't going to let it go.

Chris moved into the guest room, and Trunk was glad to see his brother was truthful about the amount of drinking he did. Trunk wasn't against people having a few, but after what they'd seen as kids, it was better if they both stayed away from alcohol.

Hulk was assigned security duties for Abbie and seemed to think he had to update Trunk on her condition. He called every evening after Abbie went to sleep for the night and her parents left.

"She's been quiet tonight. She said she's fine, but something is bothering her, I can tell. Maybe you should drop by and talk to her. She's still calling out to you in her sleep," Hulk told him a week later.

"Don't start, Hulk. Any word on when they're releasing her?" Trunk had to know.

"She's out of ICU. They had her walking around today, but I think she'll be here for another few days," Hulk explained.

"Has she remembered anything?" Trunk asked.

"For a guy who doesn't want me to keep him in the know, you ask a lot of questions, buddy." Hulk chuckled.

"Yeah, maybe I'll go over and tell Caroline who owns the house she lives in," Trunk retorted.

"Bastard," Hulk grumbled.

"Asshole," Trunk replied.

"She still doesn't remember anything from the last few years. That fucktard dropped by a few times and gets pissed when we won't let him in. I like that nurse, Bish. He's good people. I watched him grab that preppy ass by the back of the neck yesterday and push him onto an elevator." Hulk chuckled.

"I thought he was in the ICU?" Trunk inquired.

"Keith asked to have him and another guy assigned to Abbie as her personal nursing staff. He's also offered them a job with *NES*. Don't tell Darren or Claire. Keith said they would want to pay more money if they knew. He's already got shit for giving them a discounted rate." Hulk laughed.

"Blue-collar pride, I guess." Trunk smiled.

"Yeah, by the way, your pride needs to get your ass here to see her. I haven't seen a smile on her face since I got here," Hulk told him.

"It's better this way. Thanks, Hulk." Trunk hung up the phone before his friend could say another word.

He was relieved Abbie was getting better, but it bothered him that Chad was trying to force himself on Abbie. If he truly loved her, the asshole should give her some time to heal. From what Trunk knew, the doctors thought the memory loss was temporary.

"Why is it better this way?" Chris asked as he propped his shoulder against the door jamb.

"Do you always intrude on private conversations?" Trunk asked.

"Do you always answer a question with a question?" Chris raised an eyebrow.

"Seems to run in the family." Trunk chuckled.

He wasn't ready to talk about Abbie to anyone else. He had to get over her before he could talk about it. Since it had been more than six years and he was still hopelessly in love with her, he figured he'd be an eighty-year-old man before that happened.

Nazareth's song was right. *Love Hurts.*

Chapter 10

Abbie was tired of being cooped up in the tiny private room at the hospital. She'd woken up two weeks earlier, and she was ready to get out of there. The doctor seemed happy with her progress and said she could go home that day. Of course, he would need to show up to release her. Since it was after one in the afternoon, she was starting to get pissed.

"Two weeks I've been here. Two freaking weeks. Every morning Dr. Sunshine comes in and wakes me up at o'dark stupid when he's doing rounds, but the day he's going to let me go home, where is he? Who the fuck knows?" Abbie complained.

"I don't think his name is Dr. Sunshine and what exactly is o'dark stupid?" Billie laughed.

"O'dark stupid is the time before normal people open their eyes, and does Dr. Asshole sound right?" Abbie huffed.

"I dropped by to see my happy-go-lucky friend. Is she here by the way?" Dana asked as she sat on the foot of Abbie's bed.

"Bite me," Abbie returned.

"Come on, Abbie. You're lucky to be alive." Billie sat next to her on the bed.

"I know, Billie. I should be glad to be alive, and I am. I'm just not happy being stuck in this place. I want to go home. I want to get my memory back. I want to know why the hell I would have agreed to marry a guy like Chad." Abbie blew out an exasperated breath.

"Honey, we don't even know why you were dating that idiot," Dana retorted.

"He's a dick, if you ask me," Hulk grumbled from the corner of the room.

"Is that your opinion, or are you answering for a friend?" Abbie raised an eyebrow.

"Strictly mine, but I've got friends who don't think much of the guy either." Hulk lifted his light blue eyes to meet Abbie's glare.

"Are you ever going to tell us why Ben suddenly turned you over to Bruce?" Billie asked.

"Who knows," Abbie lied.

She remembered why Trunk left. Abbie was still in a state of confusion over his statement and couldn't wait to get out of the hospital so she could talk to Sandy. If anyone could find out something, it was her. Sandy was known to find out things people didn't want anyone knowing.

"Bruce, do you know?" Dana turned to the large man pretending to read a book.

"Nope," Hulk responded without looking up.

"Liar," Billie snorted.

"Forget it. I don't care." Abbie sighed.

"I'll see what I can find out when I get back to Hopedale," Billie told her. "Maybe I can talk to Emily. She'll get it out of Keith."

Emily was Keith's wife and, from what Abbie saw, had her husband wrapped around her finger. Then again, she didn't remember the last few years and who knew what had happened during that time.

"So, you have two babies?" Abbie smiled at Billie.

"Yes, they're the sweetest girls you've ever met. Maggie is five, and Aria is two." Billie held up her phone.

The picture on her phone showed Mike and Billie, with two little girls standing between them. They were holding hands, and Abbie felt a twinge of jealousy in the pit of her stomach. She was happy Billie had found the love of her life and had two beautiful children. It was just that Abbie wanted it too.

"They look just like you." Abbie forced a smile.

"I hoped they'd have the O'Connor blue eyes. They have the dimples, though." Billie looked down at her phone with a huge smile.

"I'm so glad after all that shit you went through that something positive came out of it." Abbie sighed.

"It'll come back, Abbie." Dana took Abbie's hand.

"I don't know. It's been two weeks, and all I get are flashes that make no sense." Abbie didn't know if they were memories or dreams.

"What do you remember?" Billie asked.

"I remember the fire and being here in the hospital. I remember getting brought home and having security with me all the time." Abbie closed her eyes. "I remember leaving Hopedale the night we were celebrating that asshole got arrested."

Abbie let her thoughts go to when she arrived home and how Trunk growled in her ear, how his scent made her tremble with want for him. They made love until they were both breathless, and she was happier than she thought possible.

"I think she's lost in that X-rated memory again." Dana laughed.

"Shut up," Abbie grumbled.

It was over an hour when the doctor finally showed up and discharged her with a list of rules longer than her arm. She wasn't allowed to go to work for at least another week, which was fine because she didn't know what was going on at her office.

Billie looked after everything, and another agent who they'd hired a few months earlier helped to take up the slack caused when Abbie was injured. It made her uneasy because she didn't even know the guy, but according to Billie, he was great.

Hulk pulled into her driveway, and she groaned. Her parents' car was in the driveway as well as a few other vehicles. Abbie wasn't in the mood to deal with a crowd of people at that moment.

"I'll give you a thousand dollars to pull out of here and take me somewhere they can't find me." Abbie grabbed Hulk by the arm.

"They'd find us, trust me." Hulk chuckled.

Her father was on the other side of the car before Hulk turned off the vehicle. He looked like he was about to pick up a fragile piece of glass as he pulled open the car door and held out his hand.

"Careful, Monkey," he said as she stood up.

"I'm fine, Dad." Abbie sighed.

They walked up to the front door, and it opened as if by magic. She'd expected to see her mother as well as Billie, Dana, and Dana's mother, Brenda, but she didn't expect the rest of the guests.

Nanny Betty was in the kitchen with Kathleen, Alice, and Tom Roberts. Tom was Betty's boyfriend, or he was, but Abbie had been told the couple got married recently. One of the many things Abbie didn't remember.

"Dere she is. Come sit and get a bit a grub in ya," Nanny Betty ordered.

"Thanks, but I just want to lay down." Abbie exhaled.

She couldn't understand how a ten-minute drive from the hospital to her house could make her so exhausted. She was the type of person who could get four hours of sleep and then work for eighteen hours.

"Ya go lay down. I'll bring ya up a plate." Nanny Betty waved Abbie away as she scurried around the kitchen.

"I'm sorry, but you know how she is," Billie whispered.

"It's fine. It's nice to feel like part of their family." Abbie smiled.

"You've been family for a long while, but you might regret saying that." Billie laughed.

"Let's get you up to your room." Abbie's mother wrapped her arm around Abbie, and they made their way upstairs.

She settled in her room, and her mother left the bedroom. Abbie asked Billie to get a replacement for the stolen phone but not to tell anyone. Abbie desperately wanted to call Sandy, and since Hulk was with her all the time, she didn't get a chance to use a phone in the hospital.

"Did you get me another phone?" Abbie asked Billie.

"Yes, and all your info is downloaded to it. Thank God for iCloud." Billie pulled a box out of her purse. "But if you tell anyone I got it for you, I'll deny it. You're not supposed to be working."

"It's a phone. I'm allowed to have a freaking phone. Maybe I want to play a game or catch up with the news I can't remember," Abbie grumbled as she scrolled through her contacts.

She found Sandy's number and quickly typed a message before Billie could see anything. Billie was scrolling through her own phone, so Abbie sent Sandy a quick text.

Abbie: When you get a chance, can you drop by my house to see me?

It took less than a minute for Sandy to respond, and she wasn't surprised to see her sarcasm coming through in her text. Sandy was a lot like Abbie, and it was why they got along so well.

Sandy: I wasn't sure if you knew who I was. Need to give you a knock in the head to get that brain working again. I'll drop by whenever you want.

Abbie: As soon as you can and bring your laptop.

Sandy: On the way.

Abbie blew out a breath as she glanced up to see Billie staring at her. She'd never kept anything from either of her best friends, but since they knew Trunk, she wanted confirmation that what he told her was true before she said a word.

"Everything okay?" Billie asked.

"It will be." Abbie forced a smile.

"I'm so glad you're okay. I don't know what I'd do if I lost you." Billie's eyes filled with tears, and she hugged Abbie.

"Don't start that shit. I'm fine, and when they find the prick who did this, I want five minutes with him to find out what he did with my damn car," Abbie grumbled.

"You'll never change." Billie chuckled.

Sandy arrived less than thirty minutes later, and Abbie asked everyone to leave so she could talk to Sandy alone. She felt terrible for putting the hurt expression on Billie's face, but she didn't want her to hear her conversation with Sandy.

"What's with all the secrecy?" Sandy plopped down on the bed with her laptop in hand.

"I honestly don't know if we're friends or not. I remember meeting you, and I liked you right away, but I feel more comfortable asking you to do this stuff than I would asking Smash," Abbie whispered.

She knew her friend, and chances were Billie was outside the door trying to eavesdrop. Abbie was probably paranoid, but she didn't want to sully Trunk in any way. No matter what, she still cared about him tremendously.

"I'm assuming you're whispering because you know Billie as well as I do." Sandy eased off the bed and pulled open the bedroom door.

The hallway was empty, and Abbie relaxed. She was satisfied she could talk freely with Sandy.

"What's up, girl?" Sandy's brow furrowed.

"We're friends, right?" Abbie wanted to make sure.

"Yes, we're good friends. Although the rest of the girls don't like it when we drink together." Sandy smirked.

Abbie chuckled because she did remember seeing Sandy drunk once, and the woman didn't care what she said or to who. Much like Abbie was.

"I need you to look up something for me." Abbie pulled out a piece of paper with Laurie's name on it.

"Sure, whatever you want." Sandy took the paper and froze. "Except this."

"Why?" Abbie asked.

"I just can't." Sandy handed her back the paper.

"Is it because the man that killed my sister is Ben's stepfather?" Abbie met Sandy's eyes.

It was hard to read her expression, but Sandy's shoulders squared, and she swallowed, making it clear she knew about Laurie and what happened.

"He told you?" Sandy seemed surprised.

"Yes, but is it true?" Abbie asked.

"It is, but the asshole was a bastard. Trunk was horrified when he found out. He thought it would be better to break things off before things got serious," Sandy told her.

"He said that?" Abbie asked.

"Not in those words. Trunk believes you wouldn't be able to look at him the same if you knew the truth," Sandy explained.

"Why would I blame Ben? He didn't do anything. It was his stepfather," Abbie said.

"It was whose stepfather?" Her mother's voice startled Abbie and Sandy.

"Mom, I… sorry, just something I heard about a friend." Abbie glanced over her mother's head.

"Monkey, I know that face. What's wrong?" Her father stomped into the room.

"Nothing, Dad. Sandy and I were just catching up." Abbie lied.

"Yeah, catching up." Sandy smiled.

"Abigale." Her father used the same tone that used to make her tell him anything she'd done wrong.

"Okay, I wanted Sandy to look up something on the man who killed Laurie," Abbie blurted out.

"Why the hell would you want to know about that piece of dirt?" Her father growled.

"I don't remember a whole lot on what happened to him over the last few years," Abbie lied.

"I'll tell you about Jerry Stamp. That man should have been charged with a whole lot more. He killed one of our daughters and almost killed the other and her friend. Not to mention he'd left his house that day after beating his wife and leaving her for dead. If it weren't for one of his kids running to a neighbor, the poor woman would have died." Her mother didn't get angry often but talking about Jerry Stamp seemed to bring it out.

"Those poor kids never had a chance. Hopefully they didn't end up like their old man," her father grumbled.

"They didn't," Sandy said and then pressed her lips together.

"How would you know?" Abbie's mother asked.

"I told you I asked her to look things up for me," Abbie interjected.

"Yes, it turns out both boys are doing very well. One is a fireman, and the other is working for a…" Sandy stopped.

"Works for a what?" her father asked.

"I can't remember now," Sandy replied.

"Why don't I believe you?" Her father narrowed her eyes and glared between Sandy and Abbie.

"It doesn't matter, Dad. They got away from him, and they're doing well." Abbie shrugged.

Abbie wanted to talk to Trunk, but how was she supposed to get him to come to see her. Especially if he had decided it was better if they stayed away from each other. She understood why he felt that way, but she didn't blame him. She did wonder how her parents would feel about it.

"Dad, would you talk to the man's children if you had a chance, or his wife?" Abbie asked.

"They didn't do anything, and if they turned out as well as Sandy says, then I've got no grudge against them. They were lucky to survive that bastard." Her father sounded genuinely sorry for Trunk and his family.

"I thought someone said they moved out to the west coast, but I don't know if that's true." Her mother shrugged.

"Sandy can find out for us." Her father pointed to Sandy's laptop.

"I can if you want." Sandy glanced at Abbie.

Abbie shook her head slightly to let Sandy know it wasn't the time. Abbie needed a conversation with Trunk before she told her parents anything, and she prayed they were as understanding as they said.

"Maybe another time. I'm drained, and I'd like to get some sleep." Abbie faked a yawn.

Her parents took the hint, and Sandy told her she'd call later. She couldn't do anything until she talked to the one man who could answer all her questions. The next morning, she woke up and reached for her phone. She stared at Trunk's number and wondered if she called, would he answer?

Chapter 11

Trunk sat on the back porch of his house with his feet propped up on the rail. It was still chilly, but thankfully the month of May brought sunlight. He was able to sit outside, get some air, and have a little silence. Chris wasn't hard to live with, but Trunk had lived alone for a long time. His brother was a bit of a chatterbox, and since Chris was on his three days off, it was difficult to get some tranquil time.

The doctor released Abbie from the hospital the previous day and it killed Trunk that he wasn't the one taking her home. Hulk sent texts to let him know how she was doing but other than that, he had no idea what was going on with her.

Keith informed him the police found Abbie's car earlier that morning parked behind an abandoned building on Portugal Cove Road. The car was wiped clean, and they didn't find any of her stolen items. They didn't tell Abbie yet because they wanted to go over the vehicle again.

The thing that terrified him was whoever attacked her knew where she lived. Trunk didn't like the fact that the asshole who stabbed her could possibly try to access her house. Keith assured him Abbie and her house were secure. All locks were upgraded and codes on her alarm system changed, not to mention her parents and Hulk were there.

He'd learned to live without her over the last six-plus years but after spending time with her again, he missed her more than ever. She didn't remember all the times he'd blown her off after their night together. If she did, she'd know what an asshole he'd been to her. He ignored most of her calls, but when he did answer them, he was short with her. When she gave up, Trunk was relieved, but it hurt more than any beating his stepfather ever gave him.

Trunk thought once he and Abbie could finally be together, he'd spend his life with her, but destiny had different plans for them. By some sick twist of fate, his past linked to hers in a way that made it impossible for him to find happiness with Abbie.

Trunk sipped the cup of coffee that had grown cold, much like how his heart felt. As he stared into the trees at the back of his house, his phone vibrated in his pocket. He fumbled in his jean's pocket and pulled it out, and his heart jumped in his chest. Abbie's number flashed on his screen and although he wanted to answer, he knew he couldn't.

Trunk sent the call to voicemail and placed the phone back in his pocket. Seconds later, it buzzed. He pulled it out again and saw a text from Abbie in all capital letters.

Abbie: PICK UP THE PHONE, BUTTHOLE.

Trunk threw his head back and laughed. That was the Abbie he knew and loved. She knew he always had his phone within reach. He wanted to send a return text, but he didn't. When she called again, he hit ignore.

Another buzz.

Abbie: Ben, I swear I will get in the car and come to Hopedale if you don't answer the fucking phone.

Trunk sat up straight. If she decided to do it, nobody would stop her. Not even Hulk. Trunk's finger hovered over her number but before he could tap it, she called again.

"Hello," Trunk answered.

"Hello? That's all you can say?" Abbie shrieked.

"It's the way I answer the phone, Abs," Trunk retorted.

"I need to talk to you." Abbie seemed to ignore his sarcasm.

"Talk," Trunk replied.

"Face to face." She wasn't giving him a choice by the tone of her voice.

"I think over the phone is fine." Trunk knew being close to her would be a mistake.

"I will get in the car, Ben. I swear to Jesus," Abbie warned.

"Why? We've got nothing to talk about." Trunk should've known that wouldn't fly.

"The hell we don't. Now you've got two choices. Either you come here, or I'll go there." Abbie was a master with ultimatums.

"You can't drive. You don't have a car," Trunk reminded her.

"I'll call a fucking cab," Abbie shouted.

"Jesus, calm the fuck down." Trunk pulled the phone from his ear. "Fine, I'll be there in the morning."

"Nope, tonight," Abbie pushed.

"Can't I'm drunk," Trunk lied.

"I call bullshit on that So, I guess I'm calling a cab." Abbie ended the call.

"Fucking woman." Trunk tapped her number.

"Was that so hard?" Abbie answered before it rang a second time.

"I'll be there in thirty minutes." Trunk sighed.

"If you're longer than that, I'll be calling a taxi." Abbie ended the call again.

Since it was Friday, traffic would be a bitch. Everyone in the city seemed to be preparing for the weekend. The drive from Hopedale to St. John's was ten to fifteen minutes, but it could take longer if he got stuck in gridlock. Trunk knew one thing, if he didn't get to Abbie's house in thirty minutes, she'd call a cab.

Thankfully, Chris was in his room when Trunk rushed out of the house. He didn't have time to answer any questions, but he did send his brother a quick text to say he had an errand to run.

Twenty-nine minutes later, he pulled into Abbie's driveway and was greeted at the door by a pissed-off Darren. From the expression on the man's face, Trunk wondered if Darren knew his secret.

"What the hell are you doing here? I thought you quit." Darren snapped.

"I called him." Abbie stood in the middle of the stairs with her phone in her hand. "I was just about to make that call."

"Why did you call him?" Darren asked.

"I need to talk to him about something," Abbie told her father. "Can you come up here, Ben?"

Before Trunk could answer, Darren slammed the door in Trunk's face so hard that it was surprising the window didn't shatter. Luckily, he stepped back before it hit him in the face.

He could hear Abbie shout at her father through the closed door. Darren should know he would never win an argument with his daughter. It was why it struck Trunk funny when he heard Darren comment about Abbie's stubborn streak.

Trunk leaned against the doorjamb as he waited for Darren to concede to Abbie because, that's how the conversation was going to end. After a few minutes of whispering, Claire opened the door and motioned for Trunk to enter.

"I'm sorry, Ben. Darren is upset because of something we were just told." Claire gave him a soft smile. "Abbie is upstairs."

"Is everything okay?" Trunk asked as he glanced into the kitchen.

Billie, Sandy, Darren, and the guy who worked for Abbie sat around the kitchen table going through papers. All of them looked worried, and Trunk wondered if it had something to do with what happened to Abbie.

"It's some stuff going on at Abbie's office, and they don't want to concern Abbie while she's still recovering. Especially since she won't remember anything about it," Claire whispered.

"Let me know if there is anything I can help with," Trunk told Claire.

"Right now, you need to go up and see why Abbie just told her father to back off." Claire sighed.

"I'll see what I can do." Trunk smiled and made his way to Abbie's room.

Trunk paused at the opened bedroom door. Abbie stood beside her bedroom window with her back to him. Her long brown hair hung down to the middle of her back in soft waves and he ached to run his fingers through it. He remembered how silky it felt, and the scent of lilacs still reminded him of her.

"Are you going to stand out there all evening?" Abbie asked.

Trunk stepped inside the room and closed the door behind him. Whatever they had to talk about, he had a feeling she didn't want the conversation to be heard. If they were going to discuss what Jerry did, he didn't want anyone to hear the discussion.

"You look great." Trunk leaned against the closed door.

"Really? You're going to start with small talk." Abbie turned around and crossed her arms over her chest.

"You called me, Abs. I don't know what this is about." Trunk mimicked her stance.

"Then you've either got to be the dumbest man in the world, or you're trying to bullshit me." Abbie narrowed her eyes.

"What do you want me to say?" Trunk shrugged.

"I want to know why you didn't tell me. Why you ran away and didn't tell me about your stepfather?" Abbie met his gaze with eyes so intense and focused he could hardly breathe.

Trunk couldn't look away from her, but it was hard to find an answer to her question. The reason he didn't tell her was because he never wanted to see hatred in her eyes. A lot of good it did because the look on her face was like a punch in the chest.

"Ben, I want a fucking answer." Abbie raised her voice.

"What do you want me to say? The last thing I wanted anyone to know was that vile bastard was married to my mother and that I called him Dad." Trunk shook from wanting to hold her so badly.

"You're not him," Abbie said with such intensity that her voice echoed in her room.

"I'll never be like him." Trunk growled.

"Why would you think I'd blame you for what he did?" Abbie tossed her hands up in the air but winced and grabbed her side.

"Calm down, will you? You're still not healed from nearly being murdered." Trunk pushed off the door and moved toward her.

"I am calm," Abbie returned as she eased down on the bed.

"Jesus, I wouldn't want to see you upset." Trunk scoffed and crouched in front of her.

"Ben, how could you walk away?" Abbie asked, and the tears in her eyes was like a knife in the chest.

"It was the hardest thing I ever did in my life," Trunk admitted.

"I want to hate you right now, but I don't how to turn off these feelings. I'm missing almost seven years of being without you. To me, my feelings for you are still there," Abbie whispered.

"Abs." Trunk dropped his head and blew out a shaky breath.

"You let me go, and I was so desperate I said yes to a marriage proposal from a guy with a huge stick up his ass." Abbie huffed.

Trunk lifted his head and smiled because she'd just described Chad exactly the way he saw him. At that moment, it was hard to remember how he ever had the strength to stay away from her. He loved her more than he could ever imagine.

"I'm sorry, Abs," Trunk whispered as he touched her hand.

"Oh, 'cause that makes everything better." Abbie pushed his hand away and stood up.

"You wanted to talk to me. What do you want me to say?" Trunk stood up.

Abbie turned away and wrapped her arms around herself. She trembled, and Trunk fisted his hands at his sides to hold down the urge to pull her into his arms. He wanted to make all her pain go away.

"If the situation was reversed, do you think you could see past what my father did?" Abbie whispered.

Trunk allowed her words to bounce around in his head. He didn't know how to put himself in her shoes because he couldn't think of one thing about Abbie that would make him not love her. Nothing would kill how deeply he felt for her.

Trunk placed his hand on her shoulders and turned her around to face him. She didn't raise her head to look at him, so he put his finger under her chin and lifted it until her eyes met his.

"There's nothing anyone could have done to make me stop…" Trunk swallowed hard.

"Stop what?" Abbie murmured.

"Stop loving you," Trunk whispered.

"Then why do you think I would stop loving you?" Abbie placed her hand against his cheek.

Her touch was like a warm blanket that made everything wrong with his life melt away. Every painful memory of being beaten or kicked by a cruel bastard didn't seem so horrific when she was close.

"I saw the pain in your eyes when you talked about your sister. I didn't want you to look at me and be reminded of that agony every time you saw me," Trunk whispered.

Abbie stared into his eyes, and it was as if she could see into his soul. He couldn't hide all his doubts and pain, and it made it difficult to breathe. When a tear ran down her cheek, he tugged her into his arms.

"I'm sorry, Abs." Trunk pressed his lips against the top of her head.

"I want to hate you right now." Abbie sniffed but clung to him.

"You have every right to," Trunk replied.

"I can't. I love you too damn much. You big idiot." Abbie tucked her head into his chest.

Trunk smiled because she was right, he was an idiot for letting her go. It was the first time he could take a deep breath since the night he left her. Holding her made him feel alive, and it was hard not to brush all the reasons they couldn't be together away when the one person who made him feel whole was wrapped in his arms.

"I... I love you too, Abs," Trunk murmured.

Abbie tipped her head back and gazed up at him. Trunk cupped her face and glided his thumbs under her eyes, wiping away the moisture there. As he got lost in the emerald green of her eyes, he lowered his head.

One soft brush of his lips against her cheek and then her nose. Abbie sighed, and her eyes fluttered closed as he kissed her soft, plump lips. The taste of her brought him to life. Trunk deepened the kiss as Abbie flicked her tongue against his, and he growled into her mouth.

Trunk knew he had to stop before things got carried away, but ending the kiss was like stopping oxygen. Still, he built up every bit of strength he had and pulled his lips from hers. Abbie's eyes fluttered open, and she smiled.

"That, I remember." She sighed.

"We shouldn't do this. You're not exactly free." Trunk stepped away and ran his hand over his bald head.

"You mean that pompous ass who keeps blowing up my phone? No, thank you. I've got no interest in him." Abbie stepped toward Trunk.

"You're engaged to him, Abs. You don't remember right now, but you must love him if you agreed to marry him," Trunk reminded her.

"Yeah, then where's the ring?" Abbie wiggled her fingers.

"You were robbed," Trunk reminded her.

"Look, I don't know why I would say yes to him, but I'm not going to marry him. I. Love. You." Abbie poked him in the chest.

Trunk's heart felt as if it was about to pop out of his chest just hearing her say the words, but she still didn't remember how she felt about Chad. He couldn't take a chance of getting close and then possibly lose her when her memory returned.

"Abs, you can't say that. You don't remember how you feel about Chad," Trunk covered her hand where it lay in the middle of his chest.

"I know how I feel now, and I can't see loving anyone more than I love you," Abbie told him.

Trunk stared at her. He'd dreamed of hearing her say those words to him and look at him the way she was at that moment. There was one big problem. Chad. As much as Trunk disliked the guy, he knew what it was like to lose Abbie and he wouldn't want anyone to live through that agony. Still, deep down Trunk was sure nobody loved her as much as he did.

"Fuck." Trunk growled.

"Tell me about your stepfather," she said out of the blue.

"I don't want to talk about him." Trunk turned away from her and walked to the window.

"I know he almost killed your mom," Abbie whispered as she stepped behind him.

"Did Sandy tell you that?" Trunk needed to have a long conversation with Sandy.

"No, my mother did," she replied.

Trunk turned around and stared at Abbie. Did she already tell them about Jerry? Was that why Darren was so angry when Trunk arrived? If she did, then Abbie's father wouldn't take kindly to his daughter being with Trunk.

"You told them?" Trunk asked.

"I didn't tell them anything. My mother and father heard about it after Laurie died," Abbie explained.

Trunk practically held his breath, waiting to hear what Darren and Claire thought. Few people knew about his past, mostly because he didn't want to talk about it. Once they moved to Corner Brook, his mother didn't want to discuss anything that happened in St. John's with Jerry.

"Ben, I asked you to come here because I wanted you to know what that man did has nothing to do with the type of person you are. You were a kid who was abused by a drunk." Abbie cupped his cheek.

"He was looking for me," Trunk admitted.

"Why?" Abbie smoothed her hand down the side of his beard.

"Chris broke a window, and I took the blame. Jerry wanted to punish me for breaking the glass. I ran away before he could, and he got in the car to search for me." Trunk blew out a breath.

"Again, you were a kid. Why are you carrying the guilt of something he did?" Abbie held his face between her hands.

Trunk didn't have an answer. He'd always felt guilty because he didn't protect his mother, and it didn't matter that he was a child at the time. His mother told him once he always had a protective instinct. It was why every job he ever had was keeping people safe. *NES* wasn't his first security job, but it was the best.

"In my dreams, sometimes, I can hear Mom begging him to stop hitting her." Trunk drew in a shaky breath.

"I'm so sorry you had to deal with such an evil person," Abbie whispered and pulled him into her embrace.

Trunk wrapped his arms around her while he tried to keep from falling apart. Abbie was the first person he'd ever told about his nightmares and it was like a weight off his chest.

"Sorry, to interrupt, but you need to come downstairs, Abbie," Billie said as she opened the door a crack.

When Billie stepped into the bedroom Trunk could tell by the expression on her face something was wrong. His stomach churned and a since of dread overpowered him.

Chapter 12

Abbie wanted to throw something at Billie until she turned and saw her face. Billie had a particular expression that told Abbie when her friend was stressed or upset about something.

"What's wrong?" Trunk asked.

"The police are downstairs," Billie told them.

"Which one of your relatives are here?" Abbie scoffed.

Billie's in-laws seemed to be almost half of the Hopedale division of the Newfoundland Police Department. Although from the way Billie's brows were knit together, something told Abbie the police weren't here for a social call.

"Abbie, they're here to arrest you," Billie told her.

"I'm sorry, what?" Abbie gasped.

"What the fuck are you talking about?" Trunk moved Abbie behind him.

"Abbie, they're charging you with fraud and forgery," Billie said with a crack in her voice.

Abbie felt as if the room started to spin and her skin prickled with fear. There was no way she heard Billie correctly. Fraud and forgery? Abbie would never do such a thing.

"That's impossible." Abbie could barely hear her own words.

"We got an anonymous tip, and we have proof. Abbie, you need to come downstairs." James O'Connor stepped into the room behind Billie.

Billie's brother-in-law was involved with law enforcement. Since he was wearing his badge and weapon, he was clearly on duty and there to arrest her.

Abbie trembled as her eyes darted back and forth between James and Billie. It had to be a mistake. There was no way this was happening. If it was true, then what kind of person had she become over the last six and a half years? It was hard to believe she could have changed into a person who would do something illegal.

"James, come on. You know this can't be right." Trunk pulled her into his side.

"I'm sorry, Trunk, but we have to take her in." James pulled out his handcuffs.

"James, is that necessary? I mean, it's Abbie." Billie's eyes filled with tears.

"Look, I don't want to do this, but it's my duty. I would rather take her in than send someone she doesn't know." James walked toward her.

"No." Trunk pushed Abbie behind him.

"Trunk, don't make me arrest you too," James warned.

"Ben, stop. James is just doing his job. If I did this, then I deserve to be arrested. I just wish I remembered if I did." Abbie stepped around Trunk and held out her hands.

"For God's sake, James, she still has stitches. Can you forgo the handcuffs in this case?" Trunk's voice cracked.

"Are you in pain, Abbie?" James asked as he nodded his head.

"No…" Abbie stopped when she realized what he was trying to do. "Maybe a little."

"Then, as long as you come with me willingly, I won't cuff you and make you more uncomfortable." James rested his hand on her shoulder and guided her out of the room.

"This is fucking bullshit," Trunk roared from behind her.

Abbie blinked back the tears as James led her downstairs to where her parents stood in the foyer. Her mother was pale with tears in her eyes, and her father looked as if he could gut someone. Tyler and Dana stood behind them, looking confused as James escorted her out the door to the waiting SUV.

"I brought an unmarked car so it wouldn't draw the attention of the neighbors," James told her when he opened the back door.

"Thanks, James. I know this isn't your fault." Abbie sat in the vehicle.

James nodded as he closed the door and walked around the SUV. Abbie glanced at the front of her house as tears spilled down her cheeks. Her father held her mother in his arms, Billie, Dana, and Tyler stood with their arms around each other, but it was Trunk's expression that caused a sob to escape from her lips.

Trunk's face twisted with rage, and his hands fisted at his sides. He seemed ready to rip someone apart, and it upset her. The last thing he needed was to get in trouble because of her, especially if she wasn't innocent.

"Billie is sending a lawyer to meet you at the station," James said, drawing her attention away from the people she loved.

"Okay." Abbie wiped the tears from her cheeks.

She could end up in jail for something she didn't do or didn't remember doing. Abbie closed her eyes and tried to will the forgotten memories to return. Was this the reason her brain blocked out such a huge chunk of her life?

Chapter 13

Trunk was ready to rip someone's head off and shit down their neck. There was no way Abbie was guilty. If there was one thing he knew for sure, it was that Abbie was one of the most honest people he knew. She would never jeopardize her career or her company.

After James drove off with her, Trunk stomped into the house behind everyone. He needed to get ahead of all this before she went to jail for something she didn't do, because she was innocent.

"Sandy, find out who called in the tip," Trunk practically shouted as he stomped past Keith.

"She's already on it, Trunk," Keith informed him.

"She didn't do this, Rusty." Trunk turned to see Abbie's father and mother looking completely shattered.

"I'm with you, but from what James said, it's not looking good," Keith told him.

"Someone is setting her up, and I've got a feeling I know who," Trunk said with a growl.

He turned to walk out the door, but Billie grabbed his arm. He spun around and was about to tell her to let him go. When he saw the pissed-off expression on her face, he stopped.

"I'm coming with you," Billie told him.

"No. I need to have a serious conversation with someone." Trunk growled.

"I know where you're going, and you're not going there without a witness." Billie walked around him and headed out the door.

"If you're going to see that piece of shit, I'm going too," Abbie's father growled.

"I never trusted that asshole. He stole a sale out from under Abbie, and he was always asking to use her computer." Tyler waved his hands in the air.

"What do you mean?" Trunk asked.

"This guy called Abbie more than a month ago and set up an appointment to see her. When I called to confirm the appointment for her, the guy said he went with another agent, and Abbie told me it was Chad," Tyler explained. "That night, she wanted to confront him and then she…"

Tyler Travis worked for Abbie and Billie at their real estate office. Trunk didn't know him well, but he seemed loyal to Abbie. The look on Tyler's face told Trunk that the young guy deeply cared for Abbie, and he was shaken by what happened. Trunk didn't know much about the guy, but from what Billie said, he fit in with the agency and was in the process of taking the real estate exam.

"Do you think he could have something to do with it?" Dana asked.

"I wouldn't doubt it," Tyler grumbled.

"You said he used her computer." Trunk turned to Tyler.

He knew how much a person could do if they got into someone's personal computer. Sandy could do things he couldn't even imagine. It was possible Chad knew how to maneuver his way around Abbie's personal files and set her up.

Trunk's body stiffened. Chad might have something to do with Abbie's attack as well. He wondered if the police checked to see if Chad left the restaurant after Abbie. James would definitely look into it, but Trunk wanted to mention it, just in case.

"I don't know if he did it himself, but its possible he hired someone." Darren's voice was low and lethal.

"Aren't we jumping to conclusions? He proposed to Abbie, and she accepted," Billie reminded them.

"But did she? She doesn't remember. How do we know he isn't lying?" Tyler asked.

The guy was right. Chad listened outside the hospital room before Justin caught him. He might have heard Abbie say she didn't remember anything. There was one way to find out the truth.

"Let's go." Trunk stomped out of the house, with Billie and Darren right behind him.

The downtown traffic didn't make his mood any more pleasant, but the office building where Chad worked was in the middle of the bustle. Trunk drove around the block three times before he found a parking spot near the building.

"Maybe we shouldn't talk to him at work," Billie said as they walked through the large glass doors of the RD Building.

"I don't want him to take off when he finds out the police arrested Abbie. If he's involved, he'll be in the wind." Trunk stepped on the elevator.

The doors opened into a large bright reception area. The entire building belonged to the Donovan family, but *Donovan's Commercial Development Corporation* or *DCM Co.* resided on the tenth floor. According to Billie, Chad was one of *DCM's* top employees, or at least it was what he told Abbie.

"Do you know where his office is?" Trunk asked Billie.

"No, Abbie and I have never been here." Billie looked around the area, seemingly awestruck.

"Abbie has never been to his office?" Darren sounded surprised.

"No, Chad said it was unprofessional because they were in a similar business. It didn't make sense to me, but Abbie wasn't bothered by it." Billie shrugged.

Trunk stalked up to the large glass desk in the middle of the reception area. The young woman seated there spoke into a microphone connected to a headset. When she glanced up and locked eyes with Trunk, her expression was almost comical. Her eyes grew wide, and her mouth dropped open several times before she finished the call.

"I'll transfer you," the young woman squeaked and tapped a couple of buttons on her keyboard before she turned her attention back to Trunk. "Umm… Can I help you, sir?"

"I need to speak with Chad Grady," Trunk demanded.

"Chad?" The girl tipped her head and looked at him in confusion.

"He does work here, correct?" Billie stepped next to Trunk.

"Well, yes, but why are you looking for him?" The girl glanced back and forth between Billie and Trunk.

"We need to speak to him about his fiancé," Billie explained.

"I'm sorry. Did you say fiancé?" The girl seemed astonished by the knowledge that Chad was engaged.

"Yes, he's engaged to one of my best friends," Billie explained.

She didn't say a word and seemed as if she was waiting for a punch line. When she saw they were serious, she stood up and removed her headset.

"If you'll have a seat there, I'll need to speak to Mr. Donovan before I let you speak with Chad." The girl scurried down the hall behind her.

Trunk saw her knock on a broad set of double doors, and seconds later, she walked into the office. She was in there for what seemed like a long time, making Trunk even more concerned that Chad was hiding something.

"Do you think that bastard is already married?" Darren whispered.

"Something's fishy," Trunk returned.

The receptionist returned and motioned for them to follow her. She led them to the office and pushed open the double doors. Trunk, Billie, and Darren walked through, and the receptionist closed the doors behind them. The large office had windows from floor to ceiling down one side of the room, giving them an unobstructed view of the waterfront.

Trunk glanced around the large office and started to wonder why they were left alone in the room. Before he voiced his concerns, a door on the opposite side opened. A man walked into the room, but it wasn't Chad.

The gentleman was about Darren's age and dressed in what looked like a luxurious, dark pinstriped suit. He nodded to them as he closed the door behind him and confidently walked further into the room.

He was tall with dark hair streaked with gray and receding slightly. His dark eyes studied Trunk, Billie, and Darren as he stopped behind the glass desk and motioned for them to sit down in the chairs.

"We don't need to sit," Trunk told the man. "We need to speak to Chad."

"I'm sorry. I didn't get your name." The man sat back in his leather chair and steepled his fingers.

"I didn't tell you my name," Trunk replied as he crossed his arms over his chest.

"Well, why don't we start there. My name is Cole Donovan." The man stood up and held out his hand.

"Everyone calls me Trunk. This is Billie O'Connor and Darren Martin," Trunk replied.

"Trunk? That's an interesting name. Nice to meet all of you. I'm the COO of *Donovan's Commercial Development Corporation.* I understand you have the impression Chad is engaged to your friend." Cole sat back in his chair.

"I'm not under the impression, he told us he's engaged to my daughter, and now she's in trouble. We want to talk to him. Now." Darren stepped closer and braced his fists on top of the desk.

"When did you speak to Chad?" Cole tilted his head.

"What the hell is this? Chad is your employee, and his personal life is none of your business. Where is he?" Trunk snapped.

"Chad is more than my employee. He's family, and I'm protective of my family. I don't want you scaring him." Cole didn't seem the slightest bit intimidated by Trunk.

"Look, Mr. Donovan, I understand you're worried about Chad, but Abbie is in trouble. She's accused of doing something she couldn't possibly have done." Billie stepped between Darren and Trunk.

"I don't understand any of this. I've never heard Chad mention anyone named Abbie, and he tells me everything." Cole did seem confused.

"Can we please talk to him? You can stay in the room if you want, and if he's okay with it," Billie begged.

"Oh, I'll be staying in the room, but you've got to promise not to intimidate him. He gets anxious easily." Cole stood up.

"I promise," Billie said.

"I'll get him." Cole nodded and left the room.

"What the fuck? Chad gets anxious easily?" Darren scoffed. "That bastard is arrogant, not anxious."

"Something isn't right," Trunk murmured to himself.

He walked around the room and checked out some of the photos on the credenza against the wall. There were dozens of

165

pictures of what looked like family pictures. Trunk was about to pick up a photo when Cole walked back into the room.

He held it open, and Trunk expected to see Chad walk behind him. Instead, a young man followed Cole, clinging to his hand. It wasn't Chad. The man who entered with Cole had a disability and stared at Trunk as he sat in the chair next to Cole.

"What is this? Where is Chad?" Darren asked but his tone was calm.

"This is Chad." Cole pointed to the chair next to him.

"He isn't Chad Grady," Trunk replied.

"I am Chad Grady." The young man nodded.

"We're not playing games, Mr. Donovan," Trunk said as calmly as he could.

"Neither am I. Chad is my nephew, and he works here under a program for the developmentally delayed," Cole explained.

"I bring the mail and lunch," Chad said with pride in his voice.

"That's right." Cole smiled lovingly at the young man.

"Mr. Donovan, the Chad Grady we're referring to is around my age. He told my friend he works here as an agent," Billie explained.

"Please, call me Cole. Do you have a picture of this guy?" Cole asked.

"I don't." Billie shook her head.

"Are you with the police?" Cole asked.

"No, but we're working with them to figure this out. If I could have your number, I can send you a photo when we speak with Abbie," Trunk explained.

"What's Abbie's last name?" Cole tilted his head.

"Martin," Darren answered.

"The real estate agent?" Cole's eyes grew wide with surprise.

"You know her?" Trunk asked.

"Yes, I've met her. She's a wonderful person. Now I know where I know you from." Cole pointed to Billie. "You're her business partner."

"Yes, I am," Billie admitted.

"I don't know who this guy is, but I'd like to help if I can. I heard Abbie was hurt a few weeks ago and I'm glad she's okay. Here's my business card. When you get a photo of this guy, send it to me, and if I know him, I'll happily give you his name. I don't like anyone using my nephew's name to dupe people." Cole stood up, and Chad mimicked him.

"Thank you, Cole. I'll get it to you as soon as I can." Trunk shoved the card into his wallet.

"It was nice to meet all of you." Chad walked up to each of them and shook everyone's hand.

"It was great to meet you too, buddy," Trunk smiled at the young man.

"Uncle Cole calls me buddy too." Chad grinned.

"That's right, buddy," Cole gave his nephew a smile that showed every bit of love and affection he had for the young man.

Trunk, Billie, and Darren were quiet as they left the building. Trunk was pissed that Chad scammed Abbie, and it convinced him the asshole was using her. The problem was they didn't know his real name or where to find him. To top it off, they had no way to prove Abbie wasn't responsible for the fraud. It looked like Sandy and Smash had some digging to do

.

Chapter 14

Abbie sat in the small room where she was escorted after being fingerprinted and photographed. James refused to put her in a cell with anyone else, so she sat alone on the bunk with her hands folded in her lap.

Her lawyer hadn't shown up yet, and Abbie's heart raced as she heard the men and women in the lockup shouting at the police officers. She didn't want to spend a night in the place, or worse, she could be there longer. She didn't know if she would survive something like that.

It seemed like hours since she left her house, but when she glanced at the clock, she'd been there over an hour. Abbie couldn't imagine what it would be like to be there for days, weeks, or years.

A huge lump formed in her throat as her eyes filled with tears. How could someone think she would be responsible for fake house sales? She didn't even know how that was possible, especially with all the information needed by lawyers, financial companies, plus the buyer would have to sign everything.

"What the fuck is going on?" Abbie sighed.

She tapped her fingers against the side of her head, hoping it would shake something loose, and her memories would return. There was no way she'd be able to heal if she couldn't sleep, and Abbie seriously doubted sleeping in the small cell would be possible.

"Abbie, your lawyer is here." James opened the cell door.

"Thanks." Abbie forced a smile as she stood up and followed James.

"Jason is a good lawyer," James told her.

"I hope so because this is going to be hard to figure out when I don't remember a thing from the last few years." Abbie walked into a small room.

A man with light-brown hair sat with his back to her and turned around when James called him by name. Abbie recognized him from the celebration at Sean's house. Jason Brenton was one of Mike's best friends.

"Hello, Abbie. I wish we were meeting again under better circumstances." Jason held out his hand.

"You and I both." Abbie shook his hand.

"I'll let you two deal with this." James nodded and left them alone in the room.

Jason flipped through a bunch of papers while Abbie sat quietly. When he looked up, he gave her a friendly smile.

"The good news is, you won't be spending the night here. I've got you released on your own recognizance. Since you're a business owner with close ties to your community, and you've never been in trouble before, it was pretty easy to get you out. You'll have a curfew and won't be allowed to leave the city." Jason pushed some papers across the table.

"I know I didn't do this," Abbie told him.

"We'll deal with that later. Right now, I just want to get you out of here." Jason smiled.

"Why am I not on the way home, and why wasn't I in court?" Abbie asked.

"Your release papers needed to be filed. I appeared on your behalf at court, but you'll have to be there for future dates." Jason stood up as someone knocked.

Abbie glanced up to see her mother with James. She immediately wrapped Abbie up in a comforting hug, making it almost impossible to keep the tears from falling.

"Let's get you home," her mother whispered as Jason led them out of the room.

Her mother was quiet as they drove back to Abbie's house. All the things she had when James arrested her were in a plastic bag sitting on her lap. Her phone was buzzing continuously, but she ignored it.

The soft country music on the radio soothed her, and Abbie closed her eyes as she tried to block out everything else but the music. Abbie didn't know the song or the artist, but it was calming.

Abbie sat in the middle of an empty room. It was bright, but she could hear someone shouting for her. She didn't know where the voice was coming from, and she turned to find a door. She was surrounded by slate-gray walls and when she tried to shout, nothing came out.

Abbie took a step forward, but someone or something was holding her back. An arm wrapped around her neck, and she struggled against the hold. The more she struggled, the tighter she was held. Then she heard a low, sinister voice murmur in her ear.

"Payback."

"Abbie," her mother shouted.

Abbie's eyes flew open, and she gasped for air. She glanced around and calmed when she realized she parked in the driveway sitting in her mother's car.

"Honey, are you okay?" Her mother cupped Abbie's cheek.

"Yeah, I guess it was a dream." Abbie pressed her hands against her chest and took a deep breath to calm her racing heart.

"You must be exhausted. Let's go inside and get some supper," her mother said as they got out of the car.

Abbie nodded as her mom helped her inside the house. She wasn't hungry, but her mother wouldn't give up until she ate something. The problem was how could she eat when she felt like vomiting.

She'd eaten half a sandwich when her father arrived with Trunk and Billie. Her dad was furious, but Trunk looked ready to kill someone. Still, seeing him calmed her.

"Abbie." Billie ran to her, and hugged Abbie so tightly that it was almost hard to breathe.

"Jason managed to get me out," Abbie told them as Billie released her.

"You won't have to go back because that prick you were dating isn't who he says he is," her father said after he kissed her cheek.

"What do you mean?" Abbie asked.

"The place he said he worked has a Chad Grady, but he's a young man with Down's Syndrome and the owner's nephew," her father explained.

Abbie's eyes focused on Trunk. He stood next to the counter with his phone to his ear, talking quietly to someone. There was something about the way he stood that told her he wasn't getting the answer he wanted.

"Abbie, do you have a picture of Chad?" Billie asked.

"I have no idea. I don't even remember him." Abbie shrugged.

"What about your phone?" Billie sat next to her.

"You can check it. It's over on the counter." Abbie pointed next to the coffee pot.

Abbie's head pounded, and she wanted to help them, but how could she when she didn't know what was going on? With the news Billie just gave her, she felt like a complete idiot. She wanted to figure out how the hell she could allow someone to con her so easily.

"Sandy is working on finding out who your Chad is." Trunk crouched next to her.

"He's not *my* Chad," Abbie complained.

"Sorry." Trunk ran a finger down the side of her face.

Abbie sighed and closed her eyes. His touch was warm, and it dulled the pain in her head. She wondered how he did it, but at that moment, she was just glad for the pain to ease.

"Abs, you look tired," Trunk whispered.

"That's putting it mildly." Abbie sighed.

"Maybe you should take a hot bath and go to bed." Her mother smoothed her hand down over the top of Abbie's head.

"Sounds like heaven." Abbie smiled up at her mother and then turned to Trunk. "Are you staying here?"

"He didn't stay at the hospital. Why would he stay here?" her father snapped.

"Darren, that's enough," her mom chastised.

"I'm not going anywhere, but there is something I need to talk to your parents about before I agree to stay." Trunk stood up and turned to them.

"I don't think this is the time, Ben." Abbie grabbed his hand.

"You're in the situation because I wanted to hide something. They need to know before we can think about making it work." Trunk squeezed her hand.

Her mother and father exchanged glances and then turned back to Abbie. It was as if they were preparing themselves for the worst, and maybe they wouldn't be okay with the fact Trunk's stepfather killed Laurie.

"If anyone is curious, there isn't one picture of Chad on Abbie's phone or in her iCloud," Billie interrupted.

"Sandy's working on it," Trunk said.

"Okay, I'll leave so you guys can talk." Billie started to leave the kitchen.

"You might as well stay, Billie." Trunk turned to Abbie's parents. "Darren, Claire, you might want to sit for this."

"Ben, are you sure about this?" Abbie's heart pounded.

"Yes." Trunk sat at the table next to her.

Her father and mother sat across from them, and Billie was on the other side of Abbie. It was difficult to stay calm when she didn't know how her parents were going to react to what Trunk was about to tell them.

When Trunk dropped his hand on her knee, she realized it was bouncing up and down. When she met his gaze, he mouthed the words, "It's okay," to her and Abbie covered his hand with hers.

"What's going on?" Billie asked.

"This is difficult for me to disclose to anyone. Not many people know, and it's the reason I decided to stay away from Abbie," Trunk began.

"You know since the day I met you, that's the most I've heard you say at one time," Billie interjected.

"You're about to hear a lot more," Trunk returned.

Abbie hoped Trunk was doing the right thing by telling her parents. They said they didn't blame Jerry's family, but saying it, and actually facing the family were two different things. Her father wanted to kill Trunk's stepfather and didn't mince words when the subject of Jerry Stamp came up.

"Darren, Claire, I don't know how to say this, but to just put it out there and go from there," Trunk began.

"Do you think we don't know?" Her mother smiled.

"It's so obvious." Her father scoffed.

"What are you talking about?" Trunk asked.

"Ben, we've known for a long time how you feel about our daughter, but we never knew why you didn't act on it or why Abbie would enter a relationship with someone like Chad, or whoever he is. She was so obviously in love with you." Her mother reached across the table and touched Trunk's arm.

"I would much rather see my daughter with you than that prick she's been with," Darren said.

"I hope you still feel that way when I tell you this. The truth is I love Abbie more than I could ever tell you. I stayed away because I didn't want to cause her grief." Trunk glanced at Abbie, and she nodded.

They needed to get it out in the open and start with a clean slate. Losing her sister was the hardest thing her family went through, but nobody could blame Trunk.

"Ben, what is it you're hiding?" her mother asked.

Trunk took a deep breath, and his hand tightened on Abbie's knee. She could see the struggle in his eyes as he turned to face her, and she wanted to tell him to forget it. It didn't matter because she loved him no matter what.

"My stepfather... his name... Jerry Stamp," Trunk's words came out barely above a whisper.

At first, her parents stared as if they didn't understand what came out of his mouth. Abbie watched them process the information, and the second her father put it together.

"He's the one who..." her father stammered.

"He... he killed Laurie," her mother whispered.

"Yes," Trunk answered.

Her father stood up and walked out of the room. A second later, the front door slammed, and Abbie felt a knot in her stomach tighten. Her mother quickly went after him, and Abbie blew out a nervous breath.

"I'm sorry, Abbie," Billie said, breaking the silence.

"Don't be sorry, it's not going to change my feelings for Ben," Abbie told her friend.

"Abs, we can't be together if it upsets your parents. I love you, but I couldn't do that to..." Trunk's words stopped when the front door opened again.

Her parents walked into the kitchen with a small shoebox. Abbie had seen it in the trunk of her father's car for years, but he would never show her what was inside it. All he would say was it would be returned to the owners one day.

"Stamp was a mean bastard. He's lucky some of my neighbors got to him before I did." Her father placed the box on the table. "The day Laurie died, I found this stuff on the ground next to the car. It was in a bag where he fell out. I swore one day I'd ensure his family got this back."

Her father removed the cover and pushed it toward Trunk. Inside was some jewelry, cash, and what looked like an old flask. Trunk reached inside, and his hand shook as he picked up the silver bottle.

"My mother had this. It belonged to my grandfather. It was the only thing Jerry didn't break or sell because Mom used to keep it hidden in our closet and told us never to tell him where it was." Trunk ran his thumb across the letters on the front of it.

"How did he get it then?" Abbie asked.

"He must have beat her until she couldn't take it. That day… she almost died." Trunk's knuckles turned white as he gripped the flask.

Chapter 15

Trunk stared at the flask. He hadn't seen it since he was a boy. After they moved, he'd asked his mother about it, and her eyes filled with tears. She told him it was lost in the move, and he believed it since many of their things had not made it to Corner Brook.

He pulled it into his chest as he glanced into the box again. There were some pieces of his mother's jewelry he hadn't seen in a long time. Others he didn't recognize.

"Why did he have this stuff?" Trunk murmured mostly to himself.

"Would your mother have given it to him?" Abbie asked.

"No. He got this because he beat the living shit out of her." Trunk swallowed the lump in his throat.

"He almost killed your mother that day," Claire whispered.

"He was probably going to sell it." Darren's tone was cold.

Trunk glanced up at Abbie's father with his heart thudding in his chest. He couldn't read the man, but he thought Darren wouldn't be okay with Abbie and him together. Trunk couldn't blame the man, but he was curious why Darren kept everything for so long.

"Why didn't you get rid of this stuff?" Trunk asked.

"I threw it away at first, but the day after Laurie died, the police came to tell us the bastard put his wife in hospital, and she was lucky to be alive. They told me the kids were with a neighbor and were safe. I dug through the garbage and pulled it out. I wanted to return it over to your mother at the trial, but she never showed. It's been in my trunk ever since." Darren tapped the box with his finger. "I've had three different vehicles since then, and this box moved into each one."

"Dad, why didn't you ask the police to give it to her?" Abbie asked.

"I don't know. I guess I hoped giving it back to her myself would give me some peace. I know it sounds stupid." Darren eased down into the chair across from Trunk.

"Thank you, Darren. I'll give it to my mom." Trunk placed the items back in the box and replaced the cover.

"You're not him, Ben." Darren dropped his hand on top of the box.

"No, I'm not." Trunk would never do what Jerry did.

"I would never blame you or your mother for what he did," Darren went on.

"Thank you." Trunk lifted his eyes to look at Darren.

"I know we don't know each other well, but what I do know is you're an upstanding man with a huge heart. All I ask is you treat my daughter the way she deserves. I would never blame you for something your stepfather did. If that were the case, I'd be paying for the crimes of my father too." Darren's eyes filled with tears.

"Dad, what are you talking about?" Abbie asked.

"You never knew my father, Monkey. He died before you were born. He was a raging alcoholic who enjoyed beating my mother and me. He died when he fell down the stairs, drunk, right after he raped my mother." Darren swallowed and closed his eyes.

"Dad," Abbie gasped.

"She had the nerve to tell him to get out of the house. He decided to teach her a lesson. That's what he called it when he hit either of us." Darren blew out a breath.

"I'm sorry, Darren." Trunk finally figured out why he felt a kinship with Abbie's father.

"For a while, I went wild because I didn't know how to deal with the pain of everything. They used to call me Hammer because I'd nail any girl who would open their legs." Darren smirked.

"Ugh." Abbie gagged.

"It's how I pushed down all the pain of my childhood. If I hadn't met Claire, God knows where I'd be. She gave me the kick in the ass I needed to get myself together." Darren wrapped his arm around his wife.

"My mother was the one who kept us in line. She gained a lot of strength after we went to Corner Brook. I give her credit for both Chris and me not being in trouble or ending up in jail," Trunk admitted.

"As long as you take care of our daughter, Ben, we would never prevent her from being with the man she loves." Claire gave him a soft smile.

"Thank you for that." Trunk nodded.

"Why in the hell did I not know any of this before now?" Billie slapped Trunk's arm.

"I'm surprised you didn't. Sandy's known for a while." Trunk smirked at Billie.

"Wait until I get home, she's getting a call from me." Billie crossed her arms over her chest.

"Sandy knows a lot of things about the guys. Don't expect her to spill the details unless they give her permission," Trunk told Billie.

"Let's have a bite to eat and forget everything for a while." Claire smiled.

"Sounds wonderful," Abbie said.

After supper, Darren, Claire, and Billie left. Abbie's parents hadn't gone home since Abbie got out of the hospital, but since Trunk assured them he wasn't going anywhere, they felt comfortable leaving.

Trunk helped Abbie to bed and waited while she got ready. When she was in bed, he lay next to her and wrapped her in his arms. Trunk listened to her deep, even breathing, and the sound lulled him into a deep sleep.

The soft buzz of his phone woke him from the best night's rest he had in years. Abbie was still softly snoring, and he eased out of bed, grabbing his phone before he left the room.

"Hello," Trunk answered.

"Hey, Trunk," Keith replied.

"What's up?" Trunk could tell by Keith's tone that something wasn't right.

"It's that prick. He's flown the coop," Keith told him.

"What do you mean?" Trunk growled.

"Sandy is still trying to figure out who the ass is. When James went to question him at the address Billie gave us, he was in the wind. The apartment was empty, and the landlord said the guy didn't even tell him he was leaving," Keith explained.

"Son of a bitch." Trunk growled.

"Also, the bank account where the money from the fraudulent sales was supposed to be deposited is drained," Keith went on.

"How is that possible? Wasn't there a freeze put on all her accounts until this was over?" Trunk asked.

"It looks like the money transferred out before the police got the tip. James is looking into it, but the good news is, Abbie is in the clear. James said Abbie was in the hospital when the money was transferred out of the account," Keith told him.

"At least we don't have to worry about that anymore, but are they going to keep looking for that ass?" Trunk asked.

Then there was the person who attacked her. It was starting to look more and more like it wasn't random, and since the person knew where Abbie lived, Trunk was starting to think she'd be safer in Hopedale.

"You know they will," Keith said.

"Are there any leads on her attack?" He knew the answer but still had to ask.

"No, they found some fingerprints in the car. One set was Abbie's, but the other isn't in our system," Keith explained.

"That's no fucking help." Trunk blew out a breath.

If the prints weren't in the system, it meant that the person was never arrested and never worked a government job. If that were the case, finding the bastard would be much more difficult. Everything in Trunk's body told him everything would lead to the man they knew as Chad Grady.

Chapter 16

Abbie sat up in the bed and glanced around the room. She could hear the soft rumble of Trunk's voice from downstairs, and she relaxed. She'd been dreaming all night, but she was beginning to think they were memories. Many of the visions were things her family told her happened over her missing years, which she'd forgotten.

The last dream made her jolt up in the bed. She told Chad off and left him at a table in a restaurant. Then she hit the button on her key fob. The memory of an arm around her neck woke her.

"He didn't propose," Abbie whispered to herself.

Abbie closed her eyes and tried to force the memory to return. When flashes started forming, she knew she told Chad to fly to hell. She just couldn't remember why.

"What the hell did he have planned?" Abbie whispered.

"What did who have planned?" Trunk's voice caused her to open her eyes.

"I think my memory is coming back. Chad didn't propose to me the night I was stabbed. I was pissed at him and ended things," Abbie explained.

"What else do you remember?" Trunk asked.

"I remember someone wrapping their arm around my neck and then…" Abbie stopped.

The memory of the knife penetrating her skin and falling to the ground was hazy, but she remembered the pain. Abbie reached around, and touched the raised scar still healing on her side. It was sore, and she winced as her hand ran across it.

"I remember someone in dark clothes jumping in my car and speeding off." Abbie swallowed hard. "He left me there to die."

Tears started before she could stop them, and Trunk pulled her into his arms before the first sob escaped. Abbie clung to his shirt and allowed all the fear, sadness, and anger she'd held in for the last few weeks flow. Someone left her on the ground as if she was nothing but a piece of garbage. Plus, the man she thought cared about her hadn't even come to her rescue.

Chad wasn't even who he said he was. Abbie didn't understand how he got everything he needed to set her up. He was the only person she could think of who would do something so vile.

Billie certainly wouldn't do that to her, and something told her Tyler wouldn't either. She'd had Sandy do a background check on the young man before she hired him.

Abbie sat up straight as more memories of what happened over the last few years started to flow. She pulled back from Trunk and stared into his eyes. He'd left her. He pushed her away and made her feel as if she'd been a nothing but a one-night fuck.

"Abs, what's wrong?" Truck cupped her cheek.

"When 'Love and Hate Collide,'" Abbie murmured.

"What?" Trunk looked confused.

"Def Leppard." She smiled.

"You lost me, Abs." Trunk chuckled.

"You hurt me so much, and I would listen to that song all the time because it was exactly how I felt. I hated that I loved you, and I loved to hate you. The song fit perfectly," she whispered.

"I'm so sorry." Truck's agony was written all over his face.

"I know why you did it, but I'm starting to remember how much it hurt every time I saw you." Abbie blew out a huge breath.

"I wish I could go back and change it, baby. I can't, but I can tell you from here on out, I'll do everything I can to show you how much I love you." Trunk held her head with his large hands and pressed his lips against her forehead.

"Show me now," Abbie whispered.

"Abs, as much as I want to, you're still healing." He tucked a piece of hair behind her ear.

"I want you to make love to me. Ben, please. I need you to show me." Abbie laid her hands against his chest.

Trunk was quiet, and Abbie was beginning to think he wasn't going to do anything. She wanted to be close to him and forget, even if it was for a short time. She'd spent so long dreaming of being in his arms again.

"Abs." Trunk leaned in and brushed his lips against hers. "If you have any pain at all, you need to tell me."

"I will," she murmured against his lips.

"I mean it. One twinge, and we stop." Trunk stared into her eyes.

"I promise," Abbie gave him a soft smile. "But you have to make me a promise too."

"What's that?" Trunk asked.

"Don't leave again." She swallowed hard.

"Abs, I'm not going anywhere ever again." Trunk took her hands in his and placed them over his heart. "You're what keeps this beating, and if I let you go again, it would stop."

"Ben, I love you. I have since the first time I saw you." Abbie leaned forward and pressed her lips against his.

Trunks arms slipped around her, and he deepened the kiss, taking her breath away. His kiss was slow and gentle as his hands lightly caressed her back. Her heart raced as his tongue slipped inside her mouth and swirled against hers.

When Abbie moaned, Trunk gently lowered her to the bed, never breaking the kiss. Abbie slipped her hand under the hem of his T-shirt and smoothed her hands against his firm abdominal muscles, causing them to flex under her touch.

Trunk was hard in all the right places, and she could compare his body to the carved statues she'd seen when she traveled to Greece. The difference was his package was a lot larger than those figures.

Trunk groaned as she dragged her nails gently down his chest and around to his back. His lips moved to her cheek, down her neck, and he slipped his large hand under her shirt. The warmth of it on her skin caused goosebumps to explode over her skin.

"Are you cold?" Trunk lifted his head with concern written all over his face.

"God, no." Abbie sighed.

Trunk reached behind his head and yanked off his shirt. She always found it sexy when men did that, but Trunk made it look even more erotic. After he tossed it to the floor, he sat on the edge of the bed. He pulled Abbie up gently and maneuvered her until she stood between his legs.

"Are you okay?" He unhurriedly raised the hem of her shirt.

"Yes," she breathed as his lips pressed against her abdomen.

His tongue circled her belly button as he leisurely pushed her shirt up and over her head. She'd removed her bra before she went to bed, so Trunk had a full view of her naked torso.

"Your breasts are fucking beautiful." Trunk cupped them in his hands and kissed each one tenderly.

Abbie's head dropped back, and a moan escaped as he kissed and sucked each of her sensitive nipples. With each flick of his tongue, she could feel the delicious ache between her legs increase.

Trunk ran his hands down her sides and slipped his thumbs inside the waistband of her pajama bottoms, gradually pulling them down over her hips as he teased and sucked on her breasts.

He took Abbie's hands and kept her steady as she stepped out of her clothes, then pulled her close until she straddled his thighs, wearing just her panties. Trunk captured her lips and lay back with her on top of him.

His rock-hard erection pressed against her core, and she could feel it throb even through his jeans. She pressed her heat against him, causing a deep groan to emanate from his lips. Trunk gripped her by the waist and raised his hips to meet her.

"This would be so much better if your jeans weren't in the way," Abbie complained.

"It really would." Trunk shot up, so he was sitting with her on his lap.

Abbie scrambled off his thighs, and Trunk quickly disposed of his jeans and boxers, freeing his engorged cock. Trunk reached for the waistband of her panties and yanked them down over her hips before he tugged her toward him.

"I want to taste you." He moaned and ran his nose against the top of her sex. "You smell so damn tasty."

Before Abbie could respond, his tongue slipped between her folds and flicked against her tender nub. Her legs trembled and she thrust her hips forward as he sucked and licked her pussy. When two of his fingers slipped inside her, he sucked her hard clit into his mouth, triggering a gasp of pleasure.

"Don't… oh, don't stop, Ben." Abbie panted as she thrust against his fingers.

Within a few seconds, her body trembled when he took her over the edge. Trunk slammed his fingers into her and nipped her engorged nub, making her cry out in pleasure. Trunk drew out her orgasm until her legs buckled and then held her until she could catch her breath.

"That was fucking beautiful." Trunk pulled her gently onto his lap and captured one of her nipples between his teeth.

"I want you inside me." Abbie pressed her wet heat against his thick cock.

"Condom." Trunk panted as his dick slipped between her folds.

"Drawer," Abbie whispered in his ear.

Trunk fumbled in the drawer of the nightstand while Abbie sucked on his earlobe. When he pulled back from her, he ripped open the package, and she watched him slip the latex over his swollen head.

When he was covered, he gripped her gently around the waist and she shifted until she hovered above his cock. Abbie lowered onto his hard shaft, and as he slipped inside, he moaned. Abbie wrapped her arms around his neck, and she dropped down until she had all of him filling her.

"That's it, baby," Trunk urged.

Abbie sucked and licked her way down his neck and back to whisper into his ear. Trunk loved dirty talk. She'd discovered that the first time they were together. Anytime she would describe what she wanted to do, his eyes dilated, and he'd groan.

"You like me riding your cock, don't you, Ben?" Abbie murmured into his ear.

"Fuck, yes," Trunk growled.

"You like feeling my pussy slide over your dick," Abbie continued.

"God, don't stop, Abs." Trunk panted against her breast.

Abbie tried to increase her speed, but he gently flipped her over and eased her onto her back. For a moment, he stayed that way as he looked into her eyes.

"Did I hurt you?" Trunk whispered.

"No." Abbie touched his cheek.

"Promise?" Trunk turned his face and kissed her palm.

"Promise." She lifted her hips, and he groaned.

Trunk thrust his hips forward, slowly at first, but when she began to tell him how hot she was and how much she wanted him to come for her, his thrusts became faster.

"That's it, Ben. Fuck me, bury that cock inside me," Abbie urged.

"Abs, I'm not going to last much longer. Please tell me your okay." Trunk grunted as he thrust into her.

"Fuck me, baby." Abbie grabbed his ass, and he pushed deep into her.

Abbie screamed his name, and seconds later, Trunk's body shook above her. She dropped her arms to her sides as she tried to catch her breath. Trunk held himself above her as if he was afraid to put too much weight on top of her.

"Are you okay, Abs?" Trunk brushed his lips across hers.

"Ben, are you going to ask me that every single time we do this?" Abbie sighed.

"Until you're healed." Trunk smiled.

"That's going to get on my last nerve," Abbie warned.

"I'm sure it will." Trunk chuckled as he gave her one quick kiss.

When he jumped up and made his way to the bathroom, Abbie rolled over on her side and sighed. She hadn't felt so happy in a long time, but considering what loomed over her, she shouldn't be so calm.

She spent a year with a man who lied to her about where he worked and who he was. Abbie couldn't shake the feeling his lies connected to the person who left her for dead in a parking lot. She needed to get the truth out of that bastard.

Abbie sat up in the bed and snatched her phone off the nightstand. The first thing she would do was confront Chad or whoever the hell he was. Abbie didn't care what everyone said. She wanted to give him a piece of her mind.

Abbie tapped Chad's name and put the phone to her ear. She didn't hear a ring. All she heard was a message saying the phone was out of service. Abbie tried the supposed office number she had for him, again the number was out of service.

"That sneaky fucker," Abbie spat.

"What did I do?" Trunk chuckled as he returned.

"Not you. I tried to call Chad, or whoever he is." Abbie grumbled as Trunk sat next to her.

"What did he say?" Trunk asked.

"Nothing, both numbers are out of service." Abbie dropped her phone on the table next to the bed.

"Abs, don't worry about him. The cops will get that piece of shit, and until they do, I'm going to be your personal shadow." Trunk lowered her back on the bed.

"Well, I guess something good did come out of it." Abbie smiled and wrapped her arms around his neck.

"Are you okay?" He ran his hand up and down her sides.

"Ben, I swear I'll slap you if you ask me again." Abbie narrowed her eyes and grabbed his head between her hands. "Stop worrying about me being in pain."

"I'll never stop worrying about you, Abs." Trunk hugged her body to his. "I love you too much."

"I love you too." Abbie smiled.

"Our new theme song is now Van Halen's, 'I Can't Stop Loving You,' okay?" Trunk smirked.

"Well, if you can't stop, I won't complain." Abbie rolled over on top of him.

They made love a second time, and Abbie happily snuggled in his arms. She ran her finger over one of the beautiful tattoos

Trunk had inked on his body. On his chest, there was a phrase she'd heard before, but she couldn't remember where.

"*Do not go gentle into that good night. Rage, rage against the dying of the light,*" Abbie read. "Why does that sound familiar?"

"It's from a poem by Dylan Thomas. He was a Welsh poet." Trunk ran his hand up and down her back.

"I suck at poetry. What does it mean?" Abbie asked.

"Are you asking because you want to see if I know what it means?" Trunk chuckled.

"Maybe a little, but I do suck at poetry." Abbie grinned.

"It means always fight to live. I don't know if that's the right meaning, but it's what it means to me. When I was a kid, the woman who lived next door to me read that poem to me once, and it just kind of stuck. This was my first tattoo," Trunk explained.

Abbie smiled. Nobody would ever take Trunk as a lover of poetry, but it seemed he was, or at least, he liked one specific poem. Her favorite was the star he had below his navel and the two flaming skulls on each hip. For some reason, she found them so sexy.

Abbie ran her finger around the edge of the star and giggled when he squirmed under the light touch. He grabbed her hand and linked his fingers with her.

"Is this payback for teasing you?" Trunk chuckled.

This is payback.

Abbie jolted up in the bed and gasped as the voice echoed in her head as clear as she'd heard it that night. The words her attacker whispered in her ear. Then he thrust the knife into her body.

"Abs, what's wrong?" Trunk sat up.

It took a moment for her to be able to speak because she was struggling to control her breathing. Trunk held her until she calmed enough to tell him what had her so freaked.

"My attack, it wasn't random. It was revenge," Abbie whispered.

Chapter 17

Trunk didn't sleep much during the night, and neither had Abbie. The memory of her assailant's words kept her waking with nightmares, and Trunk held her until she calmed. She wouldn't let him call James or Keith in the middle of the night and made him promise to wait until a decent hour.

Abbie sat at the kitchen table, holding the cup of specialty coffee she usually enjoyed every morning. It was the only coffee she seemed to like, and since she lived alone, it was easier for her to use the Keurig pods, although, she hadn't even taken a sip since he made it.

Trunk paced the kitchen as they waited for James' arrival. Keith sent someone to Abbie's office to check on Billie and Tyler and decided Trunk was definitely too close to the situation, so Hulk was on the way to Abbie's for extra security.

"Ben, for fuck's sake, will you sit down? You're making me dizzy with your pacing," Abbie complained.

"Who would want revenge on you, Abs?" Trunk leaned over the table.

"How the hell would I know? I don't work for the mob," she snapped sarcastically.

"Did you take a house away from another agent?" Trunk sat in the chair across from her.

"I would never do that and stop playing cop. James will be here as soon as he can." Abbie pushed her cup back, rested her elbows on the table, and folded her hands under her chin. "I wouldn't undercut another agent. I have too much integrity to do something like that."

"I'm sorry to push you. I hate to think someone wants to hurt you." Trunk took her hands and held them between his.

"You know the night I ended things with Chad, I was pissed because he bragged about a sale. One that he ripped out from under me. He said when we got married, I wouldn't have to work," Abbie's memory seemed to be returning.

"Fucking dick." Trunk shook his head.

"Yes, he is," Abbie agreed.

Trunk brought her fingers up to his lips and kissed them. His stomach knotted when he thought about how close she came to death. There was no way he would have survived if she hadn't made it.

"Did you ever feel as if there's something you need to remember, but you can't? I know a lot of my memory has returned, but there's still something I can't put my finger on." Abbie was frustrated.

"It will come to you when you're ready," Trunk assured her.

"I want to go back to work." Abbie sighed.

"I don't like the idea of that," Trunk replied.

"It's a good thing it's not your choice now, isn't it?" Abbie pulled her hands from his and reached for her cup.

"Stubborn woman," Trunk grumbled.

Abbie lifted the mug to her lips and stopped. Her eyes widened, as she lowered it back to the table. Her eyes flicked back and forth as if she was reading something.

"Did Billie leave the files here from the fake sales she found?" Abbie jumped to her feet.

"I think they may be in your study. I put everything in there when everyone left yesterday," Trunk replied.

Trunk followed Abbie as she hurried to her den in the back of the house. She practically ran to her desk and frantically shuffled through a bunch of papers piled on top. The more she searched, the more frustrated she seemed.

"What are you looking for, Abs?" Trunk asked as she opened and closed the drawers in her desk.

"I had a bunch of folders for potential clients. I just can't get my brain to remember where I had them." Abbie dropped into her office chair and pressed her fingers against her temples.

"Why are you looking for them?" Trunk asked.

"If the fake files have those names on them, then I know he's responsible for it. He was the one who gave me the client names," Abbie told him.

"We'll mention it to James when he gets here, and if we can't find them here, we'll talk to Billie." Trunk walked around the desk and crouched next to her.

Abbie sat up straight, and her face paled. For a moment, Trunk thought she would pass out, but she turned to him with wide eyes.

"Abs, what's wrong?" Trunk could see her panic.

"My purse was stolen." Abbie gasped.

"It was, but they didn't find it when they found your car." Trunk didn't know why she was suddenly so frantic.

"Did anyone cancel my credit cards?" Abbie asked.

"I don't know. You call your mom, and I'll call Billie." Trunk tapped the screen on his phone and put it to his ear.

Chapter 18

Abbie quickly called her mother, praying someone had the presence of mind to cancel all her cards. She didn't have a lot, but the two she had she used for business. Abbie started using them for bills to keep her head above water. That memory returned as she was showering that morning.

"Abbie, is everything okay?" her mother answered.

"Mom, did you happen to cancel my credit cards after I was mugged?" Abbie didn't want to tell her parents that her attack may not have been random.

"I think Billie did that. She and Dana said they would take care of all of it," her mother told her.

Abbie breathed a sigh of relief, but she was afraid to relax too much until she was sure. She still didn't like the fact her attacker had all her information, but if it was a setup, he knew where she lived anyway.

"Billie canceled everything," Trunk informed her.

"I hope they were able to cancel everything," her mother sounded panicked.

"It's okay, Mom. Billie took care of it." Abbie reassured her mother.

Abbie gave herself a mental pat on the back for her great idea to share all her personal and professional business with Billie. It was something they decided when Billie joined her agency. At first, Billie worked as Abbie's assistant, and then she got her real estate license. It was when they became partners and reopened as *A and B Realty*.

"I just got a text from James. He's here." Trunk took her hand.

Abbie felt a nervous flutter in her stomach, and it wasn't a pleasant one. She didn't feel comfortable with the knowledge someone attacked her as an act of revenge. It didn't make sense since she wasn't involved in anything shady.

"Hey, Abbie. How are you doing?" James asked when Trunk led him into the living room.

"I'm hanging in there." Abbie smiled when Trunk brought the cup of coffee she'd left on the table.

"Good to hear. I wanted to formally let you know all the charges against you are dropped. I am deeply sorry for putting you through that." James sat in the armchair across from her.

"You were doing your job, James. I understand." Abbie tucked her feet under herself and folded her hands around the cup.

"So, this is what we have so far. That account was opened online in your name, but when the money was transferred out, you were still in the hospital. The man we know as Chad is a ghost and we haven't been able to find any photos of him. Sandy is checking through the wedding videos and pictures from Pam's wedding and Nanny Betty's reception as well," James explained.

"He had tons of pictures on his phone, but he never let me take photos with mine," Abbie remembered as she sipped her coffee.

"Couldn't you get prints from his apartment?" Trunk asked.

"The landlord had the place professionally cleaned. Our techs found some prints, but mostly partials and those we did check came back to employees of the cleaning company." James sounded frustrated.

Abbie knew how he felt. How could a man fool her so long without her suspecting he wasn't who he said he was? The funny thing was they were at a party with the man who was supposed to be his boss. Nobody seemed to think Chad was out of place, and he made small talk with a lot of people.

She did remember she was never with him when he was talking to other people. When he was close to her, he would steer them away from the crowd. How could she be so stupid?

"Abs, what's with the face?" Trunk tipped her chin up with his finger.

"I feel like a complete idiot for not seeing he was a con man." Abbie sighed.

"Don't say that," Trunk whispered.

"Trunk is right. He's probably done this before, which means he knows how to get away with a lot," James assured her.

"How did you meet him?" Trunk asked.

Abbie thought back to the first day she'd met Chad Grady. It was a little over a year earlier at a convention in central Newfoundland. She'd been there alone because Billie was still on maternity leave.

Fourteen months earlier…

Abbie closed the door to her hotel room and tucked her clutch under her arm as she made her way to the elevator. She checked her phone to see which suite she had to meet some of the agents from St. John's.

The elevator doors opened, and as she stepped on, she heard a man shout. She peered out and saw an attractive man run down the hallway toward her. She pressed the button to hold the doors until he stepped on the elevator.

"Thank you," he said.

"You're welcome. Which floor?" Abbie asked.

"Third. I'm trying not to be late for a meet and greet." The man chuckled.

"For the Newfoundland Association of Realtors?" Abbie would never have pegged him as an agent.

"Yes. You too?" He smiled.

"Yes, I'm Abbie Martin of A and B Real Estate in St. John's." Abbie held out her hand.

"Chad Grady of Donovan's Commercial Development Corporation in St. John's." Chad shook her hand.

"You're a developer? Why are you at a meet and greet for realtors?" Abbie didn't know of many developers who came to the conventions.

"Mr. Donovan insisted we start to work more with all realtors and hence sent me here," Chad explained.

"Cole Donovan is a huge name in commercial development. Is he getting into residential as well?" Abbie asked as the elevator doors opened.

"You never know with him." Chad motioned for her to walk off ahead of him.

"Well, here's my card. If he is looking for an agency that gives a personal touch to their clients, tell him to call me." Abbie handed Chad her business card.

"I'll make sure he gets this. I might use it myself as well." Chad winked as he pulled open the door of the suite.

Abbie wasn't attracted to the man, but she needed a way to get over Trunk. Maybe dating someone she wouldn't normally go for would help her do that.

"I hope you do." Abbie smiled and left Chad at the door to go meet her friends.

She watched him a lot over the next few hours, and they did bump into one another a couple of times. She noticed he tended to talk to the female agents from the smaller agencies, and several of them gave him their business cards.

Hopefully, he was intrigued enough by her to ensure she got any business he had. Working with a developer like Cole Donovan would be a huge boost to her agency.

Present day...

"He never gave out business cards," Abbie said.

"What?" Trunk seemed confused.

"Agents give out cards like candy. I give out hundreds a month, but I can't remember ever seeing a business card with his name on it." Abbie shook her head because her vision was fuzzy.

"Probably because he didn't work for Cole." Trunk shrugged.

"Cole?" Abbie narrowed her eyes as she tried to focus on Trunk.

"That's what Cole Donovan told us to call him," Trunk said.

"You met Cole Donovan?" Abbie didn't know where Trunk and someone like Cole would cross paths.

"Yes, me, Billie, and your dad went to his office to talk to Chad," Trunk explained.

"When did you do this?" Abbie started to feel lightheaded.

"Abs, we told you this yesterday when you were released from jail." Trunk's brow furrowed.

"Yesterday?" Abbie's head pounded, and everything began to spin.

"Abs, are you…" Trunk's voice faded, and everything went black.

Chapter 19

"Abbie." Trunk jumped to his feet as Abbie slumped over on the sofa, and her cup slipped from her hands, crashing to the floor.

"I'll get an ambulance," James told him.

Trunk checked for a pulse and blew out a breath of relief when he felt one. He called her name over and over, but she didn't respond, and she wasn't waking up. He was frantic because he didn't know what the hell happened. She'd seemed confused before she passed out, and he wondered if it had anything to do with her head injury.

By the time the paramedics arrived, Abbie had been unconscious for almost twenty minutes. He hopped in the ambulance and prayed as he watched Abbie's chest rise and fall. As long as she was breathing, it meant she was fine.

James called Abbie's parents when the ambulance left her house, and as Trunk waited for them to arrive, he paced the waiting room outside the Trauma Unit. He was relieved when he saw Dr.

Kramer on duty because he knew Abbie would be in competent hands.

Adam Kramer was a friend of the O'Connor family, and he assured Trunk he'd let him know as soon as he had answers. It was torture waiting for news, but the same thing kept spinning around in his mind. Abbie was recovering from a head injury. All he could think about was maybe the injury was worse than the doctors originally thought. Her memory was returning, but it was possible she had some internal bleeding on the brain.

"Sweet Jesus, don't take her from me," Trunk whispered.

"Ben." His brother's voice surprised him.

"What are you doing here?" Trunk asked.

"I was at *Jack's Place* when Billie and Mike got a call from James. I came here with them." Chris sat and dropped his hand on Trunk's shoulder.

Mike said he would check in on Chris while Trunk was staying at Abbie's place just in case his brother needed anything. Not that Chris needed a caretaker, but it seemed like he'd barely moved in when all the shit with Abbie started.

"She'll be fine, Ben," Chris said.

"We thought she *was* fine," Trunk whispered.

"Maybe she's just exhausted," Chris suggested.

Trunk didn't answer because she had been restless while she was sleeping, but he knew that wasn't it. Abbie's speech slurred, and she seemed to have issues focusing right before she passed out.

When Claire and Darren arrived, Trunk filled them in on the situation. Not that he knew a whole lot, because Adam hadn't come out to give him any information.

Trunk started pacing and was ready to run into the room where they brought Abbie to demand answers. It seemed as if they'd been there for hours, but when he glanced at his watch, it was an hour later. When he looked up, Adam had entered the waiting room.

"Adam, is she okay?" Trunk asked.

"She's okay, but I need to speak with her family," Adam told him.

"I'm her mother, and this is her father. Is she okay?" Claire gripped Trunk's arm and linked into her husband's as well.

"She's stable and starting to regain consciousness. I did blood work, and I just got the results. She had Ketamine in her system," Adam explained.

"Ketamine?" Trunk asked.

"Yes." Adam nodded.

"Where the hell would she get Ketamine?" Darren snapped.

"It's a sedative a lot of veterinarians use. Some people use it recreationally, and some jerks will use it on women for shitty reasons," Adam explained.

"She's been with me since yesterday. She took Ibuprofen but nothing else. She hasn't been out of my sight," Trunk told Adam.

"I don't know what to tell you except she ingested it somehow. I don't know Ms. Martin well, but is it possible she's taking it on her own and took a little too…" Before Adam could finish, Darren grabbed him by the lab coat.

"Don't you dare finish that sentence. My daughter has never taken drugs in her life. She doesn't even like the fact that I smoke weed on occasion." Darren was pissed.

"Darren, let go of the doctor." Claire grabbed her husband's arm and pulled him away from Adam.

"I don't mean to upset you, but sometimes people can be sneaky when they have an addiction," Adam explained.

"Adam, I promise you Abbie is not doing any kind of drugs. Check your previous blood work when she was here a few weeks ago." Trunk knew without a doubt Abbie would never touch drugs.

"Then someone drugged her," Adam said.

"I don't know how. She's been with me." Trunk shook his head.

"All I can tell you is what came back on the reports. I'm going to keep her for a day, maybe two. You can come in to see her, but she's pretty out of it." Adam motioned for them to follow him.

"Darren, you and Claire go ahead. I want to check something." Trunk told Abbie's parents as he grabbed his brother's arm.

"Where are we going?" Chris asked Trunk as they headed out of the hospital.

"Abbie hasn't been out of my sight. If she was drugged, then there's something tainted in that house. I'm going to get James to bring in a crew to check everything she's put in her body today." Trunk hopped in Chris's truck.

"Call him and tell him to meet you at Abbie's place." Chris pulled his truck out of the parking lot.

Trunk placed a quick call to James and was relieved when he found out James was still at Abbie's place. James said he would get a team there right away.

Fifteen minutes later, Trunk stood in Abbie's kitchen. He showed the forensics team everything Abbie used, ate, or drank that day. He headed to the living room when he noticed Abbie's cup under the coffee table. As he reached to pick it up, he remembered she'd had coffee right before she passed out.

"James," Trunk shouted.

"What's up?" James asked as he entered the living room.

"She was drinking out of that cup before she fell over. It's all she had today that I didn't have as well." Trunk pointed to her mug.

"But I saw you drink coffee too." James pointed at the mug on the coffee table.

"Abbie doesn't drink regular coffee. She uses those pods on the counter. Come to think of it, she didn't have anything else today." Trunk bent over to pick up the mug.

"Don't touch that, Trunk. I'll get someone to test it," James told him.

They headed into the kitchen, and James sent an officer into the living room to retrieve the mug. James went to the box of Keurig pods on the counter and pulled on a pair of gloves. Trunk remembered the one in the garbage, but when he turned to retrieve it, another officer already pulled it out of the bucket.

"Trunk, come look at this." James picked up a pod.

He pointed to a slight discoloration on the side of the small plastic cup. James asked the man searching through the garbage to hand him something sharp and then gently scraped away the discoloration. Under it, they found a small hole barely visible to the naked eye. Trunk didn't know what it meant, but James ordered the guy going through the garbage to take all the pods and test them.

"What do you think that is?" Trunk asked.

"I think someone injected these with something and covered the hole to keep anything from leaking out. Was this the first cup she had out of this box?" James asked.

"I think so. She's been drinking tea mostly, but this morning Abbie asked for coffee." Trunk nodded toward the box.

"Was the box opened?" James asked, and Trunk nodded.

He watched as James carefully checked each of the pods in the box. Everyone had the same mark, which made Trunk sick to his stomach. He'd made the coffee for her that morning.

"Do you know where she got them?" James asked.

Trunk shrugged. All he knew was they were in her cupboard, and she'd said she was in the mood for coffee when she got up that morning.

"We need to find out." James motioned for Trunk to follow him.

"Where are you going?" Chris asked as they walked out of the house.

"We need to talk to Abbie and see if she knows where she got those Keurig coffee pods." James hopped in his car. "Meet me at the hospital."

James instructed the men in Abbie's house to test everything collected immediately and for someone to stay until he returned. A young woman standing outside the house nodded, and James drove off.

Trunk got in the truck with Chris, and they headed to the hospital. Trunk didn't know if Abbie would remember when or where she picked up her coffee. Her memory was full of holes, but hopefully, she'd recall something.

At the hospital, Trunk walked into Abbie's room and sighed in relief when he saw her sipping some water. She turned toward him and narrowed her eyes.

"I'm guessing I've got you to thank for being here again," Abbie grumbled.

"If you mean he was the one to save your life, then yes," her father snapped.

"I was joking, Dad." Abbie rolled her eyes.

Before Trunk could say a word, James walked into the room, and Abbie's parents tensed. It was obvious they didn't trust James because the last time they saw him, he was arresting Abbie.

"James, what's wrong?" Abbie asked.

"I'm assuming you know what brought you here," James said.

"Yes, but I don't touch drugs. I've never even smoked a cigarette." Abbie glanced at Trunk.

"Abs, the coffee pods you drink all the time, where did you get them?" Trunk asked as he sat next to her on the bed.

"Supermarket, mostly." Abbie shrugged.

"The box that's at your house. Do you remember when and where you got those?" James asked her.

Abbie stared blankly over James' head as if she was trying to remember. When she glanced at Trunk, he knew she had no idea.

"I know they were there when I got home from the hospital. I'm assuming they were there before everything happened. There's still some pieces of my memory missing." Abbie shrugged.

"Was the box open the first time you used them?" James asked.

"You'd have to ask Ben. He made a cup for me this morning. It's the first cup I've had since I got home. Why?" Abbie glanced back and forth between Trunk and James.

"I don't have verification yet, but I think they were all injected with something. Since there was Ketamine in your system, I'm assuming that's what we'll find," James explained.

"How's that possible? I haven't been alone since I went home from the hospital last week." Abbie said. "Wait, you don't think any of my family or friends did this, do you?"

"I doubt anyone of your family or friends are responsible," James assured her.

"Did Chad have access to your house?" Trunk asked.

"We dated, of course he had access," Abbie returned.

Trunk felt a surge of anger bubble up inside but did his best to keep it from showing to anyone. He had a feeling Chad was responsible for drugging Abbie, but when did he inject the coffee pods?

She must have noticed something in Trunk's expression because Abbie grabbed his hand, and instantly the anger dissipated. There was nothing he wouldn't do to protect her, but when he didn't know what direction the danger would come from, what was he supposed to do?

"Chad wouldn't do something like that." Abbie shook her head.

"Are you sure? We already know he lied about his name and about where he works." Trunk held her hand between his.

"Why? What would he get out of drugging me?" Abbie sighed.

"What would he get out of having you attacked?" Trunk asked.

"We don't know he's responsible," Abbie returned.

"We don't know that he's not." Trunk didn't know why she would defend him.

"Ben, he's not a violent guy. He may be a liar and a thief, but I don't see what he would get out of having me attacked." Abbie was getting pissed.

"If he's not guilty, then why has he vanished?" Trunk asked her.

Abbie glared at Trunk, but she didn't respond. He knew she didn't have an answer to his question, and everything pointed to Chad. They shouldn't be calling him by that name since it wasn't his name.

"Abs, I don't want to upset you, but we've got to go where the evidence is pointing." Trunk ran a finger down her cheek.

"Trunk's right. It's looking more and more like this guy is responsible," James agreed.

Abbie blew out a breath, and Trunk knew she wanted to say something, but she kept it to herself. She probably felt horrible from the drugs, but she would tell him eventually.

"Haven't you found that bastard yet?" Darren snapped.

"We're working on it, Mr. Martin," James told him.

"How can that useless piece of shit outsmart so many people?" Darren grumbled.

"Dad, stop," Abbie told her father.

"It's okay, Abbie. It's pissing me off too. If we knew who he was, maybe we'd find him." James wasn't the only one frustrated.

Abbie suddenly sat up straight in the bed and gasped. She frantically looked around her, and when she didn't find what she was looking for, she scanned the room.

"Where's my phone?" Abbie asked almost as if she was panicked.

"Back at the house, I guess. I don't think you had it on you when the ambulance took you. What's wrong?" Trunk asked.

"I remembered something. Chad... or whatever his name is, took me to a cabin once. I have the address in my contacts. It should still be there if it uploaded to the cloud. I think everything from my old phone is on the new one." Abbie tried to get out of the bed.

"Where do you think you're going?" Darren asked.

"Abs, get back in bed." Trunk held her on the bed.

"I need to get my phone. You don't understand. He said it was his family's cottage. There were pictures of him with other people on the mantel over the fireplace." Abbie was getting way too excited.

"I'll get someone to bring your phone here. You can't go home. The doctor is keeping you here for a day or two." Her mother tucked the blankets around Abbie.

"I'll run to your house and get it. Where did you have it last?" Chris asked.

"It may be in the kitchen," Abbie told Chris. "No, it's in the den. I called Mom from there earlier."

When Chris ran out the door, Abbie lay back in the bed and calmed. She had started to remember more and more every day. Trunk prayed something would click in her brain and tell them why she was targeted by someone out for revenge.

"I should have known something was wrong when I was up there," Abbie said.

"Why?" James asked.

"I asked him about some of the people on the pictures, and he said they were family. I was with him for almost a year, but I never met any of them. The second morning I was there, he was sleeping, and I took a walk around the property. There was a sign with *Sweeney Hideaway* etched into it. It was like someone purposely covered it with branches, but when I asked Chad, he told me it was the first time he'd seen it. He did tell me it might have been the previous owners," Abbie explained.

"You don't think his family owned the cottage?" Claire asked, but her voice sounded odd.

Darren must have noticed because he stepped next to his wife and wrapped an arm around her. There was an odd expression on both their faces, but Trunk assumed they were worried about Abbie.

"I know he'd been there before because there were pictures of him all over the place. There were even pictures of him as a kid. Maybe his last name is Sweeney." Abbie looked up at James.

"We'll wait until Chris gets back with your phone, and then I'll send the information to Sandy." James smiled at Abbie. "Glad you're getting your memory back."

"Me too." Abbie sighed.

Chris was gone about twenty minutes when Trunk's phone buzzed. He pulled it out and saw his brother's number on the screen. He probably didn't find the phone and didn't know where else to look.

"Have you tried calling it?" Trunk answered the phone with a chuckle.

"Tell James to get over here. The officer who was left here is unconscious." Chris sounded calm, but as a firefighter, he was trained to remain cool in a stressful situation.

"We're on the way." Trunk ended the call.

Chapter 20

"James, we got to get back to Abbie's place." Trunk jumped up and shoved his phone into his pocket.

"What's going on?" Abbie asked.

"Don't worry. Hulk is outside your room. I'll be back as soon as I know more." Trunk kissed her and ran out of the room.

Abbie stared after him, pissed because he didn't explain. Was Chris hurt? She wanted to know. She was irritated that she had to spend more time in the hospital when she felt perfectly fine.

"I'm sure it's nothing serious," her mother, ever the optimist, said as she smoothed her hand over Abbie's head.

"Don't panic until we know more, Monkey," her father told her.

Abbie stared at him as if he was crazy. The man who used to punch people and then ask questions, telling her to relax. She snorted because, as a child, she used to think her dad was calm and cool. As an adult, she realized he was a hot head sometimes.

"Dad, you're telling me not to panic, but I can see the vein in your forehead getting bigger by the minute." Abbie chuckled.

"You stop worrying about the vein on my forehead and get some rest. I'm going to grab a coffee from the cafeteria." Her father kissed her cheek and walked out through the door.

"He's going to interrogate Hulk," Abbie scoffed.

"More than likely." Her mother smiled, but it seemed forced.

Abbie rested her head back on the bed and met her mother's eyes. Her mom looked ready to burst into tears, and Abbie felt awful for upsetting her parents again.

"Mom, I'm fine." Abbie grasped her mother's hand.

"Abbie, I wouldn't survive losing you."

A tear ran down her mother's cheek. Abbie sat up and wrapped her arms around her mother, trying hard to hold back her own grief. Abbie missed her sister, but her parents lost a child, and that was something a person never got over.

"I'll be fine, Mom." Abbie tried to sound positive, but the truth was she was frightened.

If she'd been home alone when she drank the coffee, she could have died. She argued with Trunk about who was responsible because she didn't want to believe she could be stupid enough to date someone capable of such a dreadful thing.

Trunk and James were gone more than two hours, and Trunk hadn't called or returned. Neither had her father. Abbie asked Hulk if he knew what happened, but the asshole said he didn't know. She didn't believe him, but she didn't have a phone to call anyone.

"Mom, please give me your phone," Abbie begged.

"Honey, I don't have it with me. Maybe when your father returns, he'll have his." Her mother sat back in the chair, staring at the tiny television next to Abbie's bed.

She didn't understand how her mom could remain so calm when they didn't know where either of their men had gone. Abbie was tired of lying in the hospital bed. Her daily entertainment was when the cute doctor came to see her.

Adam was a nice guy, and he had a wonderful bedside manner. She'd met him first after the fire, and except for being a huge flirt, he was a nice guy.

When he left the room, he told her if things went well overnight, he'd release her in the morning. That didn't help make her feel better. Abbie wanted to go home and see why Trunk ran out in such a hurry.

"Do you come here so you can spend more time with me?" Dana entered her room with a huge smirk.

"Yes, because I never see you." Abbie snorted.

"Maybe if you stayed out of the hospital, I'd drop by your house and have a glass of wine." Dana sat on her bed.

"I doubt that." Abbie laughed.

"Billie filled me in on the whole story. Chad is not Chad." Dana shook her head.

"Yeah, I hope when they find him, they kick his balls up in his stomach and then shove his head up his own ass," Abbie grumbled.

"That sounds like it would be painful." Dana laughed.

"Not painful enough." Abbie sighed.

"At least one good thing came out of it." Dana smiled.

"What good came out of all this?" Abbie looked at her friend like she was crazy.

"You and Ben." Dana winked.

"I'm so glad they're together." Her mother smiled.

"I wanted to kick him in the ass back then, but I guess I can understand why he did what he did." Dana shrugged.

Abbie wanted to kick his ass too, but she was more concerned about what happened at her house. Hulk had to know something.

Chapter 21

Trunk's heart raced as he ran up the front steps of Abbie's house behind James. They found Chris in the kitchen kneeling on the floor next to a young police officer. She was awake, but Chris had a cloth pressed to the top of her head, and the young officer looked annoyed.

"I'm fine. Can I get up?" she grumbled.

"Natalie, stay there until the paramedics get here," James told the woman.

"I've been telling her that since she opened her eyes. She told me I don't know what I'm talking about." Chris chuckled.

"He's a firefighter," Trunk told the girl.

"Of course, he is." Natalie sighed.

"Can you tell me what happened?" James asked.

"I was outside the door and heard something in the house. It sounded like cupboards slamming. I opened the door and called out, and I know I heard someone curse. I came into the kitchen but didn't see anyone. I checked all the rooms, but when I walked into the office, someone clocked me over the head." Natalie pushed Chris' hand away and held the cloth to her own head.

"She was in the kitchen when I got here," Chris told them.

"Where's your weapon?" James asked.

Trunk glanced down at her holster and noticed it was empty. Natalie's eyes grew big, and she sat up before anyone could stop her. When she tried to stand, she swayed, and Chris caught her before she hit the floor.

"Natalie, sit down for Christ's sake," James ordered.

"I had it in my hand when I entered the house," Natalie said as Trunk and Chris helped her to a kitchen chair.

"I'll check the house. Maybe..." Trunk was interrupted when she put up her hand.

"Maybe the asshole who knocked me out took it. I just made the biggest rookie mistake of my career. I knew I should never have joined the department." Natalie sighed.

"Natalie French, you made a mistake. You're not the first to screw up on the job, and you won't be the last, but we do need to report your missing weapon." James pulled out his phone and tapped the screen.

"How could I be so stupid?" Natalie whispered.

"Don't be so hard on yourself," Chris spoke softly.

"I should've stuck to being a receptionist for the Newfoundland Police Department." She sighed and covered her face with her hands.

Chris met Trunk's eyes, and they both shrugged. Neither of them knew how to help the poor woman. She'd made a major blunder, but she was human. Trunk decided to check the rest of the house in case, by some slim chance, it was in another room.

Trunk headed to the den and when he stepped into the room he wanted to roar in anger. Abbie's office was a disaster. Someone had torn the room apart. Trunk didn't know what they were looking for, because Abbie hadn't been able to find anything in the papers when she searched through them earlier.

As Trunk turned to leave the office, he saw something sticking out from under the credenza. He crouched to get a better look and smiled as he reached for the SIG Sauer P226 handgun. He held it by the grip and made his way to the kitchen.

The paramedics had arrived, and Natalie was trying to tell them she didn't need to go to the hospital. Trunk chuckled at the spunky woman as she argued with the frustrated paramedic.

"Natalie, I have great news." Trunk held her weapon behind his back.

"I didn't leave any bloodstains on the floor," Natalie scoffed.

"I'll tell you if you go to the hospital and be examined," Trunk teased.

"What am I, eight years old?" Natalie returned.

"She's going to the hospital, or I'll have her suspended." James stepped behind Trunk.

Natalie's mouth dropped open and closed again. It was obvious she wanted to say something, but since James was her supervisor, it wouldn't be a good idea.

"Fine." She sighed.

"If it helps. I found this under the credenza." Trunk placed her weapon on the table.

"Thank God," Natalie blew out a sigh of relief.

"You must have dropped it when someone hit you," Trunk explained.

"At least we don't have to worry about that," James said.

When Natalie was taken off in the ambulance, James, Trunk, and Chris searched the house to see if anything was missing. Natalie heard cupboards slamming, but Trunk didn't notice anything in the kitchen missing, besides Abbie's coffee pods, but the police took those.

"Natalie is a real spitfire," Chris said as he helped Trunk pick up papers from the floor of the office.

"I don't think she realizes she's a terrific officer. It's her first year on the force, and it took her a few years to get the courses she needed to be accepted to the academy," James told them.

"At least she didn't have her weapon stolen," Chris replied.

"Yeah, that would be a huge mark on her record." James walked around the office. "What was he looking for?"

"I have no idea, but I hope he didn't find it." Trunk dropped some papers on the desk as his phone buzzed. "Hello."

"You better get back here before Abbie has an embolism." Hulk chuckled.

"We had a bit of a situation here, but I'll head back shortly," Trunk told his friend.

"Okay, she's sending her mother to harass me every ten minutes, and her dad headed out shortly after you. He hasn't come back either," Hulk said.

"Did he say where he was going?" Trunk asked.

"No, told me to keep Abbie safe and practically ran out the door," Hulk explained.

"Okay. He might have had something to do at home," Trunk said, but he had a feeling Darren was on a mission.

Trunk found Abbie's phone on the kitchen counter and grabbed it before he left the house. He asked James to drop by Darren's house to see if everything was okay, because Abbie's father wasn't answering Trunk's phone calls.

After Trunk arrived at the hospital, he waited for her to yell at him, then he gave Abbie her phone. He apologized for leaving without an explanation, and after a quick kiss, Abbie sent the address of the cottage to James.

"Where is Dad?" Abbie asked as if Trunk should know.

"I don't know." Trunk shook his head.

"He left with you," Abbie accused.

"No, he didn't. I haven't seen him since I left earlier," Trunk told her.

Abbie stared at him for a minute and then turned to her mother. Both women seemed concerned about Darren's sudden disappearance. Trunk was curious himself, but no matter who called Darren's cell phone, he didn't answer.

"Maybe he left the phone in his car, and he's at home." Claire didn't sound convinced.

"Did you try the landline?" Abbie asked her mother.

"Yes, but he never answers that phone," Claire replied, but Trunk could see the woman was anxious.

"James is going to drop by your house and see if Darren is there," Trunk assured the women.

A little over an hour later, Darren hadn't returned, and James informed them he wasn't home. Trunk was worried. Since the attacker told Abbie he stabbed her for payback, maybe Darren was in trouble too.

"Ben, where is my dad?" Abbie whispered as her mother stared out the window with Abbie's phone to her ear.

"I wish I knew." Trunk sat next to her and pulled her into his arms.

"If anything happens to him…" Abbie pressed her lips together, and tears filled her eyes.

"Don't think like that, Abs." Trunk kissed her temple.

Abbie fell asleep a short time later, and Claire curled up in a chair, texting her husband. Darren didn't respond, and Trunk could see she was ready to burst into tears. He pulled out his phone, stepped outside the room, and tapped the number of the one person he knew could find Darren's phone. Hopefully, it would tell them where to find the man.

"Hey, Trunk. How's Abbie?" Sandy asked.

"She's doing okay, but I need you to do something for me," Trunk said.

"Sure, what do you need?"

"Can you track Darren's phone and get a location? He left here a few hours ago, and he's not responding to calls or texts, and he wasn't at his house. Nobody knows where he is," Trunk explained.

"James already got me on it. I'm tracking the GPS on Darren's truck, too," Sandy said.

"Have you found anything?" Trunk knew if anyone could find Darren, Sandy would.

"He's stopped on a small road in Calvert," Sandy informed him.

"Did you tell James?" Trunk asked.

"Yes, he's going after him. James said the cottage Abbie told him about is on that road."

"How would he know where the cabin is?" Trunk knew Darren left before Abbie had the address.

"Hell if I know. Maybe Abbie told him," Sandy suggested.

"Maybe. Call me if you hear anything." He ended the call before Sandy could respond.

When Trunk returned to the room, Abbie was still sleeping, but Claire stood next to the window, seemingly lost in her own world. Trunk stepped next to her, but she didn't notice.

"Claire, did Abbie give Darren the address of that cottage?" Trunk whispered so he wouldn't wake Abbie.

"No. She was waiting for your brother to come back with her phone." Claire didn't look at him.

"Why would Darren go to Calvert?" Trunk asked.

"Calvert?" Claire's head snapped up, and she stared wide-eyed at Trunk.

"Sandy tracked his phone and GPS. It shows he's near the cottage," Trunk explained.

Claire's forehead furrowed, and her eyes darted back and forth as if she wanted to remember something. After a few seconds, she grabbed Trunk's arm.

"Abbie said she saw a sign with the name Sweeney on it, right?" Claire whispered.

"Yeah." Trunk nodded.

"Oh, God." Claire choked out.

"Claire, what's wrong?" Trunk held her arm as she eased down in the chair.

"He wouldn't," Claire murmured.

"Claire, talk to me." Trunk grabbed Claire's shoulders and gave her a gentle shake.

She looked up at him, and all Trunk could see was pure terror. She glanced over toward Abbie and put her finger to her lips as she dragged Trunk out of the room. She didn't speak again until they were halfway down the corridor.

"Claire, what's wrong? You looked terrified." Trunk ducked down so he could look into Claire's eyes.

For a moment, she didn't speak but when she lifted her head to look at him, she had tears in her eyes. The sight made Trunk's gut clench.

"Darren is going to kill him," Claire croaked.

Chapter 22

Abbie woke to a quiet room and quickly realized she was alone. She threw back the covers and eased out of bed. Before she attempted to find anyone, Abbie steadied herself on her feet, then she made her way to the door.

Abbie scuffed out of the room, holding the back of her gown to prevent her ass from hanging out. She saw Hulk across from the door with his back braced against the wall. He looked up from his phone when he heard her.

"Hey, I don't think you're supposed to be out of bed." Hulk pushed off the wall.

"Where are Ben and my parents?" Abbie asked.

Hulk didn't say anything as he placed his arm around her shoulders and tried to guide her back to the bed. Abbie ducked under his arm and glared at him. He wasn't going to brush her question off like it was nothing.

"Hulk, I am not some fragile piece of glass that will break. Where is everyone?" Abbie shouted.

"I'll tell you after you're back in there." Hulk pointed toward bed.

"Don't piss me off." Abbie poked him in the chest.

"Trunk and your mom are down the hall. I guess they didn't want to wake you." Hulk motioned to the bed again.

"Where's my father?" Abbie asked.

"I don't know." Hulk again waved his hand in the direction of the empty bed.

"I'm going to put you in that bed if you don't give me some answers," Abbie snapped.

"Jesus, you're worse than Sandy." Hulk shook his head. "I'll get Trunk, but you need to get back in there."

Abbie glared at the handsome man but decided to get back in bed since she felt slightly dizzy. There was also the fact her ass was not exactly covered by the gown.

"Turn around," Abbie told Hulk.

He did as she asked and Abbie crawled back into the bed. When she pulled the blanket over herself, she gave him the okay to turn around.

"I'll be right back," Hulk said in a gruff tone. "Do not get out of that bed again."

Abbie rolled her eyes as the large man hurried out of the room. She rested her head back against the pillow and closed her eyes. How could she be so tired when she'd woke up no more than fifteen minutes earlier?

"Why are you causing trouble?" Trunk walked into the room and sat next to her.

"I thought everyone abandoned me," Abbie grumbled.

"You were sleeping, and we didn't want to wake you." Trunk glanced at his phone for the third time.

"Okay, spill it." Abbie sighed.

"Spill what?" Trunk wouldn't look at her.

"I swear I'm going to throw you out the window if you don't tell me. Where are my parents?" Abbie was starting to panic.

"Your mom is out in the hallway talking to an officer James sent here, and your dad is…" Trunk pressed his lips together.

"Ben, is my dad okay?" Abbie's stomach clenched.

"As far as I know, he's fine." Trunk stopped.

"Ben, please tell me." Abbie swallowed the lump in her throat.

Trunk took her hands in his and gave them a gentle squeeze. She didn't know if she wanted to hear anything he was about to say because she had a feeling her life was about to fall apart.

"It seems that when you said the name Sweeney and talked about a cottage, something triggered a memory with your father. He left to go to the cottage to confront Chad or whatever his name is," Trunk explained.

"I don't understand. I've never heard of anyone named Sweeney." Abbie shook her head.

"It has to do with something that happened before your mother and father were married," Trunk told her.

"So, this has nothing to do with me, and what happened?" Abbie couldn't figure out what was going on.

"James thinks your attack was an act of revenge against your father, and it's all linked to the man you knew as Chad," Trunk explained.

Abbie couldn't get her head to wrap around all that vague information. She knew her dad ran with a rough crowd in his younger years, but when he met Abbie's mother, he made a change in his life.

"Where's my dad?" Abbie asked.

"James is gone to meet him." Trunk was worried, she could tell by his eyes.

"What are you not telling me?" Abbie combed her fingers through his beard.

"Everything is…" Trunk began but stopped when she tugged on his beard.

"Please stop treating me like I'm going to fall to pieces."
Abbie narrowed her eyes.

Nothing he could tell her would be worse than the thoughts
running around her head. She never saw her father lose his shit
unless her mother or Abbie were in danger. It didn't happen often,
but her dad was protective, and if he believed Chad was responsible
for Abbie's attack, he'd act without thinking.

"Shit, he'll kill Chad or whatever the fuck his name is."
Abbie squirmed to get out of the bed.

"You and your mother think a lot alike, but you need to stay
in that bed. James will handle it." Trunk tucked the blankets around
her.

When her mother returned, Abbie knew she had been crying.
It didn't make Abbie feel any better, and her heart pounded in her
chest. There was no way she could handle something happening to
her dad.

"Mom, what's wrong?" Abbie sat up straight.

"Nothing, honey." Her mother smiled.

"Mom, you've been crying, and you look like you're about to
jump out of your skin. What's going on?" Abbie was getting pissed
off.

"I'm going to go check in with James." Trunk stood up

He kissed Abbie's lips and told her he'd be back. He put her phone in her hand and smiled. Trunk said if she needed him for anything to call. When he left the room, Abbie turned to her mother and held out her hand.

"Mom, please tell me what's going on," Abbie begged.

Her mother joined their hands and sat on the bed next to Abbie. She didn't know why but she had a feeling her mother was about to tell her something she hadn't revealed to many people.

"Honey, it's a long story. It happened before you and your sister were born." Her mother squeezed Abbie's hands.

"I'm not going anywhere until tomorrow. I've got lots of time for stories." Abbie smiled.

"Your dad loves you so much." Her mother sighed.

"I know, Mom. Tell me what's going on," Abbie pushed.

Her mom walked to the window and wrapped her arms around herself. She was silent for a long time but after a deep intake of breath, Abbie's mother began to speak.

"I had two friends in high school, Sharon and Lydia. We were like sisters. A lot like you, Billie, and Dana." Her mother turned to look at Abbie.

"I guess you must have drifted apart," Abbie interjected because she'd never met or even heard of the women.

"In my last year of high school, Lydia was dating a guy who everyone said was bad news. He was handsome, and a lot of the girls in our class were infatuated with him." Her mother turned to the window.

"Bad boys are always sexier." Abbie chuckled.

"Sometimes. Lydia had a brother who was older than us. He used to tag along with us, and he asked me out a bunch of times. I kept refusing to go out with him because he was Lydia's brother and well, to be honest, a little odd. I told Lydia about it, and she warned him to leave me alone." Her mother sighed.

"Did he?" Abbie asked.

"For a while, but after we graduated high school, a group of our friends got together and went camping. A couple of classmates' families had cottages close to where we were camping, and we'd go back and forth between the cabins." Her mother stopped and ran her hands up and down her arms.

"Isn't that the same weekend you and Dad started dating?" Abbie remembered the story of how her parents got together.

Her mother sat in the chair next to Abbie's bed and covered her face with her hands. Abbie had seen her mother at her worst when Laurie died, but she'd never seen her unsure. It made Abbie uneasy.

"We didn't start dating that weekend, but we became close. We didn't tell you everything. The second night we were camping, I was outside feeling slightly tipsy. Gary showed up at the cottage and saw me alone on the back porch. He…he…" Her mother pressed her lips together.

"Mom, did he assault you?" Abbie sat up.

"He pushed me down on the floor of the deck and got on top of me. I was screaming, and… his hands were everywhere, and he was so big…" Her mother was crying.

"Mom, you don't need to tell me everything. You were raped, and it's got to be extremely traumatic." Abbie ripped off the covers and got out of bed to comfort her mother.

"He didn't rape me." Her mother pulled back.

"But you just said…" Abbie was confused.

"A guy who was there with us heard me and stopped him, but he beat Gary. If Lydia hadn't stopped him, he would have killed Gary." Her mother blew out a breath. "Lydia and a friend of hers were hysterical and blamed me. Lydia's boyfriend was the boy who beat Gary, and he took my side. She was heartbroken."

"Was Gary or the guy charged?" Abbie asked.

"I pressed charges against Gary, and the police arrested him after he got out of the hospital. Lydia never spoke to me again, and she spread a lot of bad things about her boyfriend and me. She also turned Sharon against me." Her mother sniffed, and Abbie grabbed the box of tissues from next to her bed.

"Was Dad Lydia's boyfriend?" Abbie knew the answer.

"Yes. He got in a lot of trouble for the beating. We didn't meet again for a couple of years. People always referred to him as Hammer, but he didn't get the nickname because he nailed a lot of girls. They called him Hammer because of the night he beat up Gary. People said it looked like he was swinging a hammer when he punched Gary." Her mother sniffed.

"Okay, but, Mom, what does any of this have to do with me, and what happened?" Abbie asked.

"I didn't tell you Gary's and Lydia's last name." Her mother cupped Abbie's cheek.

"No," Abbie said.

"Their last name was Sweeney, and they had a cottage in Calvert called *Sweeney's Hideaway*." Her mother pressed her lips together.

"What?" Abbie gasped.

"The house you were in belonged to Lydia and Gary's family." Her mother whispered as she lifted her eyes to meet Abbie's.

"What are you saying?" Abbie asked.

"I think Chad is Gary's son and they targeted you because you're our daughter." Her mother looked terrified.

"Why Gary's son? He might be Lydia's son." Abbie shrugged.

"I suppose that's possible too." Her mother sighed.

"Couldn't we contact her?" Abbie asked.

"She killed herself about a year ago. She couldn't live with her guilt anymore. It was her fault Gary attacked me. Apparently, he'd been molesting her, and he promised to stop if she could make it possible for him to be alone with me." Tears streamed down her mother's cheeks.

"How do you know that?" Abbie asked.

"I got a message on Facebook from her last year. She told me everything and wanted me to forgive her. The next day there was a post from Sharon saying Lydia had killed herself." Her mother sobbed.

"I'm sorry, Mom." Abbie hugged her mother and didn't even care that her ass was hanging out of her gown.

Abbie tried to get her head around her mother's story. It was hard to understand how someone could hold a grudge for so long. Abbie found it hard to believe Chad was part of something so cruel, but if he wasn't, it would be a huge coincidence. A frightening thought hit her. If someone hadn't found her in the parking lot after the attacker stabbed her, she could have died.

"Who found me in the parking lot?" Abbie asked her mother.

"Chad told us someone leaving the restaurant found you," her mother said as she wiped her face with the tissue.

Was it possible that Chad put the drugs in her coffee pods? They were at her house before they left for the restaurant. He could have done it that night, or while she was in the hospital. Why would he have her attacked and have her coffee drugged?

Chapter 23

Trunk left a message for Abbie with Hulk. He wanted her to know he would return later that evening because he was heading to Calvert to meet James. Besides, she needed to have a conversation with her mother, and hopefully, between both women, they could think of something that would help.

James and Darren stood on the side of the road leading to the cottage. Chris and Trunk drove to Calvert together, but before they exited the truck, Trunk's phone buzzed. Their mother's number popped up on the screen, and he handed the phone to Chris.

"Here, fill Mom in. I want to find out what James has to say." Trunk tossed the phone to his brother and jumped out of the vehicle.

James and Darren were with two officers Trunk knew from Hopedale. They turned as he got out of the truck, and he could tell by Darren's expression how much pain he felt because of what happened to Abbie.

"Trunk," James greeted him.

"James. Why are we all standing here?" Trunk asked.

"Waiting for a warrant so we can search the cottage," James explained.

"I got your warrant right here. My size twelve boot," Darren grumbled.

"Darren, we can't let you do that. If you want to get the guy responsible for this, you need to let us do our job," James told Abbie's father.

Trunk could tell Darren didn't like what James said. Neither did Trunk, but he knew if he ignored James, it would end up with him behind bars. The man might be a friend, but he wasn't going to let Trunk screw up the chance of arresting someone capable of trying to kill Abbie.

"Have you gone close to the house?" Trunk asked.

"Cory walked by, but there aren't any vehicles visible, and all the curtains are closed," James told him.

Cory Fleming was Aaron O'Connor's best friend and both men had gone through the police academy together. The other man, Rick Avery, Trunk didn't know as well, but if he was at the scene, James obviously trusted the guy.

"Ben." Chris ran up next to Trunk.

"Is Mom okay?" Trunk asked.

"She wanted to know how Abbie was doing," Chris told him.

Someone contacted his mother and told her about Abbie's situation, obviously. He decided to call her after everything was over or drop by and take her to supper. Maybe take Abbie with him and allow his mother to get to know the woman he loved.

"I'll call her later," Trunk said as he took his phone from Chris.

"So why is everyone just standing here?" Chris glanced around the area.

"Waiting on a warrant so they can check out the house. We don't know if anyone is inside," Trunk explained.

"Can't you just go knock on the door?" Chris had a point.

"Chad knows all of us. He's not going to open the door if we go knock," James told Chris.

"He doesn't know me." Chris peeked around the tree to get a look at the house.

"What can you do?" Trunk asked.

"I can knock, and you can find out if he's there. I can say my truck broke down or something. Ask to use a phone." Chris shrugged.

"At least we'd find out if he's there or not," Cory interjected.

James stared at Chris for a moment then tapped something into his phone. A few seconds later, his phone buzzed, and James nodded.

"Okay, but don't go inside and put your phone in your shirt pocket. We'll do a video chat so we can see what you see." James explained.

"So, I tell this guy my car broke down, and I need to use his phone, but my phone is in my pocket. That's not suspicious at all." Chris snorted.

"Ask for a screwdriver," Rick suggested.

"That'll work." Chris nodded.

Trunk Facetimed Chris' phone, and they muted the audio. Chris positioned the phone in his pocket, then checked the sound and picture before Chris headed up the driveway. Trunk hoped they hadn't sent his brother into a hornet's nest.

Chris knocked then stepped back and turned, giving them a better view of the area. A few minutes passed, but nobody answered the door. Chris knocked again, but there was still no movement. Chris strolled around the cottage and leaned close to a window.

"Don't look like anyone is home," Chris whispered.

As he was headed back down the driveway, someone shouted from behind. Chris turned and walked toward the man, giving Trunk and James a clear view of a guy. It wasn't Chad, but Trunk had a feeling it was Gary Sweeney.

"What do you want?" the crusty older man shouted.

"I was wondering if you had a screwdriver I could borrow. My truck broke down, and I need to pop the belt back on the pulley." Chris walked toward the man.

Trunk was impressed his brother would come up with an issue with his truck so quickly. He didn't know his brother knew anything about vehicle repair. Trunk certainly didn't. It was why he always brought his vehicles to Jess' husband.

Darren was quiet while they watched the screen. The minute the man's face came into focus, Darren's whole body stiffened, confirming Abbie's father knew the older man.

"Gary fucking Sweeney," Darren growled the name.

"I might have one in the garage. Come with me." The man limped off ahead of Chris.

"Don't go in the garage," Trunk mumbled.

"Could you bring it out? I'm enjoying this great view. You've got a wonderful place here." Chris stepped back from the house.

"Yeah," the man said as he limped out of sight.

"Garage behind the house," Chris whispered.

A few minutes later, the man returned with a couple of screwdrivers. He practically slapped them into Chris' hand, and without a word, he turned back to the house.

"I'll bring them back," Chris shouted after the man.

"Don't bother. I've got too many as it is," the man snapped and disappeared into the house.

"At least we know someone is home," Rick interjected.

"Yeah, but not the person we wanted to talk to." James sighed.

Chris jogged down to the end of the driveway and made his way toward James, Trunk, Rick, Darren, and Cory. He waved the screwdrivers as he sauntered toward them.

"That guy got a major attitude, but at least you know someone is there." Chris shrugged. "And I got myself some screwdrivers."

While they discussed what to do after Aaron arrived with the warrant, a car raced out of the driveway screeching tires as it turned onto the main road. Trunk didn't see the driver, but Cory and Rick jumped in a vehicle and drove off after the car. As they left, another cruiser arrived, and Aaron hopped out, waving a piece of paper over his head.

"Here's the warrant. I'm assuming the asshole who almost drove me off the road was someone running." Aaron handed James a folded piece of paper.

"Yeah," Trunk told him.

"Let's see if anyone is in the house." James headed up the driveway to the cottage.

"Darren, you stay here with Chris. He's going to know you," Trunk told Abbie's father.

"I'll wait in my car." Darren turned and stomped off to his vehicle.

"Is he okay?" Aaron asked as they watched Darren walk away.

"Just something from the past coming back to haunt him." Trunk sighed.

"I'll stay here and keep an eye on him," Chris assured them.

Trunk nodded as he and Aaron headed up the driveway behind James. He knew if Darren decided to go after the man in the house, Chris would be able to stop him or at least give Trunk plenty of warning.

James knocked on the front door as four police cruisers pulled up. Three officers began to look around the property while the rest stood behind James, waiting for someone to open the door.

Trunk didn't expect anyone to answer, especially since someone drove off like a bat out of hell. He had a feeling it wasn't the older man and hoped Rick and Cory were able to catch up with the car.

"I told you I didn't want the screw…" The older man stopped when he realized Chris wasn't at the door. "What the hell do you want?"

"Sir, I'm Inspector O'Connor, and I have a warrant to search the premises for a man we suspect as being involved in an attempted murder." James held up the warrant.

"Just me here." The man tried to close the door, but James stopped him.

"Sir, this isn't negotiable. You need to step outside and allow the officers to enter," James ordered the man.

"This is my house. You've got no right to come on my private property." The man shook his fist at James.

"Sir, I'm going to have to ask you to step outside, or I'll be forced to arrest you," James responded.

"You can't arrest me." The man swung his fist and James grabbed it before it connected.

Five minutes later, the old man was in the back of a police cruiser, shouting obscenities from the backseat. The officer posted next to the vehicle rolled his eyes at the constant screaming.

"Did James get his name?" Trunk asked the officer.

"He gave James a name, but I don't think it's his actual name." The officer chuckled.

"What did he say his name is?" Trunk asked.

"He said his first name was, Kiss, and his last name was, my left nut." The officer smirked.

"Nice. Maybe I can get a name out of him," Trunk suggested.

"You can try." The officer opened the front door to the cruiser.

Trunk eased into the front seat and turned around. The older man glared at him with hostility. He didn't look like someone who could practically rape a woman, but of course, he was much older, and from the looks of him, he'd ended up with permanent damage after the beating.

"My name is Ben Murphy, but my friends call me Trunk," Trunk told the man.

"Good for you," he snapped.

"What do your friends call you?" Trunk asked.

"I don't have friends. Friends are nothing but backstabbing bastards," the man spat.

"Is your name Gary?" Trunk asked.

The man's eyes widened, but he quickly composed himself and glared. He wasn't going to tell Trunk anything, but it was obvious he was surprised Trunk knew his name.

"Look, the faster you cooperate with the police, the faster you'll get back to your house. We're looking for a man who's been using the name, Chad Grady. Do you know who or where he is?" Trunk asked.

The man stared at Trunk for a moment than a smirk formed on his face. He looked mean, and it reminded Trunk of the same sneer his stepfather would get after he'd beat Trunk's mother.

"I don't know any Chad," the man shouted.

Trunk wasn't getting any information, but he was about to bring up Darren's name when he noticed James walk out of the house with some photo frames in his hands. James stalked toward the cruiser and yanked open the back door. The action startled Gary, and he flinched away from James.

"Who's this man?" James asked as he pointed to a photo.

Gary didn't acknowledge James, and it started to piss off Trunk. The asshole stared ahead of him with a sly grin and ignored the questions James threw at him.

"Well, since we found your wallet, we know who you are. Gary Sweeney, and we're arresting you for obstruction of justice." James raised his voice.

"Fuck you," Gary bellowed.

Trunk got out of the vehicle and made his way toward Aaron. He'd seen the picture James showed Gary and recognized the man they knew as Chad, but he didn't know anyone else in the photo.

"He's refusing to answer James' questions," Trunk told Aaron.

"We know who he is, and that fucking dick Abbie was dating is on the pictures all over the mantel." Aaron pointed inside the house.

"Do you think it was him who drove off?" Trunk asked.

"Rick and Cory lost him, but they got the license plate." Aaron held up his phone.

"They lost him?" Trunk gasped in surprise.

"Yeah, Rick is furious. They had to hold back because the asshole flew through a residential area," Aaron explained. "I should have cut off the fucker when he flew by me."

There was nothing Trunk could do, and he was desperate to get back to Abbie. She and her mother had plenty of time to talk, and Abbie had a lot to process. According to Claire, the story Abbie heard of how her parents got together was not true. Claire and Darren didn't want Abbie to know what happened.

On his way back to Chris' vehicle, he asked James if he could take a picture of the photos. He wanted to show Abbie and her mother and let them know they made a connection between Gary and Chad.

Trunk managed to convince Darren to leave with him, but only after James ensured them he'd issued a warrant for the man they knew as Chad. His real name was Jerome Sweeney, and he'd never been in any kind of trouble before. Trunk decided to send the photo of Jerome to Cole. When he arrived at the hospital, he sent a quick text to the COO.

Trunk: Cole, we've acquired a picture of the man we knew as Chad. I've attached a photo. I'd like to know if you know either of the men in the picture.

Trunk didn't expect to get an answer so quickly and was surprised when his phone rang as he stepped inside the hospital lobby. Trunk tapped the screen and motioned for Darren and Chris to go on ahead of him.

"Hello," Trunk answered.

"Trunk, this is Cole Donovan." Cole sounded panicked.

"Hey, Cole. Thanks for getting back to me so fast. Did you recognize either of the men in the picture?" Trunk asked.

"Unfortunately, I did. I know both men." Cole's voice cracked.

"How do you know them?" Trunk asked.

"Jerome is my nephew." Cole's voice was barely above a whisper.

Trunk froze. It was possible Cole was in danger too.

Chapter 24

As her father explained what the police had found at the cottage, Abbie listened intently. The name Jerome sounded completely foreign to her especially since she thought she knew him so well. It was hard to believe he could fool her so easily.

Her father was convinced it was Jerome who escaped in the car, but it wasn't confirmed. Her mom looked scared and her eyes were filled with tears. Abbie could see her mother didn't want to hear any more.

"Dad, why don't we talk about something else?" Abbie flicked her eyes in her mother's direction.

Her father immediately walked around Abbie's bed and pulled his wife into his arms. He would do anything to protect his family, and Abbie knew the last thing he wanted was to upset anyone.

"I'm fine," her mother said.

"I know, but I needed a hug," he said with a wink.

Abbie glanced toward the entrance of her room. Her father said Trunk got a call as they walked into the hospital, and Chris left to see Fatima. Apparently, she'd been concerned about Abbie.

Abbie rested her folded hands in her lap. She was edgy and sitting in the hospital for a second time didn't make it any better. She hoped the doctor would keep his word and release her the next morning. Abbie wanted to be home and she wanted to see Trunk.

"You okay, Monkey?" Her father's voice brought her out of her thoughts.

"Yeah, I can't believe this is all a huge revenge plot to get back at you, Dad." Abbie couldn't get her head around it.

"People can do weird things in the name of revenge," her mother said in a soft shaky voice.

Before Abbie could respond, Trunk stalked into her room. When he locked eyes with her, he forced a smile and sat next to her on the bed. She was glad to see him, but she needed to know what the phone call was about.

"What's wrong?" Abbie asked.

"Why would you think something is wrong?" Truck chuckled.

"Because the pulse in your neck is pounding a mile a minute." Abbie pointed to his neck.

"Would you rather I didn't have a pulse?" Trunk smirked.

"Stop. Who called you?" Abbie insisted.

She didn't know what was happening, but Trunk's grasp on her hand tightened as he glanced at both her parents. He swallowed hard and then cleared his throat before he spoke.

"I sent the picture to Cole," Trunk explained.

"Donovan?" Abbie asked.

"Yeah, I wanted to know if he knew Chad. I mean Jerome," Trunk explained.

"That name doesn't suit him," Abbie replied.

"Asshole is a better name for him," her father snapped.

"Did Cole know him?" Abbie asked.

"Yes. Jerome is Cole's nephew," Trunk told her.

For a moment, Abbie stared at Trunk as if he was crazy. How was it possible for Jerome to be related to both Cole and the man who attacked her mother?

"Is Cole related to Gary?" Her father's rage was obvious.

"Gary was married to Cole's sister, but they divorced, and when Jerome was twelve, Cole's sister died in a car accident. Gary ended up with custody of him. Cole seemed troubled by the whole situation," Trunk continued. "He said the family begged Gary to let Jerome stay with them, but Gary refused, and Cole's family didn't want to put the kid through a custody battle."

"So, they let him go with a fucking asshole who tried to rape my wife," her dad snapped.

"Wait, Gary married Cole's sister?" her mother asked with wide eyes.

"Yes," Trunk nodded.

"Darren, we knew her." Her mother looked up at her father.

"We did?" Her father didn't seem to remember.

"Violet Donovan," her mother said.

Abbie's father stared off in space as if he was trying to remember the name. It took a few minutes, but his eyes widened, and he cursed under his breath.

"She was in the special education classes. Lydia and I used to tutor a lot of the students in that class," Abbie's mother said.

"She was developmentally delayed?" Abbie asked.

"Not really. Violet had a learning disability, but back then, people with any kind of disability were put in the same class. If you didn't learn the way everyone else did, you got stuck in that class. Violet was sweet, but she was easily manipulated. Lydia was friendly to her. Now I'm beginning to wonder if there was a reason for that," her mother said.

Abbie met Trunk's eyes. She still didn't know what it had to do with her. Why would Jerome try to kill her twice? At least everyone seemed to think it was him. Could he be that evil?

Sure, he was a bit of a chauvinist, but she'd never seen him angry or violent. He could be annoying, and if she was honest with herself, he was too boring for her. To believe he could do such horrendous things was hard to get her head around.

"My God, Gary is five years older than Violet." Her mother gasped.

"He obviously liked young girls," her father said.

"Cole said his sister married Gary. Do you think she could be convinced to marry someone who assaulted her?" Trunk asked.

"Maybe we should talk to Cole and find out how Violet ended up married to someone like Gary," Abbie suggested.

"I'll call him and get James to set up a time for an interview." Trunk pulled out his phone and made the call.

By the time her parents left to go home, it was after nine. Abbie tossed and turned in the hospital bed for what seemed like hours. She felt fine and wanted to go home to sleep in a comfortable bed wrapped in the arms of the man she loved.

Cole planned to meet Trunk and James at the police station in Hopedale after lunch the next day, and Abbie couldn't be there for the interview. It pissed her off, but James had to pull some strings to allow Trunk to be there.

She turned her head to look at Trunk. He sat in the chair, watching the late-night news, and seemed content in the small chair. When she squirmed around again, he turned to look at her.

"Do you have ants in your pants?" Trunk chuckled as he squeezed her hand.

"No, this bed is like sleeping on a bag of rocks, and it's way too small," Abbie complained.

"Looks plenty big to me. I bet I could even snuggle in there with you." Trunk stood up and kicked off his boots.

"If this is too small for me, you're certainly not going to fit in here with me." Abbie laughed as he squeezed in next to her.

"Now lay your head on my chest, and I bet you'll be asleep in no time." Trunk kissed her forehead.

Abbie thought it was impossible to get comfortable, but she couldn't help the sigh that escaped as he wrapped his arm around her and pulled her tight to his side. She was surprised how comfy the bed suddenly became, and she closed her eyes.

"Sleep, Abs. I love you," Trunk whispered against the top of her head.

"I love you too, Ben," she murmured as she drifted off to sleep.

Chapter 25

Trunk kissed Abbie as he headed out to the police station. He'd convinced her to stay at his house until Jerome was apprehended. Hulk was also bunking at Trunk's house until the situation was safe.

"So, can I snoop around and find out what makes you tick?" Abbie smirked as he opened the front door to leave.

"Snoop all you want, Abs. I've got nothing to hide from you anymore. I will warn you. My mother will be by sometime today. I asked her to come over so I could give her the stuff your dad held on to all these years." Trunk was still surprised that Darren had not thrown it away.

"Good, I can find out some stories about little Ben." Abbie snickered.

"I'll be back as soon as I can. I love you. By the way, I was never little Ben." Trunk kissed her again and winked as he headed out the door.

Hulk came around the side of the house and nodded. He'd done a perimeter check and stepped inside as Trunk hopped in his truck. He felt more comfortable with Abbie at his house than he would with her at her home. His security was better and in a town like Hopedale, Jerome would be spotted before he got near Abbie.

James met Trunk in the parking lot of the Hopedale division of the Newfoundland Police Department. It wasn't far from Trunk's house, and he could have walked there in less than five minutes, but he took the truck in case he had to run into town for something.

James was a supervisor with the department, and his twin, John, was appointed Chief of Police after their uncle Kurt stepped down when he was elected Mayor of Hopedale. James decided to take the lead on Abbie's case because she was a friend of the family.

"I found a picture of Violet in an old newspaper from after the accident." James handed Trunk the photo.

The pretty woman reminded him of someone, but he couldn't put his finger on it. Trunk felt for the family because Violet died too young. He couldn't imagine what it must have been like for twelve-year-old Jerome to lose his mother.

Trunk handed the photo back to James and glanced at his watch. It was past noon, and he started to worry that Cole wouldn't show up. When Trunk spoke with Cole the previous day, the man sounded devastated. He might not want more drama in his family.

"He'll be here," James said as if he'd read Trunk's thoughts.

"I hope so." Trunk sighed.

A few minutes later, Cole walked into James' office, looking nothing like the businessman they'd met days earlier. He wore old, faded jeans, a T-shirt, and a black leather jacket. He had a black helmet under his arm and would definitely be mistaken for a biker if someone didn't know him.

"Sorry I'm late. It's such a lovely day that when I got on my bike and drove out here, I got lost in the scenery." Cole shook Trunk's hand.

"What kind of bike do you have?" James asked.

"It's a nineteen seventy-seven Honda Goldwing. I know there are better bikes, but I bought it new, and I keep it up myself. My dad was a mechanic, and I learned a lot from him." Cole sat down next to Trunk.

"I'm James O'Connor, by the way." James shook Cole's hand.

"Nice to meet you. I met your uncle at a fundraiser a couple of years ago. He's a good man." Cole nodded.

"That he is," James agreed.

Trunk could see Cole was struggling with something, and he assumed it was the guilt over his nephew. Trunk knew having a family member who hurt someone else could be difficult to comprehend.

"So, Gary has Jerome into some terrible shit." Cole sighed.

"We can't be sure Gary is involved in any of this. Right now, Jerome is a person of interest," James explained.

"Trust me. I'd bet my life Gary is involved in this somehow. He hates our family and blames us for Violet leaving him," Cole told them.

"What do you know about Gary?" Trunk asked.

Cole's head fell back, and he blew out a heavy breath. It took a few minutes before he dropped his chin and looked at them. The pain on his face was easy to see and he swallowed before he spoke.

"Violet was the oldest of the four of us. We always watched out for her because she could be naïve and some people took advantage of that. If the doctors tested her today, they'd say she was on the Autism spectrum. She was intelligent, but because she didn't think like everyone else, the school shoved her into the special class." Cole's voice cracked.

"How did she get involved with Gary?" James asked.

"Gary's sister was a friend of hers. Violet was so happy to have a friend who treated her like one of the girls. You see, because she was in a special class, she was picked on by some students. Lydia was kind to her and invited her to parties, sleepovers, and they would go shopping. The only other person who treated Violet right was an ex-girlfriend of mine." Cole linked his fingers and placed them on the top of his head.

"But Lydia wasn't a friend," Trunk interjected.

"We found out when it was too late. Violet finished high school, and my parents wanted to find a suitable career for her. One day she told my parents she was in love and she was marrying Gary. My mother was hysterical," Cole continued.

"It sounds like Lydia was grooming Violet for Gary," James retorted.

"A couple of months after that, we found out Violet was pregnant. My father was ready to kill Gary, but he convinced Dad he loved my sister, and he promised to take care of Violet and the baby. In hindsight, my parents should've told the man to go to hell, but Violet was nineteen, and according to the law, she was an adult," Cole went on.

"I'm assuming he didn't take care of her," Trunk said.

"In the beginning, he did. He treated Violet well, but when Jerome was about three, Violet showed up on my parent's doorstep with her son, crying. She left Gary because he cheated. How he got any woman to sleep with him is beyond me. I did some checking into the asshole and he had been charged with an assault, but because a guy beat the shit out of him, he got away with a slap on the wrist." Cole's jaw clenched.

Trunk didn't say anything about Claire. Abbie's mother probably didn't want her secret told to a stranger. She'd kept it from her daughter for years, and it wasn't Trunk's place to reveal it to anyone else.

"How did he end up getting custody of Jerome?" James asked.

"My parents died within a few years of Violet returning home. My siblings and I helped her after that. She had a job, and she could drive. She was on her way to work one day and lost control of the car." He dropped his head, and Trunk could see Cole fighting back the tears.

"Is that when Gary got custody?" James asked.

"Jerome was twelve, and the judge asked if he wanted to go with his father. Since Gary never missed visitation or child support, they went with the wishes of the kid. No matter what my siblings and I told the judge, it didn't matter." Cole shook his head.

Trunk wondered why a judge would allow an impressionable preteen to go live with a man who had an assault on his record. It didn't make sense.

"Didn't they know that Gary had a record?" James asked.

"Yes. I've got a feeling there was something fishy with the case. I found out when the judge was arrested. He was involved in a human trafficking ring, but I'm assuming you're aware of the case. This guy was taken down by a young woman," Cole said.

James and Trunk glanced at each other. They were well aware of the case because Billie was the one who put herself in the line of fire. The people killed one of her friends and tried to kill Abbie and Dana as well.

"We do know the case. My brother's wife was the woman who took the head guy down," James said proudly.

"Bastards like that deserve to be hung by their balls," Cole grumbled.

"I agree," Trunk interjected.

"By the time we figured it out, Jerome was an adult and refused to see any of us." Cole sighed.

Trunk could see the sadness in Cole's eyes. The man undoubtedly felt guilty for not fighting harder to get his nephew out of Gary's clutches. Being raised by a man who tended to be violent could be detrimental to a child.

"He was a sweet kid, but there's something else you should know." Cole took a deep breath.

"What is it?" James asked.

"Jerome came to me about a year ago demanding money. I offered him a job, but he said our family owed him, and if I didn't give him what he wanted, I'd be sorry." Cole pulled an envelope out of his pocket and handed it to James.

"What's this?" James asked.

"That was a letter he sent after I refused to hand over what he wanted. He thought his mother had a huge trust fund, but my parents weren't rich, and Violet didn't have any life insurance. I told him when he came to my office, and he was furious. I got that letter shortly after that," Cole explained.

Trunk watched James as he pulled out a piece of paper from the envelope and read it. James didn't show any reaction as he offered the letter to Trunk. The letter was one page with three handwritten lines. Trunk had some trouble reading it at first because of the child-like handwriting.

Uncle Cole

I went to you when I was in need, you turned your back on me. My father was right about you, and I will never doubt him again. I will ruin you, but you will never see it coming.

Your nephew

Jerome

"So, this letter was a threat to you." Trunk handed it back to James.

"It was, but nothing ever happened. He never came to see me or contact me again. I didn't even know where he was until you sent me that picture," Cole explained.

James glanced up at the door of his office and rolled his eyes. Nanny Betty scurried into the room, and Trunk did his best to keep from laughing. She had a large bag in her arms, but Trunk didn't have to see inside to know food containers filled it.

"Nan, what are you doing here?" James asked.

"Marina told me dat ya've been here all day and had nuttin' to eat since ya left fer work dis mornin'." Nanny Betty began to empty the bag onto the desk.

"Thanks, Nan." James sat back in his chair, shaking his head.

"I brought enough fer all of ya." Nanny Betty put a plate in front of James, Trunk, and Cole. "Who's dis young man?"

"This is Cole Donovan, Nan. Cole, this is my grandmother Betty O'Connor... I mean, Roberts." James completed the introductions.

"Get some grub in ya." Nanny Betty pointed her finger at Cole.

"It smells wonderful, Mrs. Roberts." Cole smiled.

"Ya call me Nan like everyone else," she told Cole.

A moment later, Trunk's mother walked in, carrying another oversized bag. He jumped up to help and placed it on the desk. It was obvious there was more than enough food for Trunk, James, and Cole. There was possibly enough to feed everyone in the building.

"Cole, this is Fatima Murphy." James motioned to Trunk's mother.

She gasped, and for a moment, Trunk thought his mom was about to faint. Her face paled, and she stepped back until her back was against the door. Trunk reached for her, but she spun around and bolted out of James' office.

Trunk caught up with her as she stepped outside the building. When he caught her arm, she turned to face him. His mother trembled, and it reminded him of her reaction when they bumped into Jerry at the supermarket.

"Mom, what's wrong?" Trunk guided her over to a bench on the outside of the building.

"Nothing, I'm fine." She gave him a forced smile and fixed her jacket.

"Mom, you look like you've seen a ghost." Trunk could see she was anything but fine.

Before he got an answer, his mother glanced behind him, and her eyes widened. When he turned around, Cole stepped behind him with the same deer-in-the-headlight look on his face.

"Fatima," Cole whispered her name.

"What are you doing here?" Trunk's mother stood up and glared at Cole.

"I'm trying to help Trunk and James with a case. What are you doing here?" Cole asked.

Trunk glanced between his mother and Cole. There was no mistake that they knew each other, but Trunk had no idea how. His mother didn't run in the same circles as Cole, plus she'd lived in Corner Brook for years. He was about to ask how they knew each other when his mother turned to him.

"You can go inside. I'd like to talk to Cole for a moment." She smiled up at him.

"Not a chance, Mom." Trunk shook his head.

"Mom?" Cole croaked.

"Yes, this is my mother. How do you know her?" Trunk asked as he wrapped his arm around her protectively.

Cole stared at Trunk for a moment, then turned his gaze to Trunk's mom. She shook her head slightly, and Cole turned back to him.

"We met a long time ago." Cole smiled, but Trunk knew a fake smile when he saw one.

"Yeah, I was just surprised to see him." Trunk's mother chuckled nervously.

"Mom, you're not a good liar." Trunk narrowed his eyes and glared at Cole.

"Honey, Cole and I dated a long time ago," Trunk's mom told him.

"Really?" Trunk glanced down at her.

"Yeah. Your mother was my first love." Cole seemed lost in a faraway memory.

"You found another after me," his mother replied with a hint of sadness.

Her smile was not the usual friendly one, and there was something in her eyes that told Trunk, Cole was not faithful. When he glanced at Cole, he was surprised to see a frown.

"I had to kill time after my heart got shattered," Cole returned.

"Heartbreak is a terrible thing. Makes you do things you should never have done," Trunk's mother whispered.

"What the hell are you two talking about?" Trunk felt as if he needed a decoder to figure out their conversation.

"I have to go." Cole spun around and stalked off.

When Trunk turned back to his mother, he saw a tear run down her cheek and a huge knot formed in the pit of his stomach. His mother hadn't given him the full story on Cole. Before he could ask her any questions, several loud pops echoed around him, and his mother screamed.

Trunk shoved her behind the brick post in front of the building and peeked around the corner. He didn't catch the plate number because the car sped off too quickly, plus he got distracted by the man lying motionless on the ground.

Trunk ordered his mother inside as he ran toward where Cole lay on the ground. As he fell to his knees, he pressed his finger against Cole's neck and blew out a breath of relief when he felt a strong pulse. When he heard the groan, he rolled Cole over to check for injuries.

"Where are you hit?" Trunk didn't see any blood.

"I wasn't. When I heard the first pop, I dropped to the ground. I smashed my knee on the pavement." Cole sat up and grabbed his leg.

"Did you see anyone in the car?" Trunk asked as he helped Cole to his feet.

"No. Fuck." Cole winced as he stumbled.

"Let me help you inside." Trunk wrapped his arm around Cole's waist and held his weight as they walked into the building.

"That guy had balls to open fire in a police station parking lot." Cole grunted as Trunk helped him sit on a chair in the lobby.

"That, or he was just stupid," Trunk returned.

Officers flocked outside, searching the lot for any signs of the car. Trunk knew it was pointless because he saw the vehicle turn onto the road. James paced the reception area with the phone to his ear, looking livid.

"I've called an ambulance," Trunk's mother said.

"I'm fine. I'll go to my doctor when I get home." Cole rubbed his hand over his swelling knee.

"How are you getting to your doctor?" Trunk's mother asked.

"I have my bike," Cole replied.

"You can't even bend your knee right now. How in heaven's name are you going to ride your bike?" Trunk's mother crossed her arms over her chest.

"Don't argue with her. You won't win." Trunk informed Cole.

"I remember." Cole smiled.

"I also remember how stubborn you are." Trunk's mother narrowed her eyes, but there was a hint of a smile.

When the ambulance arrived, Cole didn't have the option to say no. Trunk's mom went into mother mode, and Cole got lifted into the back of the vehicle.

James sent an officer to the hospital with Cole, and Trunk promised to take care of Cole's motorcycle. Apparently, he was protective over the bike. However, Trunk was surprised by his mother's reaction when she saw it. It made Trunk more curious about the relationship between Cole and his mom.

"Are you going to tell me about Cole?" Trunk asked his mother after they arrived at his house.

"I'm not ready to talk about this." She eased down on the couch and covered her face with her hands.

"Was it that serious?" Trunk asked

He glanced up when Abbie entered the room. Trunk had called to tell her what happened, but he felt terrible when he saw the panic on her face after he got home.

"It's not the time to talk about this. You've got too much on your plate right now." His mother dropped her hands and smiled.

"Mom, even I can tell seeing Cole freaked you. Tell us." Chris sat next to her and wrapped his arm around her shoulders.

She sighed and closed her eyes. It was clear she was struggling with something and didn't know how to handle it. Trunk's stomach clenched at the thought of what Cole may have done to his mother. He might seem like a stand-up guy, but sometimes people aren't who they seem.

"Mom, did he do something to you?" Chris asked.

"He broke my heart, that was all." She cupped Chris' cheek.

"Then why do you seem so shaken by seeing him?" Trunk asked as Abbie sat next to him.

"I haven't seen him in a long time, and I didn't realize he'd returned to Newfoundland." She sat back on the sofa and linked her hands together.

"You must have cared about him a lot," Abbie said.

"I loved him." His mother smiled.

"What happened?" Trunk asked.

She stared down at her hands for a while before she finally raised her eyes to look at Trunk. Then she turned to Chris and blew out a shaky breath.

"He wanted to leave Newfoundland, and I didn't." She sighed.

Something with that statement had the hair on Trunk's neck stand up. The story was familiar, and he swallowed hard when his mother met his eyes.

"Is he…" Trunk stopped.

"Yes," she whispered.

Chris glanced back and forth between Trunk and their mother. His brother wasn't catching on to what his mother was saying. Trunk's heart thudded in his chest, realizing exactly who Cole Donovan was.

"Who is this guy?" Chris raised his voice.

"He's your father," his mother answered.

Chapter 26

The silence in Trunk's living room was deafening. Abbie watched Trunk and his brother as they tried to process what they'd heard, and from their expressions, it didn't seem as if they welcomed the news. Fatima pressed her lips together, obviously struggling to hold back tears.

Trunk sat quietly next to her and his body was rigid, but Chris' expression concerned her. His jaw clenched and his hands were fisted in his lap.

"He simply turned his back on you and left you to raise two children on your own," Chris said with no hint of emotion.

"He didn't know I was pregnant with you when he left," Fatima told her son.

"That's supposed to make it better?" Trunk spat out the words.

"Ben, we were both young. He had plans to go away to school, and I couldn't hold him back," Fatima whispered.

"Yeah, but you ended up with a man who almost killed you." Chris shot to his feet as his resentment poured out.

"Cole didn't know Jerry would be like that," Fatima said.

"Wait, did Cole know Jerry?" Trunk asked.

Fatima swallowed hard before she finally spoke. Abbie wanted to wrap her arms around Trunk's mother when tears began to stream down her cheeks. There was no doubt she loved Cole deeply.

"They were friends. Cole asked Jerry to take care of me while he went to school." Fatima sniffed.

"Are you fucking kidding me?" Chris threw his arms up in the air.

"Jerry wasn't always like that, Christopher," Fatima said.

"Cole obviously knew you had another baby if he and Jerry were such good friends," Trunk snapped.

"No. I overheard Jerry on a phone call with Cole the day I found out I was pregnant. He told Cole off for cheating on me with someone in Toronto. Jerry told him never to call again and said he'd be the one to take care of me." Fatima shook her head. "When I told Jerry I was pregnant again, he told me Cole didn't deserve to know, and he asked me to marry him."

"Mom, I'm sorry, but I can't believe you married a man when you were in love with someone else." Chris sat down again.

"I was scared, and Jerry treated me wonderful in the beginning. It was after his mother died that he started drinking and becoming violent." Fatima swiped her fingers under her eyes.

Abbie grabbed a pack of tissues from her purse and handed them to Fatima. She gave Abbie a soft smile and thanked her. Abbie didn't know the full story about Fatima and Jerry, but she knew it wasn't good.

"I think you need to talk to Cole," Abbie told Fatima.

"I can't do that. He's married and…" Fatima shook her head.

"Cole isn't married, Fatima," Abbie replied.

Abbie didn't know much about Cole Donovan, but she read an article about him a while ago. Cole got married in his early twenties, but the marriage didn't last, and he divorced the woman. He also had a daughter who was a veterinarian in St. John's.

"He married a girl we used to be friends with," Fatima said.

"They're divorced, but he does have a daughter," Abbie told Fatima.

"You boys have a sister," Fatima whispered.

"I think you should tell Cole. Keeping secrets only causes trouble," Abbie said as she met Trunk's eyes.

They knew from experience that holding back information caused more issues than it solved. She and Trunk would've been together since their one night, if he'd told her about his past. Maybe

Trunk finding out about his biological father might help him get over the guilt of what his stepfather did.

"Why would we want to tell him anything? He took off and left Mom with a toddler and a baby on the way. It didn't matter if he didn't know about me. He abandoned Ben," Chris shouted.

"I told him to go," Fatima told Chris.

"If he were any kind of man, he wouldn't have left," Chris returned.

Trunk sat back on the sofa and it seemed as if he wasn't listening to the conversation between his mother and brother. It was as if he was in a state of shock. It was almost certainly a lot for him to process.

"Ben, are you okay?" Abbie touched his hand.

"I don't know," Trunk whispered.

Before she could suggest he talk to Cole, the chime of the doorbell echoed through the house. Abbie went to answer it because the last thing Trunk and his family needed was visitors. When Abbie opened the door, she was stunned to see Cole standing on the step.

"Mr. Donovan?" Abbie glanced behind to see if anyone was there.

"Ms. Martin, I'm glad to see you're up and around, and it's Cole." Cole smiled as he shook her hand.

"Thank you and call me Abbie. I thought you went to the hospital?" Abbie stepped outside and closed the door.

"I don't go to hospitals. My physician checked my knee, and it's bruised but fine," Cole assured her.

"That's good to hear, but why are you here?" Abbie asked.

When he smiled and hitched his thumb over his shoulder, she saw the resemblance between Cole, Trunk and Chris. She glanced over his head and saw Cole's bike being lifted onto the bed of the truck.

"I won't be able to drive the bike for a while, so my brother-in-law followed me out here to pick it up." Cole pointed to the man at the end of Trunk's driveway.

Before Abbie could respond, someone stepped behind her and she turned to see Trunk. His body tensed as he locked eyes with Cole, but he didn't say a word.

"Trunk, I hope nobody got hurt at the police station," Cole said.

"No," Trunk answered coldly.

"That's good. I haven't had a chance to talk to James about the incident. Have they figured out who shot at me?" Cole asked.

"No," Trunk replied with the same coldness.

"I'm sorry, Trunk, but are you angry with me?" Cole seemed to notice the harshness of Trunk's tone.

"I think we should step inside and discuss this." Abbie motioned for Cole to go into the house.

Cole looked back and forth between Abbie and Trunk. He seemed apprehensive about entering, but when Abbie gave him a reassuring smile, he nodded.

"I'll tell my brother-in-law to take the bike and go. He followed me in the truck." Cole limped down the front steps and made his way to the man waiting at the end of the driveway.

"I don't know if this is the time, Abs," Trunk whispered.

"I think you need to get this out in the open so we can move on and find Jerome before he hurts someone else." Abbie took Trunk's hands and gave them a gentle squeeze.

"Fine." Trunk sighed.

When Cole walked into the living room, Chris didn't try to hide his hostility for the man. Abbie didn't know Trunk's brother well, but she could see he wasn't happy about Cole coming into the conversation.

"Cole, would you like something to drink?" Trunk asked.

"No, thanks. I'm good." Cole shifted nervously on the couch.

"Mom, do you want to tell Cole everything?" Trunk sat next to his mother.

Fatima looked ready to throw up, and she dropped her head. It took a little while before she raised her eyes to meet Cole's confused expression. His eyes flicked back and forth between Trunk and Fatima, but she seemed unable to speak.

"Fatima, you don't need to say anything. I understand why you were scared to tell me about the baby." Cole gave her a small smile.

"You knew?" Fatima whispered.

"Jerry told me," Cole answered.

"That bastard told you about the baby, but you still didn't bother to come back?" Chris snapped.

"Christopher, enough," Fatima chastised her son.

"Cole, this is my brother, Chris." Trunk did a quick introduction.

"I wanted to say how sorry I am about what happened with Jerry. When I came back to Newfoundland and found out what he did, I was dumbfounded. I knew he had a rough childhood, but he seemed…" Cole stopped when Chris jumped to his feet and stomped out of the room.

"I apologize for my brother. He's having a lot of difficulties dealing with all this," Trunk said.

"I can't say I understand. I'm glad you got away from your father." Cole shook his head.

Abbie listened intently to the conversation, but it was obvious Cole didn't understand what was happening. When she met Fatima's eyes, she could see Trunk's mother sensed the same thing.

"Cole, what exactly did Jerry tell you?" Fatima tilted her head.

"He called me about two weeks after I left and said he had a confession to make. He said he couldn't lie anymore, and I needed to know the truth so I could move on with my life," Cole began.

"What did he confess?" Abbie asked.

"He told me Benji wasn't my son. He said you didn't want to hurt me, so you let me believe the baby was mine." Cole's eyes filled with tears.

"Son of a bitch," Trunk said through gritted teeth.

"Am I missing something?" Cole glanced around the room.

"Cole, he lied to you." Abbie eased down next to the older man.

"What are you saying?" Cole's jaw clenched.

"Ben is your son, Cole," Fatima told him.

Cole stared wide eyed at Trunk, then turned his attention to Fatima. He stood up and limped across the room to sit next to Trunk's mother. It was as if he needed to be close to her. When she repeated her statement, he shook his head.

"I didn't know, Fatima. Jerry shattered me when he told me. I dropped out of university and went wild until my father gave me an ultimatum. I'd been running around with Rebecca, and we ended up married. I did go back to university and busted my ass to graduate. Things didn't last with Rebecca, and when we divorced, I moved back to Newfoundland." Cole seemed as if he wanted to touch Fatima's hand but was afraid.

"Why would Jerry do something like that?" Fatima shook her head.

"Obviously, he wanted you for himself." Trunk's voice sounded cold.

"He told me you were cheating on me. I heard him on the phone, but I guess it wasn't you." Fatima stared down at her hands.

"Cole, there's something else you need to know," Abbie interjected as Chris returned to the room.

He'd obviously been listening from outside the doorway because his expression had softened. Chris stood in the doorway of the living room with his hands in his jeans' pockets.

Fatima reached across the couch and took one of Cole's hands. Abbie could see there were still feelings between the couple. She felt as if she was intruding on an intimate moment, but Trunk had a tight grip on her hand as if he was afraid to let her go.

"Two weeks after you left, I found out I was pregnant again," Fatima said softly.

It seemed to take a moment before Cole realized what Fatima was telling him. The second it did, his mouth dropped open and his gaze moved to where Chris stood.

"Congrats, it's another boy." Chris waved his hands in the air in an obvious attempt to break the tension.

"That two-bit piece of shit. I'm going to hunt down that bastard and beat him within an inch of his life." Cole growled as he shot to his feet.

Abbie was shocked by the alpha side of Cole. Anytime she was in his company, he always seemed controlled, but watching him in the middle of Trunk's living room, growling like a bear, she had no doubt he was Trunk's father.

"He's not worth it, Cole." Chris shook his head. "I also want to apologize for being so rude. I grew up thinking my real father ran off and left us with a monster."

"I spent more than thirty years thinking the woman I loved betrayed me with one of my closest friends." Cole wiped his hand down over his face.

It was as if the realization of the information hit Cole at that moment. He glanced back and forth between Trunk and Chris and after a few minutes, he sat down on the couch next to Fatima again. He met her eyes and then turned his attention back to his sons.

"You have a sister… I guess she'd be a half-sister, but she's amazing. She's a veterinarian, and she lives in St. John's. I should call her…" Cole began to babble.

He stopped when Fatima dropped her hand on his thigh and smiled. It was the first time Abbie saw Trunk's mother relax since they returned from the police station.

"One step at a time, Cole," Fatima said.

"Yeah, sorry. Wow. I guess nobody calls you Benji anymore," Cole chuckled as he turned his attention to Trunk.

"Not if they don't want a black eye." Trunk laughed.

"I can see Fatima raised two wonderful men. I'm glad Jerry didn't screw that up," Cole said.

"We got away from him before he became too much of an influence," Trunk replied.

Abbie stood up to give the family some quality time together. She told Trunk she'd make some coffee for everyone and quickly exited the living room.

She stood at the counter, watching the coffee drip into the pot as if she was hypnotized by the process. Abbie was drained from everything that happened over the last couple of days, but she couldn't stop thinking about Jerome and how Cole, her father, and she were connected.

Revenge was the motive for everything, but it was all so random. Abbie grabbed a notepad and pen and began to write down everything that happened over the last twelve months that she could think of.

The one thing she remembered was Jerome never interacted with anyone at any of the parties or events if Abbie was close. He was always professional and never looked out of place. She also didn't see how the shooting was related to anything that happened to her either.

Abbie closed her eyes and put herself back at the restaurant the night she was attacked. She tried to focus on everything around her and not on the infuriating conversation she'd had with Jerome.

By the time Abbie focused on her exit from the restaurant, she was ready to give up on figuring out the connection. That was until she remembered two men off to the side of the entrance. Both men were older, and she remembered one of them had a cane. When she tried to focus on their faces, she gasped.

"Gary was at the restaurant," she whispered to herself.

"What restaurant?" Trunk's voice had her spinning around.

"I remember seeing Gary at the restaurant the night I was stabbed. He was talking to another man with a cane. I know it was him because of the picture, and I didn't put it together until now." Abbie started to pat down Trunk's pockets.

"Woman, what are you doing?" Trunk asked.

"You took pictures of the photos from the cottage." Abbie reached around and found Trunk's phone in his back pocket.

"Yes." Trunk handed her his phone.

She opened a photo with some guys standing next to a truck. All of them were holding rifles and looked as if they'd been hunting. She enlarged the picture enough to make the men's faces larger. She wanted to see if she recognized any of them. She gasped when she found him standing right behind Gary.

"That's him." Abbie handed Trunk back the phone.

Trunk looked at the screen, and his face turned completely red. She'd never seen him fly into a rage, but at that moment, it looked as if his head would explode.

"That fucker," Trunk roared.

Chapter 27

Trunk's body vibrated with anger. He couldn't believe he hadn't seen the son of a bitch in the picture before, but there he was next to Gary. Both of them smiling as if they didn't have a care in the world.

"Ben, what's wrong?" Abbie asked.

"That man is the bastard who killed your sister." Trunk tapped the screen and lifted his gaze to meet Abbie's.

"That's your stepfather?" Abbie sounded surprised.

"Yes," Trunk growled through gritted teeth.

"How does Gary know Jerry?" Abbie asked.

"Gary was married to Cole's sister, and Jerry was Cole's friend. They would meet at some point." Trunk spun on his heel and practically ran into the living room.

"Is everything okay?" his mother asked as Trunk stalked toward Cole.

"I'm not sure," Abbie replied.

"Cole, did Jerry and Gary know each other?" Trunk asked.

"Jerry was a friend of mine, and I believe he was at Violet's wedding." Cole shrugged.

"He was. He brought a girl from school. Remember?" Fatima said.

"That's right." Cole sat up straight.

"You were at the wedding?" Trunk asked.

"Yes." His mother nodded.

Cole studied the photo for a few minutes before he lifted his head. His face turned bright red as he handed the phone back to Trunk, and cursed.

"Do you think these two hatched some kind of revenge to get back at me?" Cole asked.

"And Abbie's father," Trunk continued.

"Do you remember the guy Violet married?" Cole turned to Trunk's mother.

"Yes, he owned the car Jerry drove when he worked for the taxi company." Trunk's mother studied the picture more. "He had a house on the same road where Jerry's family had a summer home."

"In Calvert," Abbie and Trunk said together.

"It's how they most likely reconnected. Is it possible they convinced Jerome to help them?" Chris interjected.

Trunk needed to contact James with the information. There was a possibility Jerome was hiding at Jerry's house. Trunk wasn't a vengeful person, but he wanted to be there when James put handcuffs on Jerome. He also wanted to see the expression on Jerry's face when he realized the lies he'd told all those years ago were exposed.

James was overjoyed with the new information. It took some convincing, but James allowed Trunk to be there when they knocked on Jerry's door. Of course, Trunk had to promise to stay on the sidelines.

Abbie didn't involve her parents because she wanted to wait until Jerome was in custody. James sent an officer to bring Gary in for more questioning. The police still had no proof any of the men were involved in the incidents, but Trunk didn't doubt it for a minute.

The house was about a kilometer from Gary's place, and the road was a mess. It was unpaved, and the gravel had sunk in some places, making driving over it like a roller coaster ride. When they pulled up to the property, Trunk exited the vehicle and made his way toward James.

"I'm going to knock on the door, and the rest of the officers are securing the perimeter of the house," James told him.

Trunk nodded and stood next to the car as the police moved in closer to the building. The officers seemed to move as one person as they surrounded the tiny house. Some disappeared behind the back and it took all his willpower to keep from following them.

Five minutes after James knocked, the front door opened, and several of the officers entered the structure. Trunk waited anxiously for them to exit with Jerome or Jerry, and it didn't take long before Jerry was escorted out of the house in handcuffs.

Trunk smirked as his stepfather rattled off a string of obscenities at the young officer. When Jerry eyed Trunk, the expression was almost comical. Before he was pushed into the back of the cruiser, he threatened Trunk.

"It's time for you to pay now, old man," Trunk yelled.

A few minutes later, another man was brought out, but it wasn't Jerome. Gary looked enraged and continuously shouted at the young officer leading him to the police car. It was impressive how the officers didn't seem to let the threats and insults faze them.

Trunk expected to see Jerome come out next, but James stepped outside and shook his head. Trunk cursed under his breath because if Jerome wasn't there, then where the hell was he?

"We searched the whole house and there's no sign he was ever there. I'll ask Gary and Jerry if they know where he is, but I get the feeling neither of those old bastards are going to help," James told Trunk.

"How long can you detain them before you have to release them or press charges?" Trunk asked.

"We can hold them for twenty-four hours. Then we have to lay a formal charge and be able to tell the judge why we're arresting them. We found some rifles in there, and if they aren't registered, we can slap that on Jerry because it's his house," James explained.

"Do you think one of the rifles was used to shoot at Cole?" Trunk was grasping at straws.

"I don't know, Trunk. We found slugs in the building, but they were from a handgun. If we find one of those in here and it matches the slugs we have, then at least we have Jerry." James sighed.

"Thanks, James." Trunk turned to leave.

"Trunk, tell Abbie and Cole they still need to be cautious. We don't have Jerome," James said.

"I'll make sure Cole knows, and I'll take care of Abbie." Trunk shook James' hand.

The entire drive home, he tried to think of a place where Jerome could be hiding. The ass was responsible for what happened to Abbie, and he had access to enough money to disappear. Maybe he already had and was on an island somewhere spending the money he'd stolen.

If he'd managed to leave, then the chances of finding him were slim. Once people got off the island of Newfoundland, they could go anywhere in the world.

By the time he arrived back at his house, Trunk was exhausted. He still hadn't had time to wrap his head around the fact that Cole Donovan was his father. He was concerned about his mother and how the news of Jerry's deception was affecting her.

When he walked into his house, he found Abbie at the kitchen table with his mother and Chris. He hadn't noticed if Cole's car was still outside, and he felt slightly disappointed that his father wasn't there.

"Cole is in the living room talking to his daughter on the phone." Abbie smiled at him.

It was amazing how she could practically read his mind. He wanted to wait for Cole before he explained what had happened in Calvert. He was too tired to repeat the story more than once, so when Cole returned to the kitchen, Trunk gave them all the details.

"Since there's nothing else we can do tonight, I'm going to hit the hay." Chris stood up and stretched.

"I should head home, as well. I've got to let the rest of the family know what's going on. By the way, Paige is looking forward to meeting both of you." Cole smiled.

"I've always wanted to be a big brother." Chris chuckled.

"With two brothers who look like you two, I don't think I have to worry about boyfriends hurting her," Cole scoffed.

"Is she having issues with someone?" Trunk went into protection mode.

"Not that I'm aware of, but she can handle herself," Cole said.

"Cole, you still need to be careful. Jerome is still out there." Trunk told his father.

"I will." Cole nodded.

"I'll walk you out." Trunk's mother stood up and followed Cole.

"I'm off to bed. Goodnight." Chris headed into the spare room.

"I think there may be some feelings still there," Abbie whispered as she nodded her head toward the front door.

"If he treats Mom well than I'm okay with it. Maybe they'll get the happily-ever-after they both deserve." Trunk wrapped his arms around Abbie. "Let's head to bed and forget everything for the night."

"I like the way you think." Abbie grinned.

When his mother was settled for the night, he and Abbie headed to his master bedroom. When he closed the door behind them, he turned to see Abbie dropping her jeans and unbuttoning her blouse. From the way her eyes burned into his, she wanted to do more than sleep.

"In a hurry to go to bed, Abs?" Trunk leaned against the door and crossed his arms over his chest.

"Uh-huh." Abbie's blouse slipped off her shoulders and fell to the floor.

"Do you need your PJs?" Trunk smirked.

"The only thing I want touching my body, is you." Abbie unhooked her bra and let it drop to the floor.

She stalked toward him, wearing a pair of white silk panties. Her breasts bounced slightly as she moved, and he licked his lips in anticipation of wrapping his mouth around her dark nipples.

"Why are you still dressed?" Abbie purred.

"I was enjoying your strip tease." Trunk slipped his arms around her waist and pulled her gently against his body.

"I'd enjoy seeing you with no clothes." Abbie tugged on the bottom of his T-shirt.

As soon as his shirt hit the floor, Trunk lowered his lips to hers and plunged his tongue into her warm mouth. Abbie fumbled with the button and zipper on his jeans and Trunk groaned when her hand slipped inside his underwear and wrapped around his throbbing dick.

Abbie devoured his mouth while she struggled to lower his jeans and boxers without releasing his cock. She stroked him gently, making his dick throb as he backed her toward the bed.

"You're so hard," Abbie moaned against his lips.

"You do that to me, baby," Trunk murmured as he lowered her to the bed.

Trunk kicked off his jeans, underwear, and socks, but his eyes never left Abbie. She watched him as her hands ran up the sides of her body and cupped her breasts. It was the most erotic thing he'd ever seen.

He grabbed the back of her legs and tugged her to the edge of the bed. Trunk lightly kissed from her knee, up her inner thigh, and to her sweet pussy. The scent of her arousal filled his senses and he nuzzled her through her panties for a moment. Then he moved to her other leg and repeated the intimate kisses from her knee up the inner thigh, back to the place he wanted to consume.

"Are you wet, baby?" Trunk murmured as he slipped his fingers under the elastic of her panties.

"Why don't you stick that tongue in there and tell me?" Abbie teased as she rolled her hard nipples between her fingers.

"Pinch those buds, Abs." Trunk pulled her panties down her legs and tossed them over his head.

Abbie wasn't bare, but she was groomed, and her dark curls shimmered with moisture from her opening. Trunk separated her folds with his fingers and slipped his tongue up and down her slit.

"Fucking delicious." Trunk groaned as he lapped at her opening.

"Oh yes." Abbie moaned.

She raised her hips off the bed and arched her back when he swirled his tongue inside her. Abbie squirmed as he continued to stimulate her swollen bundle of nerves, and her moans of pleasure made him painfully hard. The tip of his cock dripped with moisture, and he ached to slam inside her. He just wanted to make her explode on his tongue first.

"Ben... Fuck... don't stop... yes... right there... oh yes," Abbie cried out as she lifted her hips off the bed.

"That's it, give me that juice, Abs." Trunk growled and proceeded to flick his tongue rapidly inside her.

"Yes, baby. Fuck me with that tongue." Abbie panted.

Trunk loved that she enjoyed dirty talk as much as he did. She suited him perfectly in all ways and kept him on his toes. She didn't hesitate to tell him what was on her mind, whether he wanted to hear it or not. He loved her so much and being with her made him feel alive.

"Ben, yes...Fuck, yes." Abbie's hips thrust up, and her body quivered as he brought her to orgasm.

Trunk lapped every drop of her sweet juice as it dripped from her opening. She called out his name as his ministrations brought her over the edge a second time. Trunk lifted her legs onto his shoulders and gently bit each of her ankles as he reached for the condom he'd left on the nightstand.

The time it took to slip the condom over his swollen member was almost too long, but as soon as he was covered, he swiped the head of his dick between her folds, and her body shivered. Trunk slowly slipped his cock inside her, stopping just inside the opening.

"Do you want all of it, Abs?" Trunk growled.

"I want every inch of your cock. Slam it into me, Ben. Fuck me." Abbie moaned.

"I don't want to hurt you," Trunk said through gritted teeth.

"Fuck me, Ben. I need you to fuck me." Abbie swirled her hips against him.

"Jesus." Trunk held her ankles against his shoulders and pushed into her.

"God, that feels so damn good." Abbie moaned.

"Fuck, yeah." Trunk grunted as he slammed into her again and again.

Abbie slithered her hand down her body to the top of her pussy and swirled her fingers around her clitoris. The sight made him thrust into her harder and when he pushed her legs off his shoulders, she wrapped them around his hips.

Trunk cupped both her breasts and squeezed them gently as he pushed into her over and over. Abbie frantically rubbed her clitoris, and her pussy began to clench around his cock.

"Come for me, Abs. Squeeze my dick with your pussy." Trunk grunted as he thrust into her.

Abbie called out his name, and her hips lifted off the bed a second after the words left his mouth. Her legs tightened around his waist as her body shuddered. Trunk felt her squeeze around his dick, and he pushed deep into her once more as he exploded.

His body convulsed in pleasure, and he tried to keep from gripping her breasts too hard. His cock jerked as he poured inside her. For the first time in his life, he wished there was no condom between them.

He leaned down and pressed his lips to one breast, then the other, then kissed his way up her chest until he found her lips. Trunk kissed her softly and tenderly, trying to pour all his love into the kiss.

"I love you, Abs." Trunk held himself above her as he brushed his lips against her cheek.

"I love you too, Ben, so much." Abbie cupped his face between her hands.

"I'm so sorry we wasted so much damn time apart. Maybe if I had told you everything back then, you'd be safe." Trunk stared deep into her eyes.

"Nanny Betty says things happen for a reason. Maybe the reason all this happened is so you could meet your father, and your mom could find out he never abandoned her," Abbie whispered.

"Nanny Betty's words of wisdom, huh." Trunk smiled.

"She's a very smart woman." Abbie grinned.

"So are you. Not to mention, beautiful, sexy, classy, bewitching, mesmerizing, sassy, stubborn, and did I mention sexy," Trunk kissed her face with each word.

"You forgot loveable," Abbie whispered.

Trunk flipped them over, so she was on top of him and bit his lip when he slipped from her body. He cupped her ass and held her body tightly against his.

"Definitely loveable." Trunk chuckled.

"And the hottest sex you ever had." Abbie wiggled her eyebrows up and down.

"Without a doubt," Trunk agreed.

Abbie's smile faded, and she ran her hand down the side of his face, dragging her fingers through his beard. When her eyes met his again, a tear slipped down her cheek.

"Hey, what's with the tears?" Trunk used his finger to wipe it away.

"I love you so much, but I remember how much it hurt not being with you. I know I'd never survive if you left me again." Abbie's voice trembled, and his heart broke.

Trunk sat up with her on his lap. The condom lay damp against his leg, but he didn't care because he had to make her understand she would never lose him again.

"Abs, I am never, ever, going to let you go. I love you more than I could ever tell you, and I need you more than I need to breathe. You're my whole heart. Nothing or nobody is going to break us apart again. I'm. Not. Going. Anywhere." Trunk spoke softly and didn't hold back any of the emotion in his voice.

"You better not." She sniffed.

"Never. You're stuck with me, sweetheart." Trunk rolled her over onto her back and captured her lips with his.

He would spend the rest of his life, showing her just how much he loved her and make up for all the time they were apart.

Chapter 28

Another week flew by, and Abbie began to think Jerome had gotten out of the province, possibly the country. Jerry and Gary were both released from custody because there was no proof they were involved in anything that happened to Abbie.

She was also back to work, much to Trunk's dismay. He wanted to keep her home for another while, but she was going stir crazy, and it wasn't doing her savings any good either.

Billie told her they barely made the bills that month and one of her large home sales fell through because the buyers backed out. That meant she lost out on a huge commission that could have kept them afloat for a while.

"I'm heading out to show that house on King's Road. Did you want to go with me?" Tyler asked as he shoved a file into a briefcase.

"Actually, I'm waiting for a possible client to come in for a meeting, and Billie is on the way to an appraisal for the house in Quidi Vidi," Abbie told him.

Abbie checked the papers to confirm she had everything she needed. It was the first time in years that she'd been nervous when meeting a potential client. Maybe because she was scared that she'd forget something, or she wasn't as ready to go back to work as she initially thought.

Another of the men who worked for *NES* sat in the reception area, out of sight of anyone. Not that he would scare any red-blooded woman away. Hunter 'Crunch' Crawford was sexy as hell, next to Trunk of course. He was tanned, tattooed and breath takingly handsome. Not to mention, he had a body that made most women and even some men drool.

As hot as Crunch was, he didn't rev her motor when he walked into a room the way Trunk did. Still, it was nice to have something pretty to look at while she worked. Abbie waved at Tyler as he headed out of the office and then turned to Crunch.

"Hey, hot stuff. I'll be in my office. A lady is coming here in about ten minutes. Would you mind showing her into my office when she comes?" Abbie asked.

"So, I'm your receptionist now." Crunch snickered.

"Yes, and I want to see shorter skirts next time you come in,"

"Hey, that's sexual harassment." Crunch feigned shock.

"Honey, you have no idea what sexual harassment is. Ask Ben." Abbie winked and walked into her office.

Abbie organized everything she would need for when Mrs. Woodman arrived and agreed to sell her two-million-dollar home through Abbie's agency. At least the appraisal Mrs. Woodman had faxed that morning said it was the estimated value of the property.

Mrs. Woodman called Abbie directly three days earlier. Her husband had passed away and she was downsizing, which meant she needed to sell her home. According to the lady, she had no children, and the house was too big for a woman her age. She'd planned on buying a condominium once the house sold. Abbie had plenty of listings that would be suitable for an older person.

"Let's hope she's happy with me," Abbie whispered to herself.

Her phone vibrated on her desk and she picked it up. Trunk sent a text to say he'd pick her up after she finished for the day. Crunch would be heading to Abbie's house for the night in case someone tried to break in again. Of course, Trunk convinced her father the men were simply house-sitting and weren't on the clock.

Abbie knew the guys were getting paid for their time. She wondered how Keith and Bull made any money with all the discounts they gave friends and family. Then again, Abbie didn't know how many clients *NES* had.

"Ms. Martin, your appointment is here." Crunch walked into the office, speaking in a professional tone.

"Thank you, Mr. Crawford. Would you escort her in here, please?" Abbie smirked.

"I certainly will." Crunch nodded.

When he returned, he was followed by an elegant lady dressed in a black fitted dress and a pillbox hat. A black veil hung down from the edge of the hat on one side. To Abbie, it looked like something for a funeral.

Mrs. Woodman obviously had money or at least her appearance projected that to people who saw her. Abbie stood up and motioned to the chair across from her desk. There was something in the way Mrs. Woodman scanned the room that made Abbie feel as if the woman wasn't impressed with the décor in the office.

"I see you're a fan of Ted Stuckless." Mrs. Woodman nodded toward a painting hung behind Abbie's desk.

Ted Stuckless was a local artist who painted beautiful pictures of scenes around the province. His art captured the essence of Newfoundland's way of life.

"It was a gift from my parents when I opened my agency," Abbie explained.

Mrs. Woodman sat in the chair and placed her purse on her lap and slipped one hand inside the bag. She glanced over her shoulder at the office door and eyed Crunch at the reception desk.

"Could you please close the door? This is a private matter, and I would rather not be overheard by your employee, Ms. Martin," Mrs. Woodman requested.

"I assure you that your information will be more than safe here, but if it makes you more comfortable, I'll close the door." Abbie stood up.

As she shut the door, Crunch shook his head as if telling her to leave it opened. He obviously didn't want her to close it, but Mrs. Woodman was an important potential client. Abbie wasn't about to risk losing her.

"There you go." Abbie strode back to her desk and sat down.

"Thank you." The woman seemed to relax, making Abbie less anxious.

"I wanted to let you know I've looked into your home and dug up the history on it. I know the house on the property now is not the original home, but from what I can see, the appraisal is accurate. I do have three buyers who are interested in the property," Abbie explained.

"Already? That was rather fast." Mrs. Woodman raised an eyebrow.

"I've had some people requesting property in Topsail. Yours is close to a lake, and the current house is ten years old." Abbie glanced at her phone, facing up on the desk, and saw another text from Trunk.

"I'd rather you didn't pay attention to your phone while you're in a meeting with me," Mrs. Woodman complained.

"I apologize. It startled me when it vibrated," Abbie lied.

"Ms. Martin, I should be completely honest with you. I'm here for another reason as well." Mrs. Woodman pulled her hand out of her purse.

"Yes, you said you wanted to find a condo as well, I assure..." Abbie stopped when she looked up.

Mrs. Woodman had a handgun pointed directly at Abbie. Automatically, Abbie reached for her phone, but the click of the gun made her drop it back on the desk. She knew if she screamed, Crunch would be through the door in a second, but would it be before the gun went off?

"I wouldn't do that, Abbie," Mrs. Woodman sneered.

"Why are you holding a gun on me?" Abbie placed her hands flat on the desk.

"I need you to tell your friend outside we're going to look at the property I'm selling. We'll tell him my limo is bringing us and I'll bring you home." Mrs. Woodman stood up but kept the weapon directed at Abbie.

"He's not going to let me go without him," Abbie told her.

"That's too bad. I didn't want to have to shoot him, but I guess I'll have to get him out of the way before we leave. I can't have him calling the police or that boyfriend of yours." Mrs. Woodman walked toward the door and grabbed the handle.

"No." Abbie gasped.

"If he's going to be a problem, I'll have to eliminate that problem," Mrs. Woodman practically growled.

"There's a back way out of my office." Abbie pointed to the fire exit.

She ensured each private office had a fire exit. After the fire that nearly killed her and Dana, as well as the one she and Billie escaped, she wasn't going to be in that situation again.

"We can go out that way. He won't know we're gone until it's too late," Abbie whispered.

Abbie watched the older woman as she seemed to consider if Abbie was lying. The fire escape was a way out, and there were security cameras, but they weren't exactly visible to someone who didn't know they were there. At least the police could check the feed and see who took her. Mrs. Woodman wasn't going to let her take her phone, so there would be no way to track her that way.

"There better not be an alarm on the door, or I will shoot you and your friend out front." Mrs. Woodman turned the lock slowly, and the click was barely audible.

"The alarm is activated when we lock up for the night," Abbie told her as she tried to slip her phone up the sleeve of her sweater.

"Abbie, do I look stupid to you?" Mrs. Woodman held out her hand.

Abbie dropped the phone into the woman's open palm. As they walked toward the door, Mrs. Woodman dropped Abbie's phone into the garbage bucket and pointed the gun in the direction of the door. Abbie moved to the exit, and Mrs. Woodman stopped her before she opened the door.

"Quietly," she whispered.

Abbie pushed the handle and opened the door lightly, trying to be as quiet as possible. A narrow set of steps led down to the ground from her office, but when Abbie started down the stairs, Mrs. Woodman grabbed her by the back of the sweater.

"I need to get my driver to come into the alley to get us." The woman sneered.

Mrs. Woodman lifted her phone to her ear and ordered someone to come to the alley. Less than a minute later, a black car with tinted windows backed into the alley. Mrs. Woodman poked the gun into Abbie's back, and they made their way to the vehicle.

As Abbie slid into the seat, she scanned the back seat for something that would help her escape. A divider separated the front from the back, and it dropped a few inches when Mrs. Woodman got in next to Abbie.

Abbie was panicked, and she felt horrible for Crunch. She had a feeling he would be in deep shit when Trunk and Keith discovered her abduction. It wasn't his fault. Abbie shouldn't have closed her office door, and that was on her.

Before she had a chance to say anything, Mrs. Woodman grabbed Abbie's hands and placed a large plastic zip-tie around her wrists. Abbie winced when the older woman pulled the restraint a little too tight. After she wrapped a scarf around Abbie's eyes, Mrs. Woodman sighed.

"Drive. Now." the woman ordered, and the car drove off.

Chapter 29

Trunk walked into Abbie's reception area and chuckled. He was used to seeing Billie or Tyler at the desk, but Crunch behind the desk with his feet propped up on the edge was comical.

"What a pretty secretary." Trunk smirked.

"I'll have you know I'm an office administrator right now." Crunch chuckled.

"Where's Abs?" Trunk asked.

"She's in a meeting with some snob who didn't want the door left open because of her personal business." Crunch rolled his eyes.

Trunk sat down and pulled out his phone. He sent a flirty text to her and shoved the phone back into his pocket. While he chatted with Crunch for a bit, he continued to check the time.

"How long has she been in that meeting?" Trunk nodded toward the closed door.

"She went in there about forty minutes before you got here," Crunch said after he glanced at his watch.

Fifteen minutes later, Abbie was still in the office with her client, and Trunk was getting impatient. She hadn't responded to his text, but she probably didn't want to be rude to the woman in her office.

"Maybe I should knock and let Abbie know you're here," Crunch suggested.

Crunch walked to the office door and knocked. He waited for a moment, but when Abbie didn't answer, Trunk shot to his feet. When he tried the doorknob, he discovered it was locked. Without a moment's hesitation, Trunk and Crunch lifted their feet and kicked it open. The room was empty, and the fire door was wide open. The sight made Trunk's stomach tighten.

"Fuck, fuck, fuck." Crunch punched the back door over and over.

"Call Sandy and get her to check the security feed," Trunk ordered and yanked his phone out of his pocket.

"Hello," Keith answered.

"Abbie's gone. Someone took her out through the back door of her office, and her last client was a woman." Trunk paced back and forth as his heart pounded in his chest.

"Fuck," Keith roared. "I'll call James and we'll be there in ten minutes."

Trunk stalked back into the office and scanned the room for something that gave him an idea of where the woman could have taken Abbie. When he didn't see anything, he stepped out through the fire exit where Crunch was searching the alley. Trunk watched him bend down and pick up something but toss it aside a second later.

"James and Keith are on the way," Trunk told his friend.

"I'm sorry, Trunk." Crunch stomped up the steps.

"Don't do that, Crunch. We didn't know there was a woman involved in all this shit." Trunk shook his head. "We better wait in the other room. We don't want to disturb any evidence."

Trunk and Crunch made their way to the reception area and waited. By the time Keith and the police arrived, it was almost twenty minutes later. The office and the back of the building was searched but nothing was found except Abbie's phone in the trash can.

Keith did his best to keep Crunch from blaming himself for Abbie's disappearance and Trunk was doing his best not to completely panic. Abbie was smart, and she could find a way to escape.

"I should have told the woman the door had to stay open for security reasons." Crunch plowed his hands through his hair.

"Then Abbie would have kicked your ass for upsetting one of her clients," Trunk returned.

"I forgot about that fucking fire door." Crunch shook his head.

"Look, there's nothing any of us can do about what happened. We need to find her," Keith reminded them.

"Who was her last client?" James asked.

"Mrs. Woodman. Abbie said she was new." Crunch handed James a card with the woman's information.

"Harris, check out this," James shouted to an officer.

"Will do," Blake Harris nodded.

Trunk ran his hand over the top of his head and tried to keep from punching a wall. What the hell was he going to do? His heart felt as if it would jump out of his chest. He didn't know where Abbie was, or who the hell Mrs. Woodman was.

It was after midnight and six hours since Abbie disappeared. Trunk stood in the window of his kitchen, looking out at the pitch black. They had a video of the woman getting into a large black car, but it didn't have a licence plate.

James had Sandy searching for vehicles of the same type in the motor vehicle database, but she said it was like looking for a needle in a haystack. The only thing they knew was the woman's last name, and the car was a black Chrysler 300.

Abbie's parents were bunking in the room where his mother usually slept, but she'd insisted they take it. Chris was on duty for the next three days, so their mother slept in his room.

Trunk stared up at the dark clouds lazily moving across the sky. He willed them to do something to show him where he could find the woman he loved, but nothing.

"Cole called. He said he'd be by in the morning, but if we find out anything, call him," his mom said as she linked into his arm.

"Not much anyone can do. We don't know who that woman is, and I don't know where to look for her." Trunk sighed.

"They'll find her, Ben. God wouldn't put you two together only to rip you apart again." His mother cupped his cheek.

Trunk gave her a gentle hug, and as he turned to the window, he spotted the shoe box Darren gave him. With everything going on, Trunk had forgotten to give it to his mother. He reached across the counter and moved it next to her.

"What's this?" She lifted the cover.

"That's a box of things Darren found after Jerry hit Laurie. They were on the ground next to the car," Trunk told her.

She looked inside, and a soft gasp escaped as she pulled the flask out of the box. Trunk didn't miss the tears in her eyes, but she had a huge smile on her face.

"My God. I thought this was gone for good," she whispered.

"I don't know how he got it, but I'm assuming he wanted to sell it." Trunk pulled the rings out of the box.

"My rings?" His mother took them with shaking hands.

"Darren kept all this stuff so he could give it back to you one day. He said when he heard what Jerry did to you, he decided to keep it until he could return it," Trunk went on. "How did Jerry get these, Mom?"

"It's not important. It was a long time ago, and now I have it back." She hugged the flask to her chest.

"You're right." Trunk sighed.

"This flask belonged to your grandfather." She sniffed.

"I don't remember him." Trunk took the flask and flipped it over.

There was an engraving on the front, and he wiped his finger across it. Etched on the front of the silver flask were the letters *RD*. He assumed they were initials, but they weren't his grandfather's.

"What do these letters stand for?" Trunk asked.

"It stands for Ronald Donovan," she told him.

His mother ran her fingers over the letters and smiled. She looked up at him as a tear ran down her cheek. Trunk stared at her for a moment before the name registered in his brain. The flask didn't belong to his mother's father.

"This belonged to Cole's family," Trunk whispered.

"Cole took it to a party filled with Vodka one night. When it was empty, he asked me to put it in my purse. We forgot about it, and when I went home, I tossed the purse in my closet. I didn't find it until after you were born. He told me to keep it because his father never even noticed it gone." She smiled.

Trunk reached into the box and pulled out three rings. He handed them to his mother. She dropped two of them back into the box without a word. The third one she held up between her fingers.

"Mom, what's wrong?" Trunk asked.

"Those are the rings Jerry gave me," she said. "This one isn't mine, but I've seen it before. I just can't remember where."

Trunk looked at the small ring that wouldn't even fit on his pinky. It looked like the ring of a child or a woman with small fingers. It was a slim gold band with two pearls side by side. Trunk didn't know much about jewelry, but judging by the chipped band, it wasn't an expensive ring.

"Darren said everything in there was on the ground next to Jerry's car. If you don't own it, then where did Jerry get it?" Trunk asked.

"I suspected he was cheating months before…" His mother's words trailed off.

"He's a dick, Mom," Trunk reminded her.

"Maybe it belonged to another woman." She placed the ring back into the box.

"Don't you want to keep the others?" Trunk asked.

"I don't want anything he gave me." She sighed and picked up the flask. "I'll give this back to Cole."

Trunk skimmed through the jewelry, but his mother didn't seem to recognize anything else mixed among the cash. Maybe she was right about Jerry cheating, and he stole the rest of the jewelry from that woman.

His mother suggested Trunk donate the cash to some sort of charity, since she didn't want anything Jerry had stolen. It was just a few dollars, but it was better it went to someone who needed it.

The box only distracted him for a short time. Every second after that, his thoughts were focused on Abbie. He wondered if she was okay or if the woman who took her hurt her. Was she cold? Scared? Would he ever see her again? Trunk's chest pained terribly, and his stomach felt as if he'd swallowed a bag of stones.

"You'll find her," his mother whispered.

"I pray you're right, Mom." Trunk wrapped his arms around her.

"You need to get some sleep, Ben. You'll be no help to Abbie if you're falling down from exhaustion." His mother kissed his cheek.

"I'll try, Mom." Trunk sighed.

By three in the morning, he was tired of tossing and turning. He kept glancing at the other side of the bed where Abbie had been sleeping for the last week. He could still smell the body lotion she applied before she went to sleep every night.

"Abs, please stay strong. Find a way out," Trunk whispered into the quiet of the room. "God, help her get out of this and bring her back to me."

He leaned against the headboard, pulled his legs up, and rested his elbows on his knees. He kept thinking about the woman who abducted Abbie and what the purpose was. Someone already tried to kill her, and everyone believed this woman was tied up with all of it.

The person who stabbed her in the restaurant parking lot had said it was revenge. It was no doubt Gary would hate Darren for beating the shit out of him, but he would also hate Cole for what happened with Violet.

Was Jerry involved with any of it? Gary was with Jerry when James entered the house, so it was obvious they were still friendly. Jerome was Gary's son and possibly the one who tried to frame Abbie for the false house sales. Sandy was still trying to track the money, but from what Trunk knew, the account was overseas, and it would take some digging to get answers.

He needed to figure out how to put all the pieces of the puzzle together so he could find her. James sent units to the houses in Calvert, but if Jerry and Gary had taken Abbie, they'd be pretty stupid to bring her to the houses the police checked previously.

Trunk ran his hands over the top of his bald head and sighed. He felt as if he sat on the edge of a cliff, and any moment it would give way, sending him tumbling over. The edge of the cliff was the possibility Abbie would never come home.

"Fuck, Trunk. Don't let that enter your head. She's coming back. You're going to find her, and then you're going to marry her," Trunk whispered to himself.

Chapter 30

Abbie sat in the small closet she was shoved into when they stopped driving. Abbie assumed the house sat in the middle of nowhere because they drove for a long time. Since she was blindfolded, she had no idea where she was.

Someone walked her up five steps and in through a door that sounded heavy when it slammed behind her. She took sixteen paces and then was pulled to a stop by someone gripping her arm roughly. Mrs. Woodman ordered the person to shove Abbie into the closet, then the door was closed, and she heard a click.

It was then she pulled off the blindfold and was relieved to see a dim light above her. The closet was empty except for a bucket and a roll of toilet paper. She assumed they put it there for her. Clearly, they were expecting to keep her there for a while.

The zip-ties was biting into her wrists, and when she tried to gnaw through the plastic, it hurt her teeth. Abbie's heart pounded in her chest as she shifted to get into a comfortable position.

"Stay calm, Abbie," she whispered.

Abbie closed her eyes and tried to will her heart to slow down. She took deep breaths and tried to calm the panic. If she lost her composure, it wouldn't help her get out of her situation.

Abbie winced as she twisted her arms to see if she could loosen her restraints. She cursed under her breath and looked around to see if there was something she could use to break free. She looked up at a bar above her and noticed a wire hanger. Abbie struggled to her feet and grabbed one.

For a moment, she didn't know how it would help, but she pushed the hook between her hands and used her fingers to turn it toward herself a couple of times. The plastic dug deeper into her skin, and she whimpered.

"It's got to break sometime," Abbie whispered and pulled the hanger through again.

It hurt too much, and she dropped the hanger to the floor and fell to her knees. She could see blood seeping around her wrists, where the zip-ties cut into the skin, and as she stared at her arms, she blinked back the tears that threatened to fall.

"Stop it, Abbie. You can't fall apart," she murmured.

She shifted around on the floor until she found a comfortable position again and kicked off her shoes. Her wrists hurt, and she wasn't able to stretch out her legs, but at least she was warm.

Abbie rested her head against the wall and closed her eyes. She'd get out of there and get back to Trunk. She missed him so much, and she tried to think about what he would tell her to do in the situation. She was staying calm, but she was scared.

She didn't understand why Mrs. Woodman would abduct her. Abbie knew the woman had help because someone was driving the car. She assumed it was a man, especially when he grabbed Abbie by the arm. His bony fingers dug into her painfully, and she was sure she had bruises.

"Ben, I need your strength," Abbie whispered.

Abbie didn't know when she fell asleep, but she woke to muffled voices outside the closet door. They were talking in hushed tones, but she recognized Mrs. Woodman's voice and at least two men.

"The police are all over that place," one man said.

"Then it's a good thing we don't have her out there," Mrs. Woodman replied.

"They'll connect the dots. No matter what you think, these people aren't stupid," the other man interjected.

"I don't care what you think. Nobody will ever figure this out. It's not like they know my name." The woman scoffed.

"Who the fuck are these people?" Abbie whispered.

"I'm not going to jail again," one man snapped.

"Will you please stop being dramatic. Nobody will ever figure out who I am. Gary took care of that." Mrs. Woodman chuckled.

When Abbie shifted on the floor, she noticed dried blood on her skirt. Her wrists had bled while she slept, and the zip-ties cut deeper. She wanted to cry, but she refused to give in to the fear.

"Are you going to at least feed her?" another man whispered.

Abbie recognized the voice, and she wanted to scream. *Jerome.* He was there and knew she was in the closet. The fear quickly faded, and anger started to bubble up. Abbie didn't care how much it hurt. She was getting free of the restraints around her wrists.

She brought up her knees and continued to slam her arms down across them. It took a long time, but she managed to free her arms, but the ties bit deeper into her skin. She flexed her fingers and then grabbed the toilet paper.

Abbie wrapped it around each of her wrists several times, but withing a few minutes, blood seeped through the thin tissue. She wrapped more around her injuries and by the time she was done, she looked like she was wearing sweatbands. Her skin burned terribly, but she didn't care. It was the first step in escaping.

She blew out a breath and pressed her ear to the door again. Jerome argued with Mrs. Woodman about keeping Abbie locked in the closet. He seemed upset about it, but the woman told him to trust her.

"So, you're not going to feed her?" Jerome wasn't even lowering his voice anymore.

"I'll get her a sandwich. It's not like she's going to be here long anyway," the man said, and Abbie could hear the smirk in his voice.

"I'm telling you they don't have it," Jerome shouted.

"They have it, and I want it," the woman yelled.

"You're out of your freaking mind. We can't keep her here until you get some trinket you think they have." Jerome was angry, and it was odd to hear him out of control.

"Calm the fuck down," the man spat.

"No, I'm taking her home. This is insane. If I'd known this was what you were doing, I would never have agreed to it. You almost killed her, twice." Jerome seemed to be getting closer to the closet door.

Abbie huddled in the corner at the back, wondering if the man she thought responsible for her attack would be the voice of reason and take her home. She hoped so even if he was a jerk for his involvement.

"Do not open that door," Mrs. Woodman shrieked.

"This has gone way too far. You got the money, and you terrified her family. That's enough." Jerome sounded like he was right next to the closet.

Abbie heard a click, but it didn't sound like the lock. She curled up into a ball as she waited for the door to open. She didn't know what to expect, and maybe it was all a ploy.

"I said do not open that." Mrs. Woodman sounded as if she was right outside the door.

"Are you serious? You're going to shoot me if I let her out?" Jerome sounded scared.

"I will if you defy me," Mrs. Woodman sneered.

"You're just going to let her do this?" Jerome said, and Abbie assumed he was speaking to the other man.

"She has the gun," the man chuckled.

It was quiet, and Abbie prayed Jerome wouldn't endanger his life. She was angry that he was involved, but she would never want to see him dead.

"You're insane. I'm washing my hands of this and getting the hell out of Newfoundland." Jerome's voice got further away from the door, and her heart sank.

"You can go wherever you want, but keep your damn mouth closed about this," Mrs. Woodman shouted.

"Don't worry about me. I'm not going anywhere near the cops," Jerome returned.

"You're damn right, you won't," Mrs. Woodman said with an eerie tone.

Abbie heard two loud pops and a heavy thud. She knew what it was, and tears formed. She hoped it wasn't what she thought, but when the man shouted, she knew what happened.

"Why the fuck would you kill him?" he bellowed.

"Do you think he wasn't going to leave and run to the police? He'd turn us in and get some kind of deal so he wouldn't end up behind bars." Mrs. Woodman sounded as if she had simply killed a bug.

"What do we do with him?" he asked.

"Shove him out in the shed with the others, for now. We'll get rid of the bodies later tonight." Mrs. Woodman was getting further away from the closet.

Abbie gasped at the word, *bodies*. Who else did the woman kill? Abbie started to tremble because she realized Mrs. Woodman had no problem ending someone's life.

"Fine. Are you going to feed that woman? Jerome is right about one thing; you can't starve her." The man didn't sound afraid of Mrs. Woodman.

"Sure, make her a sandwich or something and give her water. We'll be gone for a while," Mrs. Woodman said.

It was quiet for a while, and then the sound of heavy footsteps getting closer to the door. Abbie pressed herself up against the back wall and waited for the door to open.

"You got that blindfold on?" the man shouted.

"No," Abbie replied.

"Put it on, or you don't get the food and water," the man said.

Abbie frantically looked around for the scarf they'd had around her eyes when they abducted her. She wrapped it around her head and sat back again.

"Okay. I have it back on," Abbie told him.

The lock clicked, and the closet brightened. She heard something thud against the floor and assumed it was the bottles of water. When he grabbed her hands, she whimpered.

"What the fuck did you do?" The man growled as he touched Abbie's wrapped wrists.

"The ties cut into my skin, so I worked my way out of them." Abbie didn't know what else to tell him.

"This is fucking great. I'll be right back. Keep that blindfold on," the man snapped.

The closet door slammed, and the lock clicked. Abbie waited for several minutes and then heard the door open again. There was a loud bang on the floor, and Abbie jerked away from it.

"That's a first-aid kit. Wrap those up better and put some antiseptic on it, so it doesn't get infected." The man slammed the door, and the lock engaged again.

When she pulled off the blindfold, she saw a large white box with a first-aid crest on the front of it. She was relieved to see bandages and antibiotic cream when she opened it. She carefully removed the toilet paper from her wrists and then cleaned the cuts as best she could. After applying the cream and bandages, she blew out a heavy sigh.

She spotted the sandwich on a plate next to four water bottles and wondered if she should ration the food since she didn't know when her abductors would return. After contemplating that she didn't plan to be there as long as Mrs. Woodman expected, Abbie decided to eat half the sandwich and take a few sips of water. She didn't want to drink too much because the last thing she wanted was to be locked in a closet with a bucket full of urine.

What seemed like hours passed, and Abbie stood up to stretch out her legs. She was relatively tall, and she had to stand close to the door so she wouldn't knock her head on the metal pipe.

She knew it was a waste of time, but she tried the door to see if, by some chance, it didn't close properly. As she expected, it was secure. She noticed a blanket on the shelf above her and pulled it down. She wasn't cold, but the floor wasn't exactly comfortable.

Abbie made herself as snug as possible and scanned the closet. There had to be some way to get out. The closet door looked solid, so she knew she wouldn't be able to slam through it without hurting herself. The pipe across the closet was locked into a bracket on each side and was solid steel. Abbie sighed as she kicked off her shoes and tucked her feet under her. She rested her head against the wall, and that was when she spotted it. A large stain on the opposite side of the closet. It looked like water damage, and the area had leaked several times since the stains were darker in some areas.

Abbie ran her hand over the damaged drywall. She knew as a real estate agent that a leak could make walls soft and easy to break through. She pushed at the darkest part of the wall, and it started to crumble. After she gave it a hard punch, she waited to see if someone would come running. When she didn't hear anyone, Abbie punched the wall again, and it cracked.

"Yes," Abbie cheered quietly.

She grabbed a water bottle and used the top to pound against the damaged wall. Abbie had done more damage with her fist, and she tossed the bottle behind her. She smiled when she saw her block heels. They were the closest thing to a hammer she had.

Abbie pounded her shoe against the wall over and over. She prayed the wall connected to another room and not an area where she couldn't escape. After what seemed like an hour, she barely made a hole big enough to put her arm through, but she could see into the next room.

The sight made her more determined to get out. Abbie pulled on her shoes and began to slam both feet against the wall with every ounce of strength she had.

Her legs tired quickly, but she managed to make the hole big enough to stick her head through and get a better look. The room had no furniture, and the hardwood floor had seen better days.

Abbie eased back into the closet and continued to kick at the wall until the hole was big enough to squeeze through. Praying she could get out before Mrs. Woodman and the man returned.

It seemed to take forever before she could crawl through the hole but when she managed to escape the closet, Abbie stood up and carefully approached the window. After almost eighteen hours in the dim closet, the daylight streaming through the window was a welcome sight.

Abbie made her way to the door of the empty room and opened it quietly. She needed to get out of the house before her captors returned. She hoped there were more homes close by, or she recognized the area.

Abbie stuck her head out of the room praying nobody was there to prevent her escape. When she didn't hear anyone, she took off her shoes and ran to the front door. As she grabbed the knob, she heard a deep growl. Abbie turned and locked eyes with the biggest dog she'd ever seen in her life. It looked like a Rottweiler and seemed as if it wanted to tear her to shreds.

"Hey, boy. I'm just going to go and leave you to your house," Abbie spoke softly as she carefully fumbled with the doorknob.

The dog took a step toward her, and Abbie froze. She didn't know if she could get out of the house before the dog had her, but she wasn't about to stay in a standoff with a dog until Mrs. Woodman returned.

"I'm sorry, boy, but I got to go," Abbie tossed her shoe over the head of the dog, and he turned long enough for her to yank open the door and get outside. "Later, Kujo."

Abbie slammed the door behind her and turned around. A smile formed on her face as she scanned the familiar area. She breathed a sigh of relief when she realized her parents' house was less than two blocks away.

As she ran down the front steps, she cursed under her breath. She had one shoe, and the pavement wasn't soft on her bare feet, but she didn't care if the road was made of razor blades. She was getting as far away from that damn house as possible.

It had to be early in the morning because she didn't see any cars driving up or down the main street. As she made her way down the block, she continued to glance back over her shoulder to make sure her abductors had not discovered her escape. When she turned the corner to the street where she grew up, Abbie ran as fast as she could to her childhood home.

Chapter 31

Eighteen hours never passed so slowly before. James had every available officer trying to find Abbie and Abbie's parents were beside themselves with worry. Trunk was surviving on no sleep and tons of coffee.

His mother was doing her best to help by cooking and making sure everyone ate. Of course, she had a ton of help with Nanny Betty, Billie, and Dana.

Sandy and Smash were digging into everything they could find on the woman they knew as Mrs. Woodman, but they assumed the name was fake, and the house she told Abbie she was selling wasn't for sale.

"Ben, you need to eat something." His mother placed a large bowl of stew on the table.

"I'll eat when Abbie is safe." Trunk sighed.

"Lad, ya ain't gonna be any good ta her if yer fallin' down from starvation. Do wat yer mudder says and eat." Nanny Betty placed a basket of fresh homemade bread on the table.

"You know better than to argue with her." Billie sat across the table from him.

Trunk nodded and reluctantly dug into the thick delicious stew. It was tasty, and he hadn't realized how hungry he was until he looked down into an empty bowl.

"Good lad." Nanny Betty smiled as she sat next to him with a cup of tea.

"I don't know how to thank all of you." Claire's voice cracked.

"Its wat family does, ducky." Nanny Betty gently patted Claire's hand.

Trunk glanced across the kitchen and watched his mother as she stared into the shoebox they'd left on the counter. She seemed focused on the pearl ring that seemed so familiar to her, and he'd noticed her picking it up several times. It was almost as if she was willing a memory to come.

Cole arrived after lunch with his daughter and an excited Chad. The young man was ecstatic to find out he had two new cousins. Paige was shy at first but happy to meet her half-brothers even if it wasn't the best situation.

"What's your mother looking at?" Claire asked.

"It's a ring that was in the box of stuff Darren had in his trunk. She says it's familiar, but she can't figure out where she saw it before," Trunk explained.

Claire joined his mother and he figured the mystery of the ring would distract the women for a little while. When Abbie's mother gasped, he shot to his feet.

"Claire, what's wrong?" Trunk asked.

"I know this ring. It belonged to Lydia." Claire held it up.

"Are you sure?" Trunk asked.

"Yes. I remember her aunt gave it to her. She'd bragged about how it unlocked her aunt's jewelry chest," Claire said.

"A ring that unlocks something?" Trunk found that hard to believe.

"It does. Watch." Claire twisted the pearls.

The pearls popped off, and under them was a small square and a star. Claire placed the pearls on the counter and pulled the two ends of the ring. They popped apart into two separate pieces.

"Well, that's different," Billie said.

"Oh, my God." Trunk's mother gasped.

"Mom, what is it?" Trunk was at her side instantly.

"Do you remember the Mahers? They lived next door to us before we left St. John's," his mother said excitedly.

"Yes." Trunk nodded.

"This was Mrs. Maher's. She showed this to me a long time ago. She gave it to her niece but took it back when she noticed her niece opened the chest and stole a pair of expensive earrings. She asked me to take it, but I was afraid because of... well, you know." His mother dropped her head.

"Yes, I remember. Lydia's mother was a Maher before she married," Claire said as she put the ring back together.

Trunk didn't know how Jerry would end up with a ring that belonged to Mrs. Maher, but it wouldn't surprise him if he'd stolen it. Trunk didn't remember a lot about how Jerry interacted with the Mahers, but he did know they didn't like him.

"Are they still alive?" Trunk asked.

"Mrs. Maher is, but she lives in an assisted living home. I go to see her every Tuesday." His mother smiled.

"Why didn't you tell me?" Trunk asked.

"I know how busy you are. I got in touch with her when I came back to St. John's," his mother explained.

Before Trunk could say anything, his phone vibrated in his pocket. He pulled it out but didn't recognize the number. He thought about ignoring it, but with Abbie missing, he couldn't take that chance.

"Hello," Trunk said.

"Ben, thank God." Abbie's voice sounded panicked.

"Abs? Jesus Christ, where are you?" Trunk shouted.

"Stop yelling. I'm at my parents' neighbor's house. I escaped from Mrs. Woodman. She killed Jerome. Just shot him…" Abbie was practically screaming.

"Stay where you are. I'm on my way." Trunk ran out of the house with Darren behind him.

Trunk called James as he sped toward St. John's because he wasn't about to wait for the police to bring her home. She might be at a neighbor's house but that didn't mean her abductors didn't know where she was.

As he stopped outside the neighbor's house, he jumped out of the vehicle and bounded up the front steps. The door opened, and an older lady stepped back for Trunk and Darren to enter. Abbie practically leaped into Trunk's arms and sobbed.

He held her tightly for a moment and released her when Darren stepped next to him. She looked up and immediately wrapped her arm around her father, still keeping the other around Trunk.

By the time Abbie calmed and was able to speak, James had arrived, and they made their way out to Abbie's parents' house. They didn't want to intrude on the neighbor longer than they needed.

"First of all, are you hurt?" James asked.

Trunk noticed the bandages around her wrists and anger raged inside him. His jaw clenched as he forced himself to keep calm until he knew what happened.

"I had zip-ties on my wrists, and they sliced through my skin when I tried to get out of them. The man gave me the first-aid kit to wrap them when he noticed," Abbie explained.

"Well, when we find the asshole, I'll thank him right before I pound the piss out of him," Darren snapped.

"I don't think that will help, Darren," James said before he turned back to Abbie.

"How did you escape?" James asked.

Trunk held her while Abbie told them of her struggle to kick through a damaged wall. He was so proud of her courage and determination to escape. She trembled as she explained how Jerome had tried to help her and how he got a bullet for his efforts.

"You have no idea who the woman is?" James inquired.

"No, as far as I knew, she was a potential client." Abbie shrugged but gave her father a faint smile when he wrapped a blanket around her shoulders.

"You don't know what she's trying to get back?" James asked.

"No, but she is convinced we have something belonging to her." Abbie shrugged.

"Abbie, I think we should head to the hospital to get your wrists checked," James suggested.

"Not a fucking chance," Abbie replied adamantly.

"Abs, someone needs to check your wrists," Trunk interjected.

"Call Dr. O'Connor or Ian, I'm not going to the hospital again." Abbie shook her head.

Since the O'Connors had two doctors in the family, Trunk knew all he had to do was call, and either Keith's father or brother wouldn't hesitate to be there for him. He understood her aversion to the hospital since over the last month, she'd ended up there twice.

"I'll call Dad and get him to meet you at Trunk's place." James nodded.

"Thanks." Abbie breathed out a sigh of relief.

"Do you know where they held you?" James asked.

"Yes, the house is not even two blocks from here. I can show you." Abbie shot to her feet.

"No," Trunk and Darren said together.

"I need to show them," Abbie snapped.

"Why don't you drive her to the house, and I'll follow. Then take her back to your place. Ian will be there to check her." James suggested

Unfortunately, Sean and Kurt took their new stepfather, for a weekend of bonding, but James assured them Ian would examine Abbie's wounds.

"Fine." Trunk sighed.

"James, there's a huge freaking dog in the house. If you go in there be careful. I think he could probably eat a human if given the chance." Abbie warned.

"I'll contact animal control too," James assured her.

Trunk's body shook as they drove up the street where he lived as a kid. When Abbie pointed to the house where the Mahers used to live, Trunk felt a cold chill run up his spine. Trunk jumped out of the truck and ran back to James.

"I know that house," Trunk told him.

"You do?" James studied the house.

"I used to live next door, and the Mahers lived there." Trunk pointed to the house.

There was no way Mrs. Maher was involved in any of this. Both his mother and Abbie's mother made the connection between Lydia and Mrs. Maher, but Trunk couldn't believe the sweet woman would be that cruel.

"Get Abbie home so that Ian can take care of her wounds. We'll get a warrant to search this house," James told Trunk.

"Don't hurt the dog. He might be a savage, but he doesn't deserve to be hurt." Abbie shouted out the window as Trunk drove away from the house.

"The dog will be fine, Abs." Darren shook his head.

"I think he was just scared," Abbie whispered but seemed mostly to herself.

By the time they arrived in Hopedale, Abbie was asleep. Darren sat in the back holding her as if she would disappear again. Trunk wasn't much better because he kept glancing back to see if she was okay.

Abbie winced as Ian cleaned her wounds and even called him a butcher a few times. After he wrapped them, he checked her from head to toe. He seemed content that she was okay and turned to Trunk.

"The cuts aren't too bad and will heal fine," Ian said.

"Not that bad, says you. Let me put zip-ties on your wrists, and you try to escape from it," Abbie grumbled.

"Easy, if you know what to do." Ian winked.

"Thanks, where the hell were you when I needed that information?" Abbie scoffed.

"Take some Tylenol if you have any pain, and don't lose that spunk." Ian chuckled.

Ian instructed Trunk to change the bandages in a day or two and to keep it clean. Other than that, she was physically fine. Ian also suggested they keep her bandages dry and if she wanted to shower, to wrap them in plastic.

Abbie managed to get a bath with her mother's help, and Trunk helped her settle into bed afterward. Trunk gave her some Tylenol for pain and sat with her until she started to drift off to sleep.

"I'm so tired of being picked on." Abbie sighed as he tucked her into his bed.

"We aren't picking on you." Trunk smiled.

"Not you. The idiots who tried to kill me twice and then kidnapped me. Why the hell do they think picking on me is going to get them what they want?" Abbie asked.

"They must have planned to contact someone." Trunk didn't want her to think they were going to kill her.

"I guess. I just want to sleep." Abbie yawned.

"You sleep, baby. I'm going to get everyone settled in for the night, and then I'll be back." Trunk kissed her forehead.

Trunk made his way downstairs and found everyone in the living room, quietly talking. Abbie's parents, his mother, Chris, Billie, Mike, Cole, and Paige, looked up when he entered the room.

"How is she?" Paige asked.

"She was falling asleep when I left the room." Trunk smiled at his half-sister.

"She's a brave woman," Cole interjected.

"Are all of you staying tonight?" Trunk asked since it was midnight and they were all still there.

"I was going to take Dad home, but Billie offered us a place to stay for the night. Dad wants to stay close in case you or your mom need something." Paige smiled.

"Why don't we go over to Billie's place? Cole and Paige can stay here," Claire suggested.

"Where's Chad?" Trunk asked, noticing Cole's nephew was gone.

"His mother came to get him," Cole explained.

By the time everyone went to bed it was well after midnight. Trunk wasn't sure where everyone was sleeping but he made his way to his room, exhausted. When he opened the door he found Abbie curled up in the middle of the bed, sobbing.

"Abs, you're safe." Trunk immediately wrapped his arms around her.

"I know. I was just thinking about Jerome. She shot him because he didn't want to be involved with her plan. He's dead, Ben." Abbie clung to him.

"I'm sorry, baby. I know you cared about him." Trunk kissed the top of her head.

"I can't believe he got close to me for that woman." Abbie blew out a breath. "Who the hell is she?"

"I wish I knew," Trunk whispered.

By the next morning, his house was a buzz of activity again. Trunk insisted Abbie stay in bed for the day, and when he told her about the crowd filling his house, she agreed.

"Trunk, I think you should come with me to talk to Mrs. Maher. She knows your family," James said.

"I haven't seen her since I was a kid, but maybe Mom can come with us," Trunk suggested.

His mother was more than willing to go with them because she didn't want them scaring the elderly woman. His mom was worried she'd become distraught if James and Trunk showed up asking a ton of questions.

The senior's home was not far from where his mother lived. She seemed to know most of the staff because several of them greeted her as they made their way to Mrs. Maher's suite.

"Let me go in first and talk to her." His mother walked through the door, leaving James and Trunk in the corridor.

"Do you think she'll be able to help?" Trunk asked James.

"It can't hurt to talk to her." James shrugged.

Trunk's mother opened the door and motioned for him and James to come inside. Trunk hadn't seen Mrs. Maher in a long time, but when he saw her, he knew he would recognize her anywhere. She had the same hairstyle and the same friendly smile.

"Well, my goodness. You boys have certainly grown up," Mrs. Maher said from her chair.

"Mrs. Maher, this is James O'Connor. He's the police officer who wants to talk to you." His mother touched Trunk's arm. "This is Ben."

"Such a handsome young man." Mrs. Maher smiled.

"It's great to see you again, Mrs. Maher." Trunk crouched and took her hand in his.

"I'm so glad you came to see me. Your mother is so proud of you and Christopher." The older woman smiled.

She raised her eyes to look up at James, and her smile faded slightly. Her grip tightened on Trunk's hand, and she motioned for James to sit.

"I understand you have questions about my house," Mrs. Maher said.

"Yes, ma'am." James smiled.

"The house belonged to Ambrose, and when he passed, I didn't want to live there without him. I couldn't bear to sell it, so I asked his nephew to take care of it for me until I decided what to do." Mrs. Maher's eyes filled with tears.

"What's your nephew's name?" James asked.

"Gary Sweeney. His mother was Ambrose's sister. When she passed away, they stayed with their father, and he passed a few years later. Gary looked after his sister," Mrs. Maher explained.

"Her name was Lydia?" Trunk asked.

"Yes, that poor girl had a lot of problems, and Gary did his best to take care of her. He had to admit her to the hospital quite a few times." Mrs. Maher shook her head. "That poor girl."

Trunk was glad Mrs. Maher didn't know why Lydia had problems. Her brother had been molesting her for years, and she was stuck with him. There was no doubt in Trunk's mind that Mr. and Mrs. Maher would have gotten her out of that situation as fast as possible.

"Do you remember when she passed?" James asked.

Mrs. Maher stared at him as if he'd spoken a different language. It was as if she didn't know Lydia had passed away, and maybe Gary didn't tell her because he didn't want to upset her.

"Lydia passed away? When?" Mrs. Maher gasped.

"It was last year." Trunk didn't like the idea of upsetting the older woman.

"That's impossible. She was here two days ago," Mrs. Maher told them.

Trunk and James shared a puzzled look, and then Trunk glanced at his mother. Mrs. Maher might not be mentally healthy, and maybe she thought it was a couple of days since she'd seen Lydia.

"Are you sure?" James asked.

"Of course, I'm sure. My body might be breaking down, but my mind is sharp as a tack." Mrs. Maher nodded.

"She has a great memory," Trunk's mother agreed.

While Trunk and his mother stayed with Mrs. Maher and tried to comfort her, James contacted Sandy and had her search for Lydia's death certificate. If Lydia wasn't dead, then she might be the elusive Mrs. Woodman.

James returned a few minutes later and sat next to Mrs. Maher. He pulled up something on his phone and then turned it toward the older woman.

"Mrs. Maher, we have a death certificate for Lydia. You said there was a woman here two days ago. Are you positive it was Lydia?" James asked.

"My eyes aren't what they used to be, but now that you mention it, I hadn't seen her in a long time. She was in a psychiatric hospital for years. The day she came here, she said she was doing much better, and Gary told her to come to see me." Mrs. Maher told them.

"I'm sorry, Mrs. Maher, but I think the woman that was here was not your niece. Can you tell me what you talked about?" James asked.

"She apologized for how she acted when I gave her my special ring all those years ago and asked if she could have it back. I told her it disappeared years ago. She asked about the jewelry chest that my Ambrose made for me. I keep my valuable jewelry in it, and when the ring disappeared, Ambrose made me another ring. I keep it in my dresser over there," Mrs. Maher explained.

"Can I see it?" Trunk asked.

"Fatima, would you be a dear and get it out of that drawer? It's in a small black velvet bag. The ring isn't worth anything. Ambrose made it out of some metal and fake pearls. He was such a creative person." Mrs. Maher lowered her head, and Trunk watched a tear run down her cheek.

"Mrs. Maher, do you still have the chest?" Trunk asked.

"All my things were stored in the attic of my house. A few months back, Gary's son came here with the box and told me I should keep it with me. It wasn't safe for me to leave it in a house where nobody lived. I asked him to hold on to it for me. He said he would keep it safe." Mrs. Maher shook her head. "I thought he was paranoid, but I appreciated him worrying about me."

Trunk was frustrated. They didn't know who the woman was, but the death certificate told them Lydia was dead. So, they had no way of knowing who was responsible.

"You should talk to Gary," Mrs. Maher said.

Trunk could see Mrs. Maher was getting distressed with all the information she'd gotten. He motioned to James to meet him outside and left his mother to visit with her old friend.

"I don't want to upset her more than she is. She didn't know Lydia was dead," Trunk whispered.

"We've got to bring in Gary and find out who this woman is," James replied.

He was right, and until they had that information, Abbie was still in danger, and so was Cole. They needed to keep everyone safe until the woman was apprehended.

Trunk's mother visited with Mrs. Maher for another hour after James left to track down Gary or Jerry. Both James and Trunk had a feeling both men were working with the woman Mrs. Maher thought was Lydia.

When they got back to his house, Trunk was surprised not to see it full of people. Abbie was in the kitchen with her father and mother talking with Cole and Chris. His brother was still dressed in his uniform since he'd just finished a three-day shift.

"How did it go?" Cole asked.

"Apparently, Gary is Mrs. Maher's nephew, and a woman visited her two days ago saying she was Lydia," Trunk explained.

"Lydia's dead," Claire said.

"Yeah, we know because Sandy pulled a death certificate." Trunk sat next to Abbie.

"Who's the other woman?" Abbie asked.

"We don't know, but Mrs. Maher said she hadn't seen Lydia in a long time, so when the woman told her she was Lydia, she believed her." Trunk sighed.

Claire grabbed her phone off the counter, and after tapping the screen several times. She held up a picture of two women with their arms linked together and smiling.

"Who's this?" Trunk asked.

"The woman on the left is Lydia, and the woman on the right is Sharon. I think they were a couple. Lydia's page didn't have a lot of pictures on it, but Sharon's did. Could the woman be Sharon?" Claire asked.

Trunk scrolled through both profiles and felt like Claire could be right. Every picture with the women looked intimate and as if they were together romantically.

"I could see why Mrs. Maher would be confused, especially since she doesn't have the best sight. These two women have a strong resemblance," Trunk said.

"Growing up, a lot of people used to mistake them for sisters. There was another girl younger than us who was always mistaken for their sister as well," Claire told him.

"Let me see the picture," Abbie said, and Trunk placed the phone in her hand.

Abbie swiped through the pictures, and Trunk wondered if she recognized anyone. After several minutes she raised her eyes to meet his and shook her head.

"Mrs. Woodman had one of those hats with a veil that hung over her eyes, but I don't believe it's either of these women. I guess I didn't get a good look at her face." Abbie shrugged.

Trunk sent James copies of the pictures from the Facebook profiles. If Lydia was dead, then it wouldn't be surprising if Sharon would be out for revenge. Especially if Lydia killed herself over the past. He didn't know if Abbie's mother was on to something, but he had a feeling they were heading in the right direction.

Chapter 32

Abbie's mother paced the floor as she frequently glanced down at her phone. James had suggested she message Sharon and ask to meet for coffee so they could catch up. James wanted to make it look as if Claire wanted to reconnect with an old friend.

It had been over two hours, but Sharon hadn't responded, and everyone was frustrated. Sandy clicked away on her keyboard, searching for something Abbie didn't understand. All she knew was there was something about pings and triangulating. It was all gibberish to her.

Trunk searched through some papers they'd found in the attic of Mrs. Maher's home, hoping by some slim chance he'd figure out who they were looking for. Mrs. Maher gave the police permission to search the house for any clues on who was involved.

The police didn't find the jewelry chest, but they did let Mrs. Maher know they recovered the original ring. She was overjoyed and told Fatima she wanted her to keep it. Trunk's mother refused, but Mrs. Maher insisted. She said when they found the box to bring it to her so they could open it together. Mrs. Maher didn't want her nephew to get his hands on it, considering what he'd done.

James said they also found three bodies in the shed behind the house. He couldn't reveal the names, but it was a woman and two men. Abbie shivered when she realized how close she came to joining the poor individuals.

Abbie stepped out on the front step of Trunk's home and took a deep breath. It was early May, and it seemed as if the snow would never disappear. It had been warmer over the past couple of days, but she still needed to wear a coat. Since Hopedale was a small town surrounded by the Atlantic Ocean, the wind off the water could be bitter on the hottest days.

"I don't think you should be out here, Abs," Trunk said in a gruff voice.

"I need fresh air, Ben." Abbie rolled her eyes.

"You can go out on the back deck." Trunk wrapped his arms around her from behind.

"I like the view out here." Abbie sighed and leaned into his body.

"Enough to move in here?" Trunk whispered in her ear.

Abbie turned in his arms and stared up at him in surprise. His lips twisted up into a smile, but he looked nervous, which was not a bit like the Trunk she knew.

"Are you asking me to move in with you?" Abbie raised an eyebrow.

"Maybe." He rested his forehead against hers.

"I have a house," Abbie whispered.

"Sell it. I know a great real estate agent." Trunk ran a finger down her cheek.

"I love my house." She used to.

"More than you love me?" Trunk murmured against her lips.

"That's not fair. You know I love you more than anything," Abbie poked him in the chest.

"Then move in with me. I know we can't do it all right now. At least until we get these bastards but give me some hope that after all this is over, you'll at least think about it." Trunk stared into her eyes.

"I'll think about it," Abbie promised.

Trunk lowered his head, and his lips barely touched hers when the front door opened. They spun around to see an excited Fatima waving for them to come inside.

"Claire got a message," Fatima said.

"Sharon?" Abbie asked.

Fatima nodded as they followed her. Abbie's mother messaged back and forth with the woman who could be responsible for the attempts on Abbie's life as well as her kidnapping, not to mention Cole's shooting and the murder of the three people found in Mrs. Maher's shed. They didn't know why she did it all, but the first step was stopping her.

"What is she saying?" Abbie asked.

"She apologized for drifting apart and not keeping in contact," Abbie's mother said.

"Is it possible it isn't her?" Abbie wasn't convinced.

"Who else could it be?" Claire asked.

"It's easy to fool people behind a screen," Sandy interjected.

Abbie's mother chatted with her old friend. From the messages, Abbie didn't see anything suspicious, and according to the woman's profile, she didn't live in the province. It was why when her mother asked to meet for coffee, Abbie was surprised Sharon agreed.

"I guess she doesn't live in New Brunswick anymore," James said.

"Maybe she's visiting," Abbie interjected.

"Abs, why are you so reluctant to believe this woman is involved?" Trunk asked.

"I don't know." Abbie shrugged.

"We need to set up a meeting," James said.

"She wants to go for coffee tomorrow." Abbie's mother showed them the screen.

While everyone worked to put a plan together to capture Sharon, Abbie slipped away and found some peace in Trunk's bedroom. She had so much running through her mind, and there was something in the back of her head telling her Sharon was not responsible.

Mrs. Woodman resembled the women in the picture, but Abbie couldn't say with certainty if either woman was Mrs. Woodman. Then again, Abbie didn't know if she could recognize her. Abbie flopped back on the bed and sighed.

Maybe she should decide about moving in with Trunk. It wasn't like she hadn't dreamed about living with him, but she wanted more too. She never thought a day would come when she would want to be someone's wife, but with Trunk, she did.

Before she made that decision, she needed to sell her house. It was great but being with Trunk was so much better. Plus, his house was in such a beautiful place, and she'd be closer to Billie. Who was she kidding? There was no doubt in her mind she wanted to live with him forever.

Abbie did need to go to her house and get some things if she stayed at Trunk's place for longer. For some reason, Trunk seemed to think it was too dangerous for any of them to be anywhere but in Hopedale, but she could be in worse places.

"Laurie, do you think you could give us a hand down here?," Abbie whispered.

The next afternoon, after a heated discussion between Abbie and Trunk, he agreed to bring her home to get what she needed. James and a team of officers headed to the coffee shop to wait for Sharon with strict instructions for Abbie and her mother to stay away. Her mother wanted to be bait, but James wouldn't hear of it, not to mention, Abbie's father forbid it.

Abbie and Trunk arrived at her house and stepped inside. A cold chill skittered up her spine, but she had no idea why. The house was cool, but something made her normally cheery house seem foreboding. When she walked into her den, she gasped.

"They destroyed this place." Abbie started to pick up some papers off the floor.

"I'm sorry, Abs. I should've had someone come clean this up." Trunk stood up a toppled chair.

"Is that blood?" Abbie noticed a dark stain on her rug.

"I think so. The officer was attacked in here," Trunk told her.

"I'm suddenly not liking my house so much anymore." Abbie shivered.

"Why don't we go upstairs and get the things you need? Then we can head back to Hopedale." Trunk wrapped his arm around her shoulder.

Abbie walked into her closet and grabbed a suitcase from the corner. She opened it on her bed and started to toss some things inside. As she returned to the closet, Trunk turned away from her dresser with a huge smirk on his face.

"I'm assuming this is something you came to pick up." Trunk held up a see-through red teddy.

"Yes, that was the main thing I came back to get." Abbie rolled her eyes.

Trunk tossed it into her suitcase and continued his search through her lingerie drawer. He would be there a while if he went through all her sexy things.

"Get out of my drawers, pervert." Abbie tossed a pillow at him.

"Hey, we can't have this stuff sitting here, not getting used." Trunk flicked the pillow on the bed.

"Whatever." Abbie laughed as she headed into her closet.

She reached for a pair of sneakers in her shoe cupboard, and the light above her flickered. As she looked up, she noticed something sticking out of the top shelf. It wasn't something she'd placed there, and she pulled it down off the shelf.

In her hand, she held a gold square box with etchings on the side and top. It looked old with intricate carving, and she ran her finger over the large *B* on top. It was then she saw the square and star inside the letter.

"Ben," Abbie practically screamed and felt awful when he ran into the closet, looking completely unnerved.

"Abs, what's wrong?" Trunk scanned her up and down as if he expected to see an injury.

"I think this is Mrs. Maher's jewelry box." Abbie held it up.

Chapter 33

Trunk took the beautiful chest from Abbie's hands and turned it over. He ran his fingers around the edges and tried to open it, but couldn't see anything to open.

"See." Abbie pointed to the star.

"It's been here, and you didn't know?" Trunk was dumbfounded.

"It was up there on that shelf. I never look up there. The only reason I did was because the light flickered." Abbie pointed to the burned-out light.

"Jerome must have hidden it here and didn't tell anyone." Trunk turned to exit the closet.

He stopped and shoved Abbie behind him when he saw the barrel of a gun. His eyes moved up the arm attached to the gun and locked gazes with an older woman. He didn't know who she was, but he had a feeling it was the elusive Mrs. Woodman.

"I knew that bastard hid it here." She smirked.

"I guess you think you're going to take this and walk out of here." Trunk held up the box.

"Not exactly. I need to get rid of both of you, first. I can't have you coming after me." The woman smiled.

Trunk studied her face. It certainly wasn't Lydia or Sharon, at least it didn't look like the women in the picture Claire showed him. So, who the hell was she?

"You know the police are looking for you." Trunk pushed Abbie back further into the closet.

"The police are looking for Sharon. As you can see, I'm not her. She's dead, by the way. She figured out that I helped Lydia die. She wanted to call the police, so I fixed the situation," she said, confirming the identity of the woman the police had found.

She reached for the jewelry chest, but Trunk tucked it under his arm. The woman lifted the gun and aimed it at his head. The last thing he wanted was to let this woman kill him and leave Abbie unprotected.

"Give it to her, Ben." Abbie tugged on his arm.

"Yes, Ben. Give me what's mine." The woman sneered.

"I'll give it to you if you tell me who you are." Trunk held up the box.

"Why does it matter? It's not like you'll live long enough to tell anyone." The woman scoffed.

"Let's just say I'd like to die knowing the truth." Trunk had no intention of letting this woman end Abbie's life or his.

"Ben, I don't want either of us to die," Abbie whispered.

The woman glared at Trunk then she sighed and backed out of through the door. She aimed the gun at Trunk as she motioned for them to come out of the closet.

"Don't try anything because I'll have you know I'm a crack shot, but I guess it wouldn't hurt to tell you both everything. It's not like I'll be going anywhere for a while. Abbie here has some nosey neighbors, so I'll have to wait until it's dark." The woman chuckled.

Trunk sat on the bed, putting himself between Abbie and the weapon. He wanted to keep all of Mrs. Woodman's attention on him, and if he saw a chance, he'd get Abbie out safely.

"You see, a long time ago I was in love with a man who promised me the world. He was older than me, but he promised to marry me one day," Mrs. Woodman said.

"I'm guessing he didn't," Trunk interjected.

"No, he betrayed me for a half-wit who ended up breaking his heart," the woman sneered.

"You were in love with Gary Sweeney," Abbie said.

"Didn't take you long to figure that out." Mrs. Woodman snorted.

"How did you know about Mrs. Maher's jewelry case?" Trunk asked.

"Gary promised I could have all the jewelry, but his stupid sister screwed it up. Her aunt took the ring back, but Lydia asked the guy she was screwing to get it back for her. He was good at getting in there since they were neighbors." The woman lowered the gun a little.

"Jerry," Trunk growled.

"Yes, you're very familiar with him, aren't you, Benji." Mrs. Woodman tilted her head.

"Yes," Trunk said with distain.

"You see Jerry, Gary, Lydia, and I knew each other from spending summers in Calvert. I lived there, but the guys would be there every summer." Mrs. Woodman went on.

"That's how you knew all of them." Abbie nodded.

"Yes, as a matter of fact, I knew your parents too. Gary thought he wanted your mother once, but Claire was more into that bastard who almost killed him." She glared at Abbie. "He could have killed Gary that night if it wasn't for me."

"I thought Lydia stopped him?" Abbie asked.

"Lydia took credit, but I was the one who called the cops. Lydia was more worried about someone finding out she was fucking Sharon inside the house," she snapped.

"You were at the party, too," Trunk said.

"Of course, I was. Everyone was there, and I was hoping Gary would come to his senses and make a move. That was until I saw him with that slut Claire." She sneered.

"My mother wasn't a slut. Gary tried to rape her," Abbie shouted.

"Is that what she told you? Honey, your mother was teasing him for months, and when he made a move, she made it look like he attacked her." The woman narrowed her eyes and glared at Abbie. "You look like her."

"I take that as a compliment," Abbie snapped.

"Why go after Abbie?" Trunk asked.

"We needed money for when we could convince the old woman to sell Gary the house. That way, we could tear it apart until we found what we wanted. When Jerome couldn't get money from Cole, we had to figure out another way. Your agency was new, and it was easy for Jerome to get into your systems. He was actually pretty smart that way. God rest his soul." Mrs. Woodman smiled.

She enjoyed telling them the intricate plan and almost seemed proud of what she did. It was blatantly obvious she didn't like Cole either because when she said his name, she cringed.

"When you got the money, why didn't you leave Abbie alone?" Trunk asked.

"Because that idiot suddenly got a conscience and wanted to return all the money before anyone noticed. He also found that box and hid it from us. I knew he was gutless, but his father thought he'd never turn on us," she went on.

"You killed him because he didn't want to hurt people?" Abbie sounded shocked.

"I got rid of him before he spoiled everything. Do you realize there is over a million dollars worth of jewelry inside that chest?" Mrs. Woodman waved the gun.

Trunk looked down at the beautiful gold chest that wasn't as big as a shoebox. He found it hard to believe it could contain so many valuable items. It didn't matter. Trunk wasn't about to let this woman take what belonged to Mrs. Maher.

"Why shoot Cole?" Abbie asked.

It was the first time Trunk saw Mrs. Woodman's confident demeanor crack a little. She looked enraged and Trunk worried that she might stop talking, or worse, snap and shoot them before they could get help. He also wanted to get as much out of her as he could.

"He ruined my life. He turned my family against me, and I lost the one person I ever loved more than Gary." She sneered.

"Your husband?" Abbie asked.

"No, my daughter," she sneered at them.

Trunk saw something familiar about the woman as he studied her. When she tucked a piece of hair behind her ear it hit him. The resemblance was too great. Mrs. Woodman had the same shape nose and mouth as well as Paige's petite stature. Mrs. Woodman was Cole's ex-wife Rebecca.

"You were married to Cole," Trunk said.

"You really are smarter than you look," she scoffed.

"Why marry Cole if you were in love with Gary?" Abbie asked.

"I married him because of Jerry. He was crazy about Fatima, but she wouldn't give him a second look because of Cole. When she got pregnant with you, Jerry thought he'd lost his chance with her, but Cole's father wanted him to go away for school. Jerry took that opportunity to get what he wanted. He told Cole he'd take care of Fatima while he was away at school." Rebecca laughed. "Cole was so easy to convince Fatima was screwing Jerry long before he left Newfoundland."

"That still doesn't tell us why you'd marry Cole." Abbie pushed.

"I got knocked up. Cole might not have been the man I wanted, but he was great in bed, and he kind of reminded me of Errol Flynn. You look just like your father." Rebecca turned her head to the side.

"Paige looks like you," Trunk said.

"Yes, but Cole took her away from me. He got mad because I left her with a friend for a month to spend time with Gary." Rebecca rolled her eyes. "It wasn't like I left her with a stranger, and she was two, so she would never remember it anyway."

"You left your child in another province." Abbie gasped.

"She was getting on my nerves, and I needed to be with Gary. That half-wit left him and took his son. I warned him about her," Rebecca sneered.

"Have you seen Paige lately?" Trunk asked.

"Very good. You figured out where I got the Ketamine. I went to see her a few months ago. I told her I wanted to rebuild our relationship. She was so happy and asked me to wait while she finished up with her work. It was amazing how easy it was to get the drugs from the cabinet," Rebecca said with a smirk.

Trunk noticed movement outside the bedroom door and assumed it was either Jerry or Gary since they were both involved. They'd possibly come to help Rebecca search the house but never expected to see Trunk and Abbie. He wanted to kick himself for being so careless.

"So, what happens after this? You and Gary are going to run away together? The man looks like he has one foot in the grave and the other on a banana peel." Trunk hoped the statement would get Gary or Jerry to show themselves.

"More like two feet in the grave now. He wasn't happy that I got rid of Jerome. He got so upset and started ranting about how Jerome was all he had left of that half-wit. He told me he would never love anyone the way he loved Violet. So I sent him to be with her." She shrugged.

The woman was out of her mind, and Trunk felt more uneasy knowing she'd already killed four people. Trunk also didn't like the fact that the person in the hallway could possibly be Jerry.

"I guess you and Jerry will be leaving the province together," Trunk glanced at the doorway.

"Nope. I wasn't giving him any of the money. Gary wanted to involve him, and I needed him for a place to stay. Jerry actually thought he'd get half the money." Rebecca laughed.

Trunk was confused. If she'd already killed Jerry, Gary, and Jerome, who the hell was outside the bedroom door? Who else could be involved? She was ranting about her perfect plan when Trunk saw Cole through the half-opened door.

For a split second, Trunk was concerned Cole was involved, but from the way Rebecca seemed to feel about her ex-husband, she would probably rather see Cole dead.

"Now, it's getting dark. I'll be leaving as soon as I tie up these loose ends." Rebecca lifted the gun and aimed it at Trunk.

Before she could pull the trigger, the bedroom door swung open, slamming against Rebecca's shoulder. She fell against the wall, and the gun flew out of her hand, sliding across the hardwood floor. Trunk lunged for the weapon as Cole grabbed Rebecca and brought her down to the ground.

"Get off me," Rebecca shrieked as she swung her fist at Cole's head.

Cole avoided the blow easily and flipped her over onto her stomach. He pinned her arms behind her back while she flailed and continued to shout obscenities at him.

"What the hell is wrong with you, Rebecca?" Cole shouted.

Before she could answer, Aaron and Cory ran into the room with their weapons drawn. Cory pulled Cole off Rebecca, and Aaron struggled to handcuff the raging woman. She threatened everyone in the room and promised they would all die by her hand.

"Ma'am, our family has survived worse than you." Aaron chuckled as he and Cory escorted her out of the room.

"I don't know what you're doing here, Cole, but I've never been so glad to see someone in my life," Abbie said as she wrapped her arms around Trunk's father.

"Fatima and I were out to supper, and she suggested we drop by here to see if Abbie needed a hand with packing," Cole said.

"Packing?" Abbie looked confused.

Trunk's mother ran into the room, looking panicked. She wrapped her arms around Trunk and squeezed him tightly. She released him enough to pull Abbie into her embrace and held them while she sobbed.

"I'm so glad we came when we did," his mother wept.

"Are you all okay?" Aaron asked when he returned.

"A little shaken, but I'm fine," Abbie said.

"We're good, A.J. Thanks for getting here in time." Trunk reached out to shake Aaron's hand.

"Your mom called emergency services, and I heard the dispatch. Cory and I were leaving an elementary school. We booted it over here," Aaron told them.

"I can't believe Rebecca is responsible for all this." Cole shook his head. "I knew she had problems, but if I hadn't seen this, I never would have believed it."

"She said she killed Lydia, Sharon, Jerry, Jerome, and Gary," Trunk told Aaron.

"That will keep her locked up for a long, long time." Aaron nodded.

"I certainly hope so," Cole said.

"Let's get out of here and go back to Hopedale." Trunk slammed Abbie's suitcase closed and tugged it off the bed.

"Let's go home." Abbie smiled up at him.

Chapter 34

It was over. Rebecca had gone through psychiatric evaluation and deemed fit to stand trial. Thankfully she pleaded guilty to five counts of murder, one count of kidnapping, and three counts of attempted murder. The judge gave her life in prison and told her he'd never met anyone so evil.

The dog in the house had turned out to be stolen from a family and was returned to them. According to James, once the dog was reunited with his owners, it was as if he was a different animal. Abbie was glad the poor thing wasn't euthanized.

A month had passed since Rebecca's sentencing, and Abbie was glad it was finally over. It meant she and Trunk could move on with their lives together. Especially since she'd put her house on the market, and it sold in two weeks, mainly because Trunk's brother bought it.

The O'Connors were also celebrating. Cora's daughter Pam had given birth to, Tara Pamela and Evan Damon during the last week of May. A week later, Billie, Nick's wife and Aaron's wife all announced they were expecting babies in the late fall. Abbie was happy for them and hoped someday soon to be announcing her own joyful news.

Abbie walked out on the front deck of her new home and took a deep breath. When she turned her head, she was surprised to see Paige sitting on the wicker chair staring off into space. Abbie's heart went out to Trunk's sister. Paige hadn't seen her mother but a handful of times over her lifetime and was heartbroken when she found out Rebecca was responsible for everything.

"Hey, why didn't you come inside when you got here?" Abbie sat next to her.

"This view is beautiful," Paige said softly.

"It really is." Abbie smiled as she scanned the horizon.

Trunk's house was on an elevated part of Hopedale, and from the front of the house, she could see most of the town. At the end of the front porch, she could see the beach and watch the sun rise and set.

"It's kind of therapeutic," Paige whispered.

"Paige, are you okay?" Abbie asked.

"I can't believe my mother would do such terrible things. How can you even talk to me, knowing what she did?" Paige had tears in her eyes.

"You had nothing to do with anything your mother did. None of it was your fault," Abbie told her.

"Dad tried so hard to involve her in my upbringing, but she always had excuses. The few times I did see her, all she wanted to do was talk about being with the man she loved." Paige shook her head. "Then, she kills him."

"I can't pretend I understand what she did, but I'm not going to let it ruin my happiness. You shouldn't either. Paige, you're a wonderful person, and you've got a great family. Not to mention two new overbearing brothers." Abbie smiled.

"They're a lot like Dad. I just don't want to remind you of her every time you see me." Paige dropped her head.

"Paige." Trunk's voice startled Abbie.

Paige looked up with tears running down her cheeks. Trunk sat next to her and took both her hands in his.

"We're not responsible for what our parents do. I'm thrilled to have a sister. You're part of my family, and I don't care who your mother is." Trunk smiled. "By the way, we need to talk about that dude who was hugging you outside the courthouse."

Paige seemed confused at first but then started laughing hysterically. She held her stomach as she tried to tell them who she was hugging.

"He's my cousin. I guess your cousin, too." Paige laughed. "He's Chad's older brother Anton."

"Good, because not just any guy is going to be good enough for my baby sister," Trunk said.

"Good Lord, the poor girl doesn't have a chance." Abbie scoffed.

"I'm a big girl." Paige smiled.

"I have a great idea. Why don't we have a dinner party and invite everyone so you can all get to know each other?" Abbie suggested.

"That sounds like a great plan," Trunk leaned forward and kissed Abbie's cheek.

Abbie left the planning of the party to her mother and Fatima. They were more than happy to put together a family dinner for everyone, and Abbie took the time to get back into the routine of working again.

Cole had been a great help and sent her a ton of clients. It was great to have a boyfriend whose father had connections. She was also relieved the money Jerome scammed was returned to the finance companies. She wasn't on the hook for it, but she didn't want to have anything like it connected to her company.

"It's so good to be back to normal." Abbie sat in the chair across from Billie's desk.

"Yes, it is. It's also nice to see that smile on your face." Billie smirked.

"I have no idea what you mean." Abbie fluttered her eyes.

"It's so great to see you happy, Abbie." Billie smiled.

"I never thought I'd be so content with someone. Ben makes me feel like… like…" Abbie couldn't think of a word to explain it.

"Like you're home?" Billie returned.

"Yeah." Abbie sighed.

"I'm so happy for you." Billie's eyes filled with tears.

Abbie finally had her forever.

Chapter 35

Trunk, Chris, and his mother walked into Mrs. Maher's room to return her ring and jewelry chest. James brought it to Trunk that morning so he could return it to Mrs. Maher. His mother was glad to have something good to bring to the older woman. The last time she'd seen them, they had to tell her about Gary and Jerome.

Trunk walked into the room, and Mrs. Maher smiled when she saw them. Trunk and Chris started visiting her once a week because she was family to them. With the deaths of Gary and Jerome, Mrs. Maher had no family left and they hated to see her alone. His mother suggested the older woman move in with her, but she refused.

"It's so nice to see you all," Mrs. Maher said.

"You too, Mrs. Maher." Chris kissed her cheek.

"We've come to return your jewelry chest. The police dropped it off today," Trunk told her as he placed it on her lap.

She stared at it with tear filled eyes before she touched it. She smiled as she ran her fingers across the etchings and the letter on the top.

"This is the original ring." His mother handed it to Mrs. Maher.

The older woman took it apart and placed the two pieces in the locks. She turned them in opposite directions until there was a soft click, and a drawer popped out of the front.

"Ambrose worked on this box for years before he could get that to work right." She chuckled.

"It's amazing." Chris sounded awed.

"He could have made a fortune making these, but he told me he made it for his one and only." Mrs. Maher pulled the drawer out and placed it on top of the box.

She lifted a piece of velvet and reached inside the drawer. She removed two rings and a pair of earrings from inside and for several minutes, she held them in her hands before she finally looked up at Trunk's mother.

"I have nobody to pass these on to, and you're like a daughter to me. I want you to have these, Fatima." Mrs. Maher placed the earrings in Trunk's mother's palm.

"I can't take these, Mrs. Maher. They look very old and expensive." His mother gasped.

"They are. They've been in my family for generations. I'm the last of them. They should go to another family to enjoy, and I know you'll take care of them." Mrs. Maher closed his mother's hand over the earrings.

"I'll take good care of them." His mother hugged Mrs. Maher.

When Trunk's mom stepped back, Mrs. Maher looked up at Trunk and then Chris. She held up a ring in each hand and smiled at them.

"These rings have also been in my family for a long time. They were supposed to go to my children, but I never had any. I wanted to give them to Gary and Lydia, but I was afraid because I knew they wouldn't take care of them. You can give this to that lady friend of yours, Ben." Mrs. Maher raised an eyebrow.

"I'll do just that." Ben smiled.

Mrs. Maher placed one ring in his hand and gave the other to Chris. The one Trunk had was truly beautiful with a square emerald in the center and surrounded by small diamonds. It didn't look like a traditional engagement ring, but it was the first thing he thought about when he looked at it.

"It may be time for, *do, do, dodo*." Chris hummed to the tune of "Here Comes the Bride."

"I think you're right." Trunk decided to propose at the dinner party.

"You better talk to Darren first. I've got a feeling he'd kick your ass if you didn't ask for his blessing." Chris chuckled.

Trunk knew it was the right thing to do. It might be old-fashioned, but it would show Darren Trunk respected him.

Two days later, Trunk's house was bursting at the seams with people. His mother and Claire invited Cole's family, as well as the O'Connors and his co-workers. It made it hard for him to get a second alone with Darren.

While everyone was busy eating and getting to know each other, Trunk pulled Darren aside and asked to speak with him privately. Darren looked concerned as they both stepped outside.

"Is everything okay?" Darren asked.

"Yes, I wanted to ask you something before I ask Abbie." Trunk reached in his pocket and pulled out the ring.

"You're proposing?" Darren stared at the ring.

"I'd like to, but I'd love to have your blessing before I do," Trunk said.

Darren lifted his head and stared directly into Trunk's eyes. He didn't say anything; he simply reached out and shook Trunk's hand.

"I'd be honored to call you my son-in-law and thank you for showing me the respect to ask for my blessing." Darren smiled.

"You're welcome, and I promise to take care of her for the rest of my life." Trunk told Abbie's father.

It took almost an hour to pull Abbie away from the group of women chatting in Trunk's living room. He stood in the middle of the crowd with Abbie smiling next to him. although she had no idea why they were both standing in the middle of the room.

"Everyone, I hope you enjoyed the evening. It's wonderful to get to know my father's family and introduce them to my extended family. There's nothing more a person could ask for than great family and great friends. Except for one thing." Trunk turned to Abbie and took her hand in his. "Abs, I know we've only been together a short time, but I've loved you since the first day I saw you. I thought letting you go was the best thing, but it was hell not being with you. I must have an angel on my shoulder helping me. because I got a second chance with the love of my life. Abs, nothing would make me happier than having you with me for the rest of our lives."

Trunk pulled the ring from his pocket and dropped down to his knee. He lifted his eyes to meet her surprised face and smiled as he asked the most important question he'd ever uttered.

"Abigale Martin, will you marry me?" Trunk held up the ring.

"I'll marry you tomorrow if I could. Yes," Abbie shouted and pounced on him knocking him to the ground.

The room erupted in cheers while Trunk slipped the ring on Abbie's finger. He pulled her to her feet and kissed her with all the love he had in his heart. She was completely his.

Epilogue

Bruce Hulk Steele stood on the front step and waited for the door to open. It was his house, but his current tenant didn't know he was the landlord. She would never have accepted the offer if she knew. She already thought he did way too much for her, but he couldn't help it. Caroline Baker had a hold on him, and she didn't even know.

The first time he saw her at the café all those years ago, pregnant, he felt an unexplainable connection to her. It was why he was so pissed when the guy she served that day thought it was appropriate to grab her.

Hulk quickly put the asshole in his place, and from that moment, he would check on her every week. He missed a few weeks when he was shot trying to protect Nick's wife, but when he recovered enough to go back to the café, she was on maternity leave.

The next time, she was arguing with a man outside the café where she worked. He was both excited to see her and pissed because the guy was giving her a hard time. When the man slapped her, Hulk saw red.

Luckily, she stopped him from beating the hell out of the guy. The man was her landlord and refused to do something about the mold in her apartment. She had two kids and her mother living with her. Which was when Hulk went into protection mode and did everything he could to help. That included a job with one of the best restaurants in Hopedale and his house.

He wasn't homeless or anything because he stayed in a bunkhouse on his boss' property. Everyone knew what he was doing for Caroline, except her. Now he was here to tell her another lie.

"Hey." Caroline smiled as she opened the door with her youngest little boy on her hip.

"Hey, Trunk said you're having trouble with the kitchen sink." Hulk stepped inside.

"Yeah, it's leaking." She sighed.

"No problem, I got my handy toolbox." Hulk smiled and headed into the kitchen.

"You're just a jack of all trades, aren't you?" Caroline laughed.

"Yeah and master of none." Hulk shrugged out of his jacket and opened the cupboard under the sink.

Caroline watched him for a moment but turned away when the phone rang. Hulk's gaze dropped to how the snug jeans hugged her round ass in just the right way. She was all woman and had curves to prove it.

"Hello," she answered the phone pleasantly.

As Hulk dug through his toolbox for a wrench, he heard a thud. When he looked up, Caroline sat on the floor, holding her son tightly and staring at the phone.

"Not again," she whispered.

Coming Soon

Fall of 2020

NES Series

Newfoundland Elite Security

Book 2

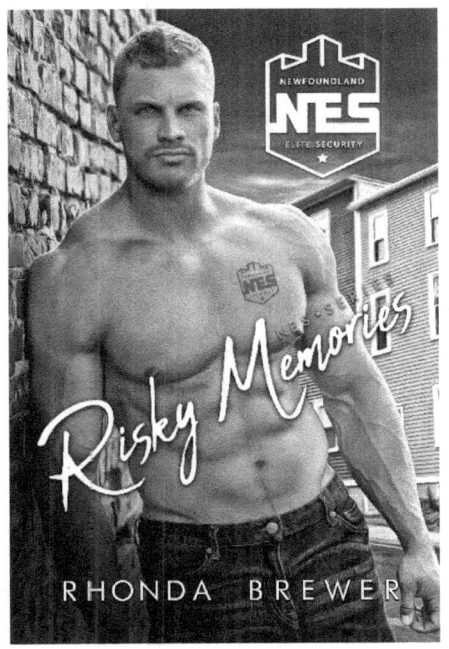

*Can Bruce 'Hulk' Steel help Caroline Baker
find out the mystery surrounding her father's
disappearance? Will she let him help when
his secret is revealed?*

About the Author

What does someone say to describe themselves? You could start by saying what others say about you. Scratch that. It doesn't matter what others think about you. So here we go.

First of all, I'm a wife and mother. I'm also a grandmother. That alone would fulfill any woman's life, and to be honest, it does. But.....

I'm also a writer, someone who loves to tell stories of love, suspense, heartache, and of course, happily ever after. For most of my life, I've written those stories for myself. A type of therapy, I suppose. I love the characters I create. They become part of who I am because there's part of me in them.

So... Now that you know this about me. I hope when you read my books and fall in love with them.

You should also know that I'm a Newfoundlander. What is that you ask? We're a proud people who live on an island off the east coast of Canada. Some people believe Canada ends with Nova Scotia. It doesn't. If you keep going east, there is a beautiful island full of amazing people and magnificent scenery. That is where my stories are set because let's face it. The best stories always come from the places you know and love.

Also check out

O'Connor Brothers Series

O'Connor Girls

O'Connor Prequel

Available on Amazon and Kindle Unlimited.

Rhonda Brewer

Keep up to date on all things new.

Follow me on

Facebook
Twitter
Instagram
MeWe
All Author
Bookbub

Sign up for my newsletter and never miss another release!

http://www.rhondabrewerauthor.com/talk-to-me

www.ingramcontent.com/pod-product-compliance
Lightning Source LLC
Chambersburg PA
CBHW071149250626
47159CB00001B/38